# AGENTS OF GRADATION

## ENDEARMENT IN INFERNO - TREACHERY IN ELYSIUM

JEASON THOMAS PARECATTIL

Made with ♥ on the Notion Press Platform
www.notionpress.com

# Contents

# Acknowledgements

To My mother who has taught me that true power lies somewhere between 'being a part of' and 'being different from' .

To Prabhjot Kaur for reading my very first drafts and guiding me to this door.

# Prologue

***"In peacetime Sons bury their fathers, when fathers bury their sons it's war and when you are at War, you keep your enemies close."***

*"One of the biggest contrasts between Humans and Animals is that animals cannot choose to be a predator or a prey, they can only act in accordance with their innate instincts. Natural order is that Predators hunt and gorge on Preys, however, from time to time, a Prey when completely outmatched and overpowered, not just loses all hope but also loses the sense of all fears, when that happens, fear is replaced by an uncontrollable rage and when the grasp of powerlessness is lost, it gets replaced by an absolute and unstoppable madness."*

CHAPTER ONE

# EARTH

"Why am I not resisting? I feel serene despite the fact that I am on the verge of death. Never thought I could be impervious to a predicament such as this. I should be angry, a few drops of sad tears would have made me feel normal but my eyes refuse to let go. Understandably, of course, I can see things are not in my control, but is my response appropriate? Perhaps, these relentless tormentors have rendered me numb to all sensations, depleting me of both physical and emotional capacity. What is this feeling called? Am I in the state they call 'The state of Absolution'? Was all of this fate? Is this where my journey ends? Was this my destiny all along?

The blood loss has weakened me, but the weakness is so peaceful. The floor is red, the walls are red, and no matter where I turn my head, I don't see another shade. Most people will find this kind of sight dreadful, but it turns out, I want to relish these final moments, I want to feel proud of everything that brought me here. My life is patting my back, calming me, and congratulating me, for finally, I have achieved the end of my journey, my culmination is here. What happens after this, what awaits further? There may be countless creations that are no more on the face of this earth, waiting for me on the other side. If that is so, I cannot wait to see them, I cannot wait for their welcome. How can I find the resilience to confront the looming spectre of mortality? But wait, there is something special about this moment, there is something different about this. What makes it special is that this very moment is not governed by those two-faces I despised, it is incorrigible by the corrupt, liars and powerful transgressors. I am glad those deceitful have no segment in my life anymore, no one can manipulate me, use me, coerce me. Even though I am surrounded by the most brutal and inhuman of the society, regardless - unlike those wolves in sheep's skin, these terrorists are true to themselves, they are what they are, brutal and monstrous and that is exactly how they portray themselves. This has to be it, this is the time, today is the day where it all ends."

Discuss the concept of being in the wrong place at the wrong time. Of course, none of it made sense. Manav is unable to recall what brought him here. "Did someone ask me to stay back for overtime? Was I even supposed to be here? Why can't I remember the reason why I stayed back? Besides, does it even matter you idiot?"

After hours of torture and no sign of outside intervention, Manav lost every remaining hope of being rescued. They say life flashes in front of your eyes just before you die, he never believed it but hoped to catch one last glimpse, a flashback of anything he wanted to grasp on to. "What a stupid fact that is! How many dead came back to life and shared their experience?" Those thoughts brought a chuckle to his face that he did not even care to control or hide. Perhaps during the final moments, fate decides what emotions are revealed and those to be kept buried. Manav seems to have lost the governance of his actions, unable to determine if he is really speaking or just ideas revolving in his mind. The terrorists, on the other hand, might have never seen someone so adamant. This one is one of those "Non-Talkers" they say about Manav, They are not particularly amused by Manav's response to the attack. He did not scream or agitate once, even when they pierced his arms with knives and battered his face and legs with the stock of their guns. For all the torture they gave him, His only retort came in the form of a high-pitched, unintelligible mutter, accompanied by a malevolent grin, as he grimly clenched his teeth, stained with the crimson of fresh blood all over it.

Terrorists feed on fear and violence, but their hunt was failing, they were going hungry today as Manav was in no mood to accept submission. Although it was not bringing Manav any good. In reality, he just incited a challenge for terrorists to come up with more ruthless ideas, "How to make his last moments so painful that he begs to put a stop," and that was their adrenaline, to see someone plead for mercy. Although, everyone in the room knew begging for life or even a glass of water was pointless. It was only a matter of time before witnessing what the voracious wild animals would serve up next. "They really are skilled at what they do, I don't see any other way this could have made any worse," Manav continues talking to himself, uncaring of the sharks surrounding him. Death is at his door, but instead of being alarmed by it, Manav is hoping that perhaps a flashback will allow him to be reminded of his lost memories, but nothing has happened so far. Perhaps it is a protective mechanism in his brain to prevent him from being reminded of his meaningless past or the meagre amount of hope that is left for his future. He is in the moment, feeling nothing but observant of his surroundings, he is in the presence of fellow-humans who are certainly not his well-wishers.

He was fine this morning, and every morning before this and unlike today, never ever bled, not one drop. "Wow, is that a red rainbow? How tiny it is, and ... why is it red?" As he gives a closer and thoughtful attention, he realises he is looking at a small column of a blood droplet surfacing down his eyelid. He could not control the laughter perceived by irony. "HA HA HA HA, Is that supposed to make me feel better? Am I supposed to see the beauty in all this savagery? I got to say I am not liking this flashback at all." The tricky-blood-rainbow did not lift up his spirits, it just gave rise to his nerves, with agitation he addresses one of the young terrorists, and shouts "Can we get it over with? WHAT ARE YOU WAITING FOR? A SIGN? Come-on let's just get it over with already, don't you want to make your superiors proud, be recognized?" Being naïve and out of frustration, He emits grating, ear-piercing sounds that resemble the raucous laughter of a hyena. Though his words possess a coherent logic within the confines of his own mind, for the terrorists, they serve as nothing more than an irksome nuisance. One of the terrorists drew Manav's attention, indignant and frustrated, this terrorist's facial expression towards Manav was strong. A few moments later, One of the seniors walks in and approaches Manav. He looks at him from top to bottom and painfully grabs his hair, with his thick accent he says. "There is a lot more to be done, patience is crucial, we are working really hard here." Then turns around and orders the younger ones something in their own language. Mockingly Manav replies "What's the delay? I thought you were good at baseless murders." Looking into their eyes with a ridiculing-relaxed smile he says, "what happened? You guys lost your touch?"

Their leader (presumably), holding his anger, approaches Manav, returning a cruel sinister smile he says, “What’s the hurry? Do you have to be somewhere?" Then he turns around keeping the same mysterious smile and walks back with everyone, leaving Manav alone and restrained.

Manav wanted to reply with a stunner but he couldn’t come up with one, he had to stop and think “Did I have to be somewhere?" Manav takes a moment. “Well nowhere usual or useful, same old routine and tasks. Isn’t everything a task nowadays, from the morning till night. Waking up, making your bed, cooking then cleaning. Even the simple act of eating becomes laborious, for I am compelled to partake in a meal despite lacking hunger. Why? Simply because it is deemed "lunchtime" by societal norms and expectations. All of these were merely a piece of work for me, I was least bothered about anything that happened around me. God! I wasted so much time like a clock. Never even designed a plan for myself, long term or short. To say the least, short term plans were to buy groceries and clean the house, long term was a bike ride planned alongside of Western Ghat roads. Oh! yeah that one...My Escapism, something I was good at. Hmm, so there are virtually some suitable things to recollect, in spite of everything. If only I had known those vistas would be the final images imprinted in my memory, I would have held them dearer, bidding a heartfelt farewell. But on the other hand, it is good to be dying imagining the splendour of Ladakh Valley and the purity of Varkala Beaches. Seems my life wasn’t that bad after all, there are some things I can say ‘Goodbye’ to." He wanted to smile for the fugacious happiness he drew for himself, although it was just for a moment but not thus far from contentment.

Disrupting his moment of tranquillity, two of the younger Terrorists return with ropes of various sizes. Before they release Manav, One of them, with a gun aimed menacingly, bares his tobacco-stained teeth, viciously he says, “Anything you try, You Die!” If hatred was a form of liquid, it would have been overflowing out of him. Whether by choice or against his will, the terrorist trembled and quivered with seething anger, locking eyes with unwavering intensity. Manav, just falling a few inches shorter than him, looks right back in his eyes, denying the terrorists any chance of receiving adequate retribution for the fear they instilled. Manav talks back at him, “Are you sure that is the only reason why I’ll die.... huh?" Perhaps it was the weight of authority from above that bound the man to silence in the face of maddening and exasperating retorts; they remained stoic, uttering no words and taking no action, they just carried out the orders given by their superiors which was to tie him upright with both hands on either side, hanging him high enough to touch the floor only with his toes, no more and no less, so that he can only balance on either hands or toes, one at a time. The idea was to tighten the blood circulation and let the internal pain do its job, at the beginning it may have looked bearable, but not during the later part when the blood bottlenecked towards his toes, shoulders and arms, that’s when the congestion spread everywhere with the consequential numbness and pain. For a moment Manav regretted his actions, his inner voice spoke, “Why am I making this harder for myself? Shouldn’t I just keep quiet and let them be, It will all be over soon anyway. All your life you never spoke a word, now is not the time to become conscious. Just die you idiot, die and make it as easy when you can, while you can." Suspended by his hands on either side, tethered to hooks embedded in the wall, he alternates between brief respites. He can endure the strain by either gripping tightly with one of his hands or relying on his toes for support, yet neither position can be sustained for more than a fleeting few seconds, his battered body was not capable enough to take his whole weight. Pain was excruciating; and kept getting worse. Trying to wander his painful thoughts, he remembers a great quote "Time is the best healer, Time eventually takes all the pain away, if not in this world then the next." "Who said that? I do not know but I have said this so many times and felt it too but only when it was in motion, today it appears time has stopped, there will not be a sunrise again or a sunset. Seems like I have been here all along, whatever I did, whatever happened to me, led me here to this moment. For all my actions, this is my penance; this is my reward. The day I was born my fate was already decided and my choices ensured it, could it have been any different? But how?" A paradox of infinite thoughts spreads across Manav's mind.

Breaking his series of thoughts, a young terrorist who Manav did not recognise approaches him just as he was about to lose consciousness, to tell him something."I have some bad news for you, your government has crossed the deadline for our demands....". Before the terrorist could utter his next words, Manav erupted into laughter so thunderous that it echoed through the room, as if he had just heard the most uproariously hilarious joke known to mankind. In defiance of the anguish coursing through him, his lips - etched with scars and cheeks - marred by countless blows, swelled with mirthful laughter, oblivious to the profound pain he should have acknowledged. The Terrorist disregarded the insult and said, "You know what it means, right?" Controlling his laughter, Manav replies,

"I admire your optimism, you waited this long just to find out that the Government failed you, I could have saved you so much time", He tried very hard, but the harder he tried, the louder he laughed. Mockingly he asks, "Did it ever cross your mind that you have kept a 'Nobody' as a hostage, I thought you were professionals, seems you guys are still learning." His laughter and every syllable spoken comes with slow pauses, making it even more annoying to listen to his slow sentences. The Terrorist takes a moment and responds, "It would be better for you to remain quiet and give up. This show of courage is meaningless, we both know what is going to happen now. I will not lie to you; you cannot endure the pain, but it will be over before your mind discovers another thought." Manav was unaffected, his laughter did not stop. Demanding attention the terrorist's voice got louder. "Now listen to me carefully, your idea of courage is misplaced, this is not the time, it will lead you nowhere but more suffering and trust me you don't want that, not with these people."

Someone would have got the impression that the terrorist's words have ultimately created worry in Manav. Everything fell so silent that you could hear the wind whistling through the broken windows. On the contrary Manav was feeling thankful and humble on the unexpected pleasantry, a drop of tear found its way out. In the past 24 hours, no one had expressed any sympathy towards him, it was a strange feeling. He did not want to be disrespectful to the last person who showed kindness towards him. Manav raises his head, looks at the terrorist, gently and respectfully smiles and nods in acknowledgement. The terrorist returns the same gesture and heads back. "Hey, Wait"!! Manav calls out. Surprised, the terrorist stops and turns back, expecting another insult from Manav, and the terrorist asks “What?" Manav takes a moment and with a smile he says, “If my maths is correct, there are nine of you, right?" The Terrorist does not care much and walks back. Manav stops him again, imploringly he says, “Hey man come on I was bored, just trying to make a conversation before I die. You'll be the last person I'll remember, please don't be offended, I'm profusely thankful for your kindness and apologetic too, in case I offended you, it was unintentional." The terrorist stops and folds his hand, looks at Manav from top to bottom and just says “OK, go ahead." Manav in a bit nervously reserved manner asks, “So.... I'm Manav, what's your name?" Terrorist looks around, checks if they are being noticed and replies,

“Mikhail” (meek-hah-eel). Manav's eyes glittered with happiness. “I got a response”, "Yay"!! he celebrates within his head.

Manav – “Nice to meet you Mikhail”, and smiles.

Mikhail – “So why were you counting us?"

Manav with a crooked smile says – “Just trying to keep myself occupied, anyhow, do you know how much time I have?"

Mikhail thinks for a moment and replies, “It won't be wise to know that."

Manav – “Why not Doctor?" and smiles followed by some childish giggles.

Mikhail – “Why would you think I'm a Doctor?" He gets a bit confused and comes closer to Manav.

Manav – “I heard them calling someone ‘Tabib’ on a few occasions which If I am not mistaken, translates to “Doctor” in Arabic, I figured if someone has to be a Doctor in the group, it has to be you. It was a long shot I know."

Mikhail expresses a gentle chuckle, looks around and says – “It wasn't for me, but you will meet him soon, but for your own sake you better hope to die of blood loss before you meet him. This man that they call 'Tabib' is not exactly a Doctor of wounds or diseases, he is famous for surgeries, in your language you may as well call him a 'Surgeon'."

Manav – "Oh! you came prepared for any on-job injuries, that's progressive."

Mikhail – "Precisely"! He replies in a taunting tone.

After a brief pause, Manav grasped the humour, and in that understanding, a tender moment of shared laughter unfolded between them. With newfound ease, the barriers between them began to dissipate, paving the way for more comfortable and open conversation. Mikhail was already sympathetic towards Manav seeing his whole body covered in darkened and clotted blood. He was getting weaker every second and his pale body did not fool anyone, even with his unbreakable wit. Concerned with his condition, Mikhail reluctantly asks, "Is there someone you want to remember right now? Do you want to be left alone while you do that?" to which Manav replied without even thinking about it.

"That is the problem, I can't remember anything significant before today. It's like I never existed before, now here I am, serving my purpose."

Mikhail was not sure how to respond to something like that, so he kept his silence for a few minutes. However, awkwardness was only growing every second. When the silence became excruciating, Mikhail tried to break it by some open-ended questions, while he was figuring it out, Manav took the first step and asked, "You still haven't answered my question, there are nine of you, right?" Mikhail looks around and with a sigh, thinking what harm can a dead man cause? he replies, "that's correct." Manav, with a deeper voice, asks, "You're not the leader, are you?"

Mikhail – "No, I'm not the leader, if 'role' is what you wanted to know, then you may as well call me the 'steward', my job is to arrange things. Keep an eye on the supplies and organise things according to plan."

Manav – "I have no idea what that's supposed to mean, looks like you are on a higher pay grade, good for you."

Mikhail, for some reason somehow was offended and got agitated with Manav's response – "You see that's it, that ignorance of yours is why we always win, that's exactly why our plans work, because your people can never interpret anything simple, Even when the truth lies glaringly before their eyes, it seems that your people have an inclination towards convoluted matters in order to deem them worthy of serious attention. It is tricky for them to grasp that a simple and unacknowledged plan is the most effective. That's why we can demand and that is why you are here." Mikhail's voice was getting louder and definitive with each phrase.

Shocked by Mikhail's sudden outburst, Manav asks – "Are you blaming me for where I am right now?"

Mikhail – "To an extent, Yes."

Manav – "Tell me what could have I done to avoid all of this?"

Mikhail – "It doesn't matter now; you can't escape from where you are."

Manav – "Something tells me you are not talking about me, anyway, what are your plans for me, 'Steward'!"

Mikhail's abrupt outburst spread over Manav, he matched his response with the same anger and sarcasm.

Mikhail – "The same for every Kafir, beheading, if you really are a man of tenacity you would know what that means."

Manav suddenly burst out laughing loudly, breaking the uneasiness and tension that had been permeating the otherwise silent room. The pathological outburst of Manav could be heard booming across the wide, unoccupied floor of the office building.

Manav – "I do not know why I find that so funny, sorry your scary speech went all in vain, Steward!"

Some of the terrorists became alarmed by his laughter; they naturally arrived at the site, but Mikhail reassured them that everything was under control.

Mikhail on top of his anger – "You are not just a denier, but you are also an ignorant fool, I am trying to help you...

Manav disregards and interrupts him disrespectfully with a stern and loud voice before he could utter another word.

"A DENIER!!?? A denier has a choice to deny or accept. A non-believer gets to choose what to believe and what not to. A man is taught where he lacks perception. I was not taught or given a choice. I was granted nothing, no father, no mother, or GOD....... Choose your words wisely... Steward"!!!

They both take a deep breath as they continue their heated exchange in the absurdity-filled room. Despite it, they maintained respect for one another. They began to settle down a little after their initial outbreak. Despite the absurdity and intensity of the situation, they were able to find common ground and settle into a more composed state.

Manav - "You say my idea of bravery is misplaced, be that as it may but your idea of belief is misplaced my friend. You're killing me only because you want to."

Mikhail – "SILENCE!! You dare question my belief? Do you have any idea how much I have sacrificed? An ignorant fool like you can never understand the diligence required to be a true believer."

Mikhail's response was so grim that it depressed the air inside the room, words that could quieten the most arrogant and ferocity that could puncture souls, However, Manav's resilience and unwavering determination proved to be unyielding in the face of Mikhail's grim response. Despite the oppressive atmosphere, Manav seemed to elicit a desire in Mikhail to release his fury, as if he understood how to thwart every onslaught that Mikhail could unleash. With unbridled intensity and a fire burning in his eyes, Manav retaliated, unleashing his own torrent of emotions. Holding nothing back, he poured out his frustrations and grievances, directing his words with laser-focused precision and emphasising with unwavering conviction. Manav's gaze locked onto Mikhail, unflinching, as he demanded answers and sought to pierce through any defences or barriers that stood in his way, while his cheeks displayed fine lines stretching over his cheeks like a wild cat, he says.

Manav – "Your sacrifices? .. Were all those your choices or forced upon you? What good are those sacrifices if they burden your soul?"

Mikhail became unresponsive, yet he maintained a proud stance, Manav continued with his interrogation.

Manav – "Who's the fool now, my friend?"

Mikhail kept his stand, and proudly he replied.

Mikhail – "I am proud of my sacrifices, and I am ready to sacrifice more for my deity. That is what I was taught and I will continue to believe in it until my last breath. At least I had the honour of illumination. What do you have? 'kafir'.

Just when Manav thought he had the psychological advantage over Mikhail, suddenly he was out of wits. He stopped for a moment and thought, “Mikhail never had the choice, but I had. What difference did it make? We both are puppets in our own world, more or less. Anyhow, it seems unwise to turn your last conversation into an argument." Manav took the first step to end the hostility between them.

Manav – “I apologise, you are right. I am in no position to comment on a life I never saw or lived. I admire that you are sure about your purpose, and I can see it now, why does that make your life better than mine."

Embarrassingly he pauses, and makes an awkward attempt to change the subject,

“May I ask for some water, Please?"

Mikhail was a bit astonished how Manav changed gears.

Mikhail – “I never took you for an ‘apologising’ kind. Did you hit your all-time-lowest for a glass of water?"

As ironic as it may sound but even in those moments of wickedness , like finding a nail in the haystack of negativity, they both find the comment amusing and chuckle for a bit. Mikhail pours some water directly into Manav’s mouth, Manav couldn’t keep balance and spills some water all over himself. Mikhail being the good samaritan, cleans and tidy him up.

Manav – “Would you believe? Today was the least amount of apologies I made. The one that I wasn’t planning to, but you got me. I guess there is a first time for everything."

Mikhail – “You’re right, first time for everything."

Then he remembers something,

“I need to go now; would you like some more water?"

Manav – “That would be great, but will you be back?"

Manav’s eyes could not hide his expectations, the deeper he looked into Mikhail’s eyes, the more presumptuous they appeared. It did not take much time for

Mikhail to figure out what Manav was hoping.

Mikhail – "I'm not sure, but I know that I have been here long enough for them to be suspicious and we definitely don't want that."

Manav – "I understand, in case I don't see you again, I Thank you from the bottom of my heart."

Mikhail just shook his head and gave him some more water. While he did that, As he drew nearer, the clarity of the situation became as apparent as crystal, intensifying as he locked eyes with Manav. In that precise instant, something extraordinary unfolded between them, an uncommon connection. Mikhail felt as though he wasn't merely gazing into Manav's eyes, but into the depths of his own soul. Peering into those innocent orbs, he detected a raw vulnerability concealed beneath the surface, with tears welling up and a valiant effort made to suppress their release, causing the ache but not to be seen. Mikhail was suddenly compelled to see through him and feel what Manav felt, It was as if he caught a glimpse of his own existence in a fleeting instant. Mikhail felt terribly sorry for Manav, as in his eyes, he could see Manav's failures and feats just as his own. Manav's vulnerability was painfully on display, however rather being uncomfortable with this experience, Mikhail felt privileged to have known someone so significantly for the first time in his life. Mikhail felt a bit estranged and alienated as this feeling of acceptance is only for countable moments. Not just Manav but Mikhail felt emotionally vulnerable too, he could feel that Manav could read him like a book, however he stood there with comfort, happy to have known and to be known. Unintentionally the whole situation resolves into both of them saying it together, "There's a first time for everything."

Mikhail – "In case we don't meet again, this was an honour. Thank you."

Mikhail changes his course, making a swift U-turn and retracing his steps. Throughout his journey back, Manav's watchful gaze remained fixed upon him, never wavering till he remained within Manav's line of sight, and when he couldn't see him any longer, he raised his head and pretended to have x-ray vision as he addressed the almighty, "Whichever one amongst you decided to take my life, I am not angry or sad anymore, you let me have this experience and I thank you. I have no more grudges, remorse or fear but a few apologies. I am ready and now I can leave this world peacefully. Hmm, so, it seems my life never belonged to me, but it was not a total waste after all. I have emptied all my second chances. But wait a minute!!! Why did I say, 'a few apologies'? what was I thinking, whom have I wronged? I was always at the receiving end, I do not owe an apology to anyone! on the contrary they should all line up, get on their knees, and beg for my forgiveness. All those who used me." Manav tried but his peace was compromised by something in his consciousness that he could not agree with. Probably the excessive blood loss plays a different game with the brain, though blood clotting helped tremendously but standing straight was not easy anymore, considering the innovative way they used to restrain Manav. Even so, he could not stop thinking about what he wasn't able to remember. After a few attempts he gave up and diverted his mind towards Mikhail, "Such a nice guy, he would have been miraculous to the society, perfect example of an 'Angel who switched sides'. I wonder what kind of life he lived, I should have asked more about my Guardian Angel. Poor guy seemed helpless and defenceless like me and unsure of his choices, a tad bit vulnerable emotionally. But the million-dollar question is what he had to pawn to trade sides."

*"Well, that doesn't seem to be an impartial question, we all have signed a deal with the devil at some point in our life. Those who claim they haven't are lying. Those cretins - lust, greed, and envy, each have their own method of infiltrating one's soul. Men Envy those who possess more luxuries and better women, and pretend not to be carrying a superiority complex; they never fail in luring others into it. I have wronged in my own measure, if not in action but in my thoughts. There were people I could have helped but my envy did not allow me to make them better, and those undeserving men I helped for the greed for something in return, for those lost causes I didn't even get a proper thanks. What was life all about, the only universal objective mankind ever had was wealth and power and more of it, a lot more of it. Money means happy life and respect, probably more important than love itself, even if people do not say it out loud but the fact is imprinted in everyone's mind that Money can buy everything. I could have bought my freedom if I only had met their demands, who would spend so much money on 'A Nobody' like me. When I die today, I will be just a number added to the 'Killed' or 'Murdered' list, they will not even say my name. I bet things would have been different had I been a politician or an actor, or a famous sports icon, they would have counter-*

*rotated the earth to bring me back from the dead. What a life!" ... In an empty room Manav smiles looking at the blank walls and false ceiling, his very own 'death-dome'. Something had changed though; he found it weird talking to himself now. He did not want to admit it but he wanted to see Mikhail one more time. Thoughts of Mikhail brought new conceptions in his mind "Have I not loved a single person in all my life? Why am I unable to recall any gestures of love? Why am I at ease welcoming death? this Is wrong, this is so wrong." He starts to panic; it seems unnatural to him that he never felt love from either side. He gave his best to remember everything about everyone, but the reflections were too many, he was unable to focus on anything significant or particular. "It appears the conclusion is I never cared about anything. From the first time when I was hit by realisations of my surroundings and the world, I just wanted to do my time and leave. So finally, I have arrived at the most significant moment in my life - The End. I want to shed a tear for someone I lost, I want to remember a moment that made my heart smile." He pushes himself so hard to remember that the veins of his forehead became visible, the blood rush started causing dizziness, when he could not take it anymore, he stops and focuses on his breathing, acknowledging the reality seemed to be the better choice. "So, what?" he says out loud. "The great Shakespeare said "All the world's a stage, all the men and women merely players"; "I played my part, I came with nothing, and am taking nothing, not even memories, I feel like I am done. At least I didn't have to go through infancy again, maybe this is my Absolution afterall."*

CHAPTER TWO

# RAIN

Manav was lost in concentration when he heard a familiar sound that alerted him of fast-approaching footsteps. Which means the terrorists are back for the culmination of all that was hatching. "Ok so that's it, my legacy is finally coming to an end." Bracing himself mentally for the impending assault, Manav's thoughts wandered to the duration and intensity of the pain, contemplating what awaited him in the afterlife. Yet, as he lifted his gaze, he was met with a heartening surprise - standing before him was none other than Mikhail. When he was back Mikhail appeared to be in a state of urgency, sweat cascading down his face. In a frantic manner, he began to speak quickly, his words stumbling from his lips "Your government called back, they have asked for an extension of the deadline." Manav did not know how to react to that, he was tiny bit shocked to learn that he is being regarded by those he thought were corrupt to the core and won't care if he lives or dies, however did not know if he should feel relieved or frustrated. "Hmm" Manav waits for a moment, "I'm assuming there is an 'and' or 'however' after that?"

Mikhail – "That was a tough guess but you are right, it's not a good sign for you, this could be a tactical approach to pin us down. They may as well be getting their snipers ready for surveillance. Our leaders have asked us to mobilise and spread out to every corner."

Manav looked clueless, "What the hell am I supposed to do?" If he had his arms untied, he would have opened them and asked.

Mikhail – "Do you want the short version or the detailed one?"

Manav – "Since I am busy stuck in between a gunfight that I have nothing to do with, short will be better."

Manav would have been proud of the superhot pinch of sarcasm he added.

Mikhail – "Short version is ... Stay where you are."

Mikhail gives Manav a taste of his own medicine and he smiles while assembling his rifle.

Manav could not help but show his agitation, there was too little information for him, but he knew that there was no point inquiring further. When have the higher authorities given clear information about anything ever? Even if the idea is as simple as to move a desk, they will write a whole essay full of things that do not matter, but the significant fact of the matter will still somehow remain unclear. "If things have come down to a Mexican Standoff, then probably Mikhail is right, and I am just a decoy." Annoyed with all the new events, Manav, in a displeasing voice says, "I'm hungry."

Mikhail's focus gets diverted from his weapon and a bit cluelessly he asks, "Oh! You want to eat?! ... right now?"

Manav sighs hopelessly and with a sarcastic smile he replies, "or you can just push open a window, I can fill my stomach with some air."

Mikhail had enough, with all the unforeseen and miscalculated events, he needed to come up with a new plan, however the circumstances have changed so many times and so frequently that he cannot keep up, with added sarcasm from Manav, his frustration crosses the limit.

Mikhail – "Will you shut up?" he shouts on top of his voice. "I will bring a bite for you, till that time just keep quiet and say some prayers with the little time you have left? Thanking the almighty might just add up some value to your life."

Manav yells back– "Thank God for what? The life I hate or the death I dread?"!

Manav's reply was so fierce that his voice echoed in the empty hall, and the word "dread" repeated till the echo faded away and nothing remained but a deadly silence, so much that their heavy breathing could be heard from any of the corners. After regaining his senses, Manav got a little embarrassed with his outbreak, he calmed himself and took a few cleansing breaths. "I will say a prayer, if it comforts you, I will say a prayer for you." Mikhail didn't move a muscle; he looked at him for a second and got busy preparing his gun. Manav waits a few minutes but still no response from Mikhail. The awkward silence became unbearable.

Manav – "I Apologise, I didn't mean to disrespect your faith...."

Manav had to stop as Mikhail interrupts him abruptly, "No need, now listen to me, all the complaints you have in mind about this world, it means you are one of the few left who haven't got comfortable with the wrongs in it and pretended that everything is perfect, you avoided bad choices and remained in your company, it doesn't mean loneliness, it means uniqueness and you chose it. Some chose wrong and some were helpless. Not all of us were lucky to have lived a life like you."

Describing Manav's emotional state as "shocked" would be a tremendous understatement. In light of Mikhail's words, just a few sentences managed to evoke within Manav a profound sense of joy and pride, surpassing any previous experience. "What 'Right' did I do? Am I hearing this correctly? Who is he? Does he know me?" Manav's mind became a swirling vortex of countless questions, each one giving rise to a multitude of branching inquiries. It was as if a never-ending web interwoven with cross-questionings, that had taken root in his thoughts, stretching into infinity. But Mikhail helped him fill in the blanks without letting him go through the pain.

Mikhail – "Don't be shocked, you did not tell me anything, neither did I try to find out about you, I have seen a lot of men die in front of me but none of them behaved like you. Every one of them tried to remember someone they loved, but you have been talking to yourself mostly, I could make out that you were alone and now you are sad about it. A dying man shows a lot of vulnerabilities, even when they try to be brave, you can feel their fear. Indifferent from them, you were mostly quizzed about death, almost as if you were welcoming it. Fear of death made you a man who looked into those butcher's eyes, you held back nothing. You were truly brave and fearless. I have never seen anyone die like you and trust me when I say this, I have seen enough."

Manav's puzzlement got even more complicated, the idea of dying soon wasn't as appealing as it was an hour earlier, he started to feel he had been neglecting a lot of positivity in his life. He was never proud of himself, mostly because his comparison of talents was based on the successes he saw elsewhere. Now it seems that all his appreciation was only for others and all the ingratitude only for himself.

Manav was experiencing a lot of remarkable and unthinkable sensations at this time, but not even his greatest imagination could have prepared him for what transpired next. Mikhail takes out a knife and takes it over Manav's head and almost whispering he says, "I know how this is going to end, there won't be any deals or truce, they are going to kill you anyway, do you want to die doing nothing or die with a chance to fight? You have a choice again in your life, but we don't have much time to decide."

Manav - "What are you talking about? how am I supposed to fight trained terrorists?"

Mikhail – "Today is your lucky day, they are trained but not highly. If you do just as I say, we just might have a chance, all of them are at their post and not together, this might just work for us. Now before you ask any more questions, do you want me to release you or not?

Manav was expressionless and unblinking but he was thinking "He's right, I'm going to die anyway. People outside are just stalling them, they are not planning a rescue mission for me and when have the terrorists fulfilled their end of the bargain??" His thought process was disturbed by the reflective light from the blade, it twinkled Manav's eyes, but rather than getting flinched, he responded in a relaxed tone.

"I hear you, I hear you, now shut up, just get me the hell out of these ropes. I sure hope I am in the easier parts of your plan."

As he was releasing Manav, Mikhail says – "Nothing is easy and there is no plan, but I have trained with them and I know their weaknesses and they know mine, we need to be very precise on every move. One of them has a faulty radio, so we get him first and get his weapons. This strategy favours the side having the guns and ammunition. We take their advantage and hope we don't get caught. We move swiftly and stealthily, employing the blade as much as we can. As I approach them, support me and be on the lookout, is that clear?"

Manav recalls a previous fantasy in which he got the impression that everything in his life had led him to this point and that perhaps this is it, die trying. Although he is pretty certain that he will die, perhaps he may not depart alone. This time, death seems fascinating. He quickly responded with a definitive "Yes,." His pursuit of this absurdity was not driven by adrenaline, but rather despair and a fear of being left alone. The realisation that he is just an ordinary man, lacking any distinctive expertise and merely conforming to societal expectations, intermittently dawns on Manav. These contemplations serve as a recurring reminder of his perceived insignificance in the grand scheme of things. He tries to cover up his anxiety with his ridiculous wit and comedy, but quickly recognises that he is not fooling anyone. They take soft, quiet steps to the next floor. Just before a stairway door, Mikhail stops Manav and asks him to remain there before giving him some brief instructions. "Now remember they are communicating on wireless, if you hear anything like a radio noise, it means you are very close to one of them. If you hear any sound, do not wait for me, hide. Keep your eyes and ears open" Manav nods but he was precarious, his heart was pounding out of his chest. Mikhail signals towards a room.

Mikhail – "One of them is in that room, but like I said they are trained, they can be only diverted for a few seconds and that might just be enough. We need those crucial seconds though. Once I go inside, take something a little heavy from that janitor's room, count till 100 and drop it right outside that room, remember, it should be heavy enough to startle a sound."

Manav nods and says – "and If you don't hear a sound till the count of 100 that would mean I'm in hiding and someone is close."

Mikhail found himself pleasantly surprised by Manav's spontaneous response and swift comprehension of the situation. It exceeded his expectations, leaving him impressed by Manav's ability to grasp things effortlessly, "Perhaps he trusts me now", Mikhail thinks for a second admiring Manav's courage and chuckles, which of course caught Manav's attention, he couldn't help but ask, "Bad plan? What's so funny?" With a warm smile Mikhail replies, "You are a quick learner, maybe after all destiny just might have a role to play, indeed."

They had no time to reflect or even bury their emotions, it was a moment to fight with what they had. After nodding and exchanging glances, they advance in harmony towards the same goal—Survival! Was all they had in their mind. Manav moves towards Janitor's room crawling like a spider, and Mikhail heads towards the station where the first Terrorist was positioned. Before they set foot in, for a fraction of a second they look at each other from a distance, As if signalling the commencement of a countdown, the ticking clock serves as a reminder that only time would reveal the outcome of their initial plan. The unknown future awaited, and the unfolding events would determine what lay at its end. Soon as Manav entered the damp and dark Janitor's room, he immediately began counting his breaths as instructed by Mikhail, while looking for something he can drop, but couldn't find anything suitable, either it was too long or difficult to carry, at this point he would have loved to find an escape route or a big safe to hide in till the madness was over. Manav's eyes catch the attention of a toolbox at a corner, he opens it up while trying not to make any sound, he finds some appliances like spanners and a hammer. Without giving much thought he chooses the hammer as the tool to create the needed distraction. Even in all the rush he did not lose the count and when it finally reached 100, realisation sunk in for him, that was the moment, he gave a few quick but deep, final reflections on the chosen tool. Once he was able to convince himself he made his way out of the janitor room but a sound coming through the corridor alarmed him. As he focused on the sound intently, his blood evaporated, heart started beating faster than his chest could cage. His tongue loses its moisture, his body froze instantaneously. He tried to verify that those noises he heard were actually footsteps getting closer and louder rather than his dread playing tricks on him. "Perhaps it was all a stupid plan, I should have just stayed there and waited for them to kill me, I have made it worse." As the footsteps come closer, he prepares himself for a fight The door opens and with all the might and vexation of his weakness, Manav steps up to attack, however,to his relief, it was the only person he wanted to see, it was Mikhail. The relief was nothing less than a breath of life. Mikhail enters and is out of breath.

Mikhail – "We have a problem." He whispers.

Mikhail was expecting Manav to get worried however to his surprise he patted him and asked him to sit down on the floor. "What is it?" Manav asks.

Mikhail - "There are two of them, Hafeez is here with Assad. We need to change our plan."

Manav - "Okay, what do you have in mind?"

Mikhail – "Let me think... I cannot take them both out, either we have to wait for Hafeez to leave and then take Assad out or we both attack now." He looks into Manav's eyes and asks "Would you like to choose for us?"

Manav's Adam's apple bobbed. He was not in a condition to stand straight, let alone fight. Nervously he says. "Shouldn't we wait for him to leave?"

Mikhail – "Let's be quiet then, he is here to check on Assad. He should leave soon."

Manav obeys, however he keeps his eyes glued on Mikhail as if he wants to say something but unable to bridge a sentence. They sit on the floor waiting to hear footsteps passing by. It was a very long wait and Manav couldn't resist breaking the uncomforting silence.

"There's no better way to prove the theory of relativity."

Mikhail – "How do you mean?"

Manav – "Hardly five minutes I waited here, but those five minutes were so discomforting, I can feel parts of my body feeling pain and numbness, I'm sweating so bad and my only wish is to see the time run faster, much faster. These five minutes would have been over in a flash, had I been somewhere else. It is like in the movie 'Interstellar', "An hour here is 7 years on Earth."

Manav smiles on his joke but then realises Mikhail did not get it, he had a blank face.

Manav – "Do you guys watch movies?"

Mikhail – "No, but I know relativity."

Manav – "Then you know what I mean."

They continue their soft whispered conversation. Mikhail still looks blank and seems not so positive as he was before. There are a million notions and reasoning processes running through his mind and time and again he looks at Manav for comfort and expecting something miraculous.

Mikhail – “Let’s stay focussed, Perhaps the duration of challenging circumstances tends to surpass our expectations, allowing us ample time to glean valuable lessons from those very experiences."

Mikhail has been avoiding eye contact, which keeps Manav wondering if something was wrong. He could not help asking,

Manav – “You look worried, till now you weren’t, are you beginning to think it was all a bad idea?"

Mikhail looks at him apologetically; he looks so red, as if Manav touched his most vulnerable nerve. Manav can see a man just on the brink of collapsing to his breaking point and erupt full of tears.

Mikhail – “There’s no going back from here. I am afraid we did not have enough time to think it through. If they find us together, they will kill us anyway. Hafeez is the best of us, everyone adores him like a mentor. He was the last one on my list. Once there is nobody to protect him, might give us a chance. He is hard to kill. Trying to survive is the only way now."

Manav – “Then why do we have to kill them, can’t we just find a route to escape, I know this place, I can find a way out."

Mikhail – “They have covered all exits. We came prepared. The only way is to go through them or hide somewhere till it is over. But hiding has its cons. It is just a matter of time until they find out you’re gone and Hafeez for what he is, will soon figure out when he doesn’t find me at my post. For the vicious man he is, I will not be surprised if he burns down the whole building to find a traitor."

Manav tries to lighten the mood. “Well, that’s too bad, I was hoping to hold a gun after you kill Assad."

Mikhail – “Hopefully you shall, it’s not that difficult. Difficulty is in facing what happens after you use them."

Manav – “Tell me about it, is it troubling to kill a bad person?"

Mikhail tries to understand his question and pauses for a moment, he looks down, while he replies calmly. Manav’s question evoked memories from Mikhail’s past that he had long tried to suppress. The familiarity of the query served as a stark reminder that there was no evading the probing nature of the question, compelling Mikhail to confront and acknowledge his past.

Mikhail – “When you’re the last person they’ve encountered, the victim always looks right in your eyes. You feel naked. The helplessness in their eyes shout out how you exploited their weakness. At times you feel you won but at times the pride of your prowess seems fake, that happens when you kill someone who didn’t deserve to die." He raises his hand and touches Manav’s shoulder. “That’s why I couldn’t see you die; I can’t bear that look anymore. The realisation that you’re the last person the victim saw before leaving this world, is unbearable, and I was ordered to kill you."

Manav – “How many have you killed?" Manav asks curiously.

Mikhail – “I’d rather not say, they are not just numbers for me, but I have killed enough poor souls who had a dying wish to see their family again when all of it was over, a pointless hope that they may survive. I never saw that in you, you were scared but you never let that fear control you. Why were you acting like you have faced worse?"

Suddenly, without a warning, Manav reaches over and covers Mikhail’s mouth with his hands signalling him to be quiet. Then he whispers.

Manav – "They're coming."

Mikhail whispers back – "I hear only one pair of boots."

The tension was so intense that they even ignored their necessity to breathe, worried that their exhaling could alert the terrorist, they focused their hearing to each footstep which sounded like it was coming closer, almost in front of their door but thankfully it passed on until they couldn't hear it anymore. After waiting for a few minutes.

Mikhail – "That might be Hafeez leaving."

Manav – "All that patience paid after all. What's the plan now."

Mikhail – "Same as it was before, but this time count only till 25. He would not anticipate anything unexpected. That surprise may work for us."

Manav's confidence was not at par, in fact he was so nervous that all he wanted was to make a run for it and see how it goes. For a moment he conspires in his mind to find another way out once Mikhail leaves, however, in such an unreliable situation where his life or death was hanging on one wrong decision, he decides if he really has to die, he won't die disloyal.

Manav nods his head and says, "I'll be ready, good luck!"

Mikhail goes again, following a plan that is so outrageous that even someone as trained as him is as unsure and nervous as Manav. These are the kind of situations when the mind narrows down itself so much that even the obvious escape route goes unnoticed and the mind has the tendency to fall prey to illusions; however, luckily for Mikhail,all his training came back hitting his senses all at once and somehow, he managed to select the most helpful. He decided to make no decision, and follow his trained protocols of the hunt.

He takes a deep breath and walks back towards the door, behind which his first obstacle stands.

CHAPTER THREE

# DESERT STORM

After Mikhail went in, it was Manav's act now. In the hopes that Hafeez or someone else won't take a stroll in the hallway during his portion of the plan, he begins counting while squeezing the wrench in his hands. His eyes widen as he concludes counting and becomes aware of what he needs to do. Slowly he crawls towards the door one step at a time, he removes his shoes ensuring his footsteps are unheard. His body goes cold, he shivers from every inch of it, the exhaled breath gets stuck just around his tonsils, his body's response is a big "NO" to everything right now, However, beating all his 'escape thoughts' and disregarding all the obstacles in his mind, he finally brings himself right outside the door. He stands straight, holds the spanner high in his hand and releases it, then flees back to his hiding spot like a startled cat. Manav does not even care to look back, he goes back into the janitor's room and hides in a dark corner, lucky for him that only HE can hear his own heartbeat, else finding him would have been a child's play. He kept the door open, just enough for a little peek. Not long after, he noticed some movement, he saw a shadow expanding under the door on the other side, expanding further in perfect sync with the sound of footsteps it was making. There it was, a muzzle of a gun slowly pushing the door open, making a creaky, groaning sound in the quited hallway, the door opens momentarily but the gunman leaves right after however, it was enough to scare all the beliefs in Manav, he backs himself as if trying to get absorbed in the walls, restless and uncertain, cursing his luck "What now?' He holds the whim with his hands, sweating profusely. "Has he made his move? Does he need my help?" The infinite but obvious questions he was surrounded with were squeaking but also exploding in his brain. After a long wait of a few minutes, he gathers his courage to crawl back to the door and look outside. He didn't hear a thing and he wondered if there was any sound at all or if fear impaired his eyes and ears. He crawls towards the door that was not even a metre away from him. He gazes outside and sees no one, not a soul, not in the hallway or at the other door. He noticed that the door was partially open, but even if it wasn't, one could see the floor beneath the door that was entirely covered in blood become crimson. Overwhelmed with fear, Manav whimpered and instinctively covered his mouth with his trembling hands. Tears welled up in his eyes, threatening to spill forth, as he battled to suppress his surging emotions. The more he fought to hold them back, the more intensively they pressed against the confines of his emotional fortitude. In all the aggravation Manav tries to breathe as slowly as possible. He removes his shirt and lies down with his chest on the cold floor in an attempt to slow down his heart rate. He tries to make himself understand that nothing is in his control now and he has to act for his own deliverance, that too on his own, no more helping hands. As he gathers his senses back, he sits himself up and thinks for a moment, "Was it really Mikhail? I never saw what happened, let's take another look." He puts his shirt back on and slowly crawls back to the door but suddenly the Janitor room's door opens, horrifying the remaining life left in Manav, the dark room brightens up, making him vulnerable again. Out of instinctual fear, Manav drags himself back towards the wall even hoping to somehow pass through it. However, he quickly realises that all that distress was completely useless, to his most pleasant surprise, and with eyes wide open, he saw a familiar image, it was Mikhail.

Manav, still grappling to regain control of his breath, gasps desperately, akin to a wild animal caught in distress. His eyes remain wide and unyielding, unable to return to their normal size. The notion that the figure before him is truly Mikhail becomes incomprehensible, defying his belief. Soon after realising it, he sobs like a baby but very gently, and at lightning speed he gets up, covers his hands over Mikhail and hugs him. The gesture surprises Mikhail, he gets inside the room, closes the door and hugs him back. Manav keeps sobbing like a little child, resting his head over Mikhail's shoulder. He wanted to tell him a lot of things that happened while he was away, but he could not conjure a sentence, too many words trying to come out of his mouth at the same time. He hardly cares how ridiculous he looks right now, maybe because he feels safe. As Manav slows down on his cries and starts getting better, he notices an unusual reaction from Mikhail, he steps back to see that Mikhail is giggling over Manav. He observes that Mikhail is trying hard to control himself and is so much in laughter right now that he could not even balance his feet. Plan was still not to alert anyone however, He seemed to be enjoying immensely, very hard to figure out if he was laughing or crying. "What happened to the brave man I left here?"

He mocks Manav, still trying to control his laughter and holding his stomach. Settling down he says, "I apologise, I just couldn't control myself, you might agree it was pretty unfamiliar for both of us."

Manav just stands there with his hands crossed, does not say a word. Embarrassment was very clear on his face.

Mikhail – "You can relax, we're fine for now."

Manav was so embarrassed, in an effort to change the subject he asked, "What happened?"

Mikhail – "I covered his mouth with my left hand and used my right hand to slit his throat. Kept his mouth shut till he anguished to death." He explains with physical gestures and then Intensely looks at Manav and says, "but you did good, the distraction worked."

Manav takes a deep breath and sits down on the opposite side of Mikhail, they both have earned a few relaxing breaths, but just a few. Mikhail hasn't forgotten the challenges ahead, that have just become more exciting.

Though it was peaceful and quiet, the silence became deadly. The sound of the ticking watch, and the wind finding its way out of the tiny little holes of the door were not unheard.

Manav – "You make it sound so easy."

Mikhail – "Over a period of time, it becomes easier. Do you have anything in mind, or shall we plan what's next?"

Manav shakes his head but asks" What about the blood on the floor? Shouldn't we clean up?"

Mikhail – "No need, it won't make a difference anyway, moreover we don't have time. Now listen carefully, Hafeez came here to hand over his wireless to Asaad which means Hafeez can be anywhere right now."

Manav – "It also means we won't hear him coming."

Mikhail – "Precisely. Stay sharp and stay together, now let us move."

Mikhail leads the way towards the room where he kept Asaad's body. On the way Manav interrupts, "What's next?"

Mikhail - "We need to keep the wireless close and monitor their conversation."

As soon as they entered the room, they had to make sure they didn't step into Asaad's blood, there was very little room to step foot on. Mikhail starts frisking Asaad's lifeless body with his eyes still open even after death.

Manav - "Can you at least close his eyes, I feel sick."

Mikhail – "Then don't look don't you remember what the father of your nation taught you? See no Evil?"

Manav does not really appreciate Mikhail's continuous mocking, however he does not react as he knows how much pressure he is under. Mikhail takes out a small sharp looking knife and hands it over to Manav.

Mikhail - "From here on it will only get uglier, it's time to dust off your baggage of emotions and get real. Moving on we are going to need back up; I need my one hand free to keep my gun up for any unexpected threats. That is where you become useful. While I grab them with my free hand, stab the knife in their throat until you can't see the metal."

Even before Manav could make an image out of it, create another thought or even utter a word, in a firm voice Mikhail continued his instructions to ensure Manav's mind doesn't wander away from their ultimate goal, perhaps that was for the best and he already recognized his role as the 'Leader' in this plan.

"Do not think, do nothing except what I tell you. Focus on what we have in front of us. All we have to do is make our move one by one."

Manav nods his head nervously but acknowledges, "So who's next?"

Mikhail - "I don't know, but we need to set a trap wherever we can't use a distraction. We have to assume that they are not aware about us yet, no such topics conversed on the wireless so far. But it's just a matter of time." He then points towards a bottle of floor cleaner and a mop. "Grab those and come with me."

They headed towards the restroom, emptied the bottle and cleaned up the mop as much as they could, considering that being an office mop, they did a pretty fine job. Very carefully they went back to the hallway where Asaad's blood was spilled all over the floor. Mikhail uses the mop to soak up the blood and wrings it down in the empty bottle. There was no scarcity of blood, the bottle was filled in a few attempts. Mikhail and Manav then grab everything they can from Asaad and swiftly but very quietly move towards the next post at the office reception that covers the main entrance.

Mikhail - "That is an important post, there could be two. As far as I know Hafeez, he must have kept Anees or Ilyas."

Manav – "Why's that?"

Mikhail – "Because they are the most ruthless of the lot. Unconcerned of crossing any limits of violence. An area that wide open, needs a big gun and big balls to handle threats of that size."

Mikhail does not cease to surprise Manav with each new information bigger, more powerful and dangerous than before. Just when his mind and body start getting used to the current threat, another more menacing and vicious obstacle fabricates. He imagines "What could be bigger than this super heavy gun with bullets the size of my middle finger?"

Manav – “What could be bigger than your gun, a Bazooka?"

Mikhail – “I wish, at least there was a chance with a Bazooka, it has a sloppy aim and takes time to reload."

Manav appeared to have given up all hope, dying the earlier way while he was roped, seemed easier now, than dying while trying to survive. It was depressing to see Mikhail exerting every effort to keep them alive while Manav acted as a clueless spectator. After a while he had enough and stopped Mikhail.

Manav – “Can I be honest, there is a lot going on that I don’t have the ability to understand and I am starting to feel light-headed, can we hide somewhere and rest for a few minutes?"

Mikhail looks Manav right in his eyes and observes him from top to bottom, He can see it is not the fear that’s troubling Manav. He is just irritated because he feels useless. He is a man of action and he doesn’t want to die without doing something about it. He wants to engage but Mikhail feels it could be premature as it is not the right time yet and Manav knows that in his heart too. Mikhail calmly replies.

Mikhail - “Of course, let’s find a hideout."

Manav quickly responds – “I know a place, follow me."

Suddenly there was a change in the air as he finally got to be a part of what he wanted to be a part of. Manav led the way and it appeared that he was regaining his confidence, which brought a cheeky little smile on Mikhail’s face.

Mikhail – “Okay, stay in front but if you hear any sound hide, if you see someone just duck, I have to shoot before they shoot at us."

Manav – “Understood."

They move through the hallways with extreme caution, making sure they don't make any noise and carefully survey their surroundings before moving further. They move through many offices and hallways, one at a time, waiting at each corner and listening for any sound that might warn them. They are fully aware that luck is not on their side and that the only way out is to leave no room for error. Manav halts at a big floor with about a hundred vacant seats. Mikhail finds it foolish, they can be seen from any direction and there are no places to hide. Being there does not make any sense to him, if the idea is to hide, that was the worst place, those cubicles cannot stop an air gun shot. How will they armour against military-grade-steel-piercing bullets? He was apprehensive.

Mikhail – "Are you sure about this place, it doesn't look safe, we can be seen and shot from any direction."

Manav – "We are not there yet."

Then he turns around to a door with access control and number pad. He takes his knife and starts detaching them from the wall.

Mikhail –"What difference does it make, there is no electricity, Tactical team has already cut down electricity and communication lines."

Manav –"Exactly, but these have battery backups which activates automatically if there is a fire alarm."

Mikhail – "But there's no fire, and if you break down one, that won't be wise for us, it will become easier for them to locate us."

Manav – "Don't worry I'm not actually starting a fire just fooling this door that there is one. The software of the touchpad has a minor flaw, when the battery overheats, the door lock determines there is a fire, and without electricity there is no other way to validate if it was a false alarm or not, it demagnetizes itself." Manav takes the lighter and puts it near the battery while Mikhail circles the surroundings, right about a minute later, the door opens. "After you, welcome to the server room."

Manav shows Mikhail in with a smile and cheeky pride. Then he puts the locks back, making sure no breadcrumbs are left to be noticed.

Manav – "Don't you feel lucky? I was about to update the software patches before your men caught me."

Mikhail – "mmm just a little bit, but we're still inside a room with glass walls."

Manav takes him on the raised floor and picks up one of the flooring, Mikhail is utterly astonished when a metal ladder was revealed to him when the 'seemingly' trap door was opened, not more than a square foot wide, going down to another chamber. Very carefully they descended to the chamber underneath the false floor.

Mikhail – "What is this place?"

Manav –"A separate backup generator just for the servers, certain companies do that to ensure servers are accessible even when the power is out."

Mikhail –"Ok now I'm impressed, and I do feel lucky. Is there a way you can contact people outside, any communication devices?"

Manav –"I'm sorry no, just some old fashioned generators, we can use the servers, but that might leave us in the open."

Mikhail –"Then I guess we can plan our next move while we picnic here for a while." He says with a smile.

Manav –"Good idea, I'll order us some pizzas."

For a brief moment, they both inconspicuously giggle in tandem, feeling like the ideal depiction of two young males. Although they are hesitant to accept it yet, they are aware of the closeness that has developed between them despite their difficult circumstances. It's like there's an elephant in the room, but it's a kind, gentle, and benign elephant. No vocal confirmation was necessary whenever they glanced at each other, they conferred the truth.

Mikhail –"I'm really sorry you had to go through all this, you seem like a good man."

Manav –"I feel the same about you."

They shook hands.

Manav –"So what is our next move?"

Mikhail –"You sure you're ready."

Manav –"I will never be ready, but I get that we are in a "do or die, now or never" sort of situation, and I have one choice, follow you and try not to die while trying."

Mikhail –"That's a good realisation, take your time." Then he hands over a pistol to Manav. "Make yourself acquainted with your new friend, it's not that difficult to use, just point and pull."

Manav takes a good look at the gun and accepts it very slowly, he explores the gun and tries to get a feel of it. He observes the label, the switch, the trigger, the nozzle and the weight.

Manav –"Is this good enough against the big guns at the reception?"

Mikhail laughs– "Ha Ha Ha, not even remotely, but we are not going against the guns, we are going against the men. We must make them lose focus, distract and then attack. I'll engage them into a conversation so that you can make your move."

Manav –"You make it sound so easy; We'll get to the part where you said, 'make my move' but before that tell me something, would a distraction be enough?"

Mikhail –"It always is, that's what we do, and it always works no matter which country we've been sent to."

Manav – "I think you do more than just a 'distraction', I didn't want to go there but your 'distractions' have cost a lot of innocent lives."

Mikhail does not react; he takes a moment of silence and then passively responds.

Mikhail – "You're right. I should have been careful with my words.

Manav – "We have a lot of common and uncommon opinions."

Mikhail – "You are correct, though, the path I chose was a form of retaliation, but when I sacrificed those who had nothing to do with my goal, I came to naught. All I ever desired was to hurt those who had harmed me and my family but I never got to anyone. and now I don't even know who they are. Are they individuals, a group, a country or a religion? I have no idea. I wish I had the fortitude to reject those erroneous beliefs that reduced me to nothing more than a tool of distraction but when I watched you facing those men head-on, the men who could harm you, something flared up in me. I can't express how sorry I am for what I did, but if protecting you is the only good I can do in this life, IT WILL BE DONE."

Manav was clueless, he felt a bit awkward for himself, he was unable to gather a proper response to show his appreciation, in fact Mikhail's words made him so nervous that the only response he could put together was based on humour, rather a self-defense. He just shakes his head with acknowledgement and says.

Manav – "That's a good speech but tell me, what if I miss the target?"

Mikhail – "Well, then let's hope that you missing your target creates a distraction, enough for me to take the shot. You seem ready. Yes?"

Manav – "On your lead, and please enough with the Military language."

Mikhail gives a few pointers about the pistol then they ascend, picking up the false ceiling enough to discreetly check if anyone is outside. After making sure it's clear, they head towards their next obstacle – The reception.

There were five ways to reach the reception. Three from the inside and two from outside - the lift and the stairway. Mikhail's best guess was that the AA-52 gun must be pointed towards the lift and stairway. He planned to enter the reception by one of the back doors, divert their attention, and then let Manav perform the tricks. Was it a long shot? Of course it was but when sands of time and life are slipping through your fingers, the mind tends to rely on the easiest options. 'Everything that sounds simple is typically too good to be true', the thought might have occurred to Manav but the inter-trust between them demanded them both to deliver. They appear a lot more easygoing than they were earlier, almost as if they have begun to relish the challenges. The biggest challenge in front of them, though, was slipping between the glass walls unseen. Modern offices are not the best venues for such an intense game of hide and seek. They eventually locate an area where they can stealthily observe the reception, but since it is still too far away or suboptimal for Manav to take a clear shot, they were faced with choosing whether to split up.

Mikhail – "This is it; this is the closest we can be right now. I will alert him of my arrival on the wireless, then try to divert him. You might not be able to get a clear shot at first so take your time and wait for the perfect moment. I'll try to give you a signal if possible but do not depend on it, trust your instincts and remember the plan."

Manav just nods and says, "Be safe."

Mikhail – "You too, be aware of your surroundings, do not depend on your eyes and ears completely."

Unsure if their strategy will succeed, they part ways, gesturing to each other goodbye, in other words unsure if they will see each other again. Mikhail leaves Manav and on his way to the reception he notifies on the wireless about his arrival. Until Mikhail arrived at the reception, Manav didn't let go of him, his puppy eyes were already missing Mikhail. He pushes aside his feelings and softly crawls on his hands and knees like a predator getting ready to strike. He analyses every position to get the best shot but second guesses every position. His mind constantly plays tricks on him into reasoning whether he was nervous or over-confident about all of it, but he held on to Mikhail's advice to follow his instincts which were truly beneficial, he hardly lost control.

Mikhail has already reached the reception and can be seen having a conversation with the terrorist posted there. Manav tries different angles crawling from one position to another, still analysing his shot. It was obvious that Mikhail cannot be there for too long since he has already broadcasted his position, there was room for everyone to wonder why he left his post unattended. Although it won't matter much in a few minutes when all of the cold-blooded murderers will be alerted after the sound of gunfire is heard throughout the entire building.

Just beside a cubicle Manav finds a good spot from where he can see the terrorist clearly enough to take the shot, when he pays attention, he remembers him. This was the one who mauled him pretty bad and hit him on his head with his gun. “Oh! I wish I could beat the crap out of him first, but since I am in a good mood today, I’ll make it quick." He looks around, evaluating if that is the best position he can be at and finally comes to a decision. He reckons a safe place and makes his move; he raises the pistol and very discreetly takes the aim. The Terrorist seems to be totally engaged in conversation with Mikhail, and Manav had his aim locked on at the Terrorist, he could not be more ready, all he had to do now was pull the trigger however just when he was about to, he notices Mikhail’s finger around the reception table signalling him to abort. Briefly paralyzed by the overwhelming surge of emotions and disbelief, Manav found himself immobilised, grappling with uncertainty and unsure of what he should do next.

A moment of "misfortune" can completely change the course of events, and that is exactly what happened when Ilyas saw movement in his peripheral vision and quickly turned towards something that was just starting to acquire momentum. Alas all the plan went into ruins, the stealth, the hunt, everything started falling apart in front of their eyes. Ilyas saw Manav completely exposed pointing a gun at him. That glare from Ilyas pierced through Manav’s courageous heart. If earlier Manav was frozen, now he was shivering like a sculpture during an earthquake. Ilyas moves to grab his AA-52 gun, which by the way as per Mikhail could puncture metal, that was now pointed at the shivering flesh and bones of Manav. All these events occur so fast within the cardboard cubicles that may as well be similar to paper in front of the gun Ilyas was holding, Manav decides to close his eyes, fully convinced that he cannot cheat death anymore. As soon as he shuts his eyes, a gunshot was heard but Manav did not feel anything, “did he miss?" Out of obvious and uncontrollable curiosity, he opens his eyes only to see Ilyas's lifeless body on the floor and Mikhail struggling with another Terrorist, possibly Anees. Mikhail was able to neutralise Ilyas but it was still not over. "Oh that is why he signalled me to abort." Anees was wrestling his way through to take aim on Mikhail and Mikhail was using all his power to keep the barrel of the gun out of his face. All of this stops as they hear another gunshot and Mikhail's face gets showered with blood and other things from what was left of Anees's head. Mikhail wipes his face and carefully opens his eyes, with all his training and experience, it did not take long to get back to his senses. However, as he caught sight of Manav, who remained frozen in the same position as when Ilyas had first spotted him, it took a moment for the realisation of what had just transpired to sink in. It was a perfect shot, as indicated by the smoke billowing out of Manav's gun. "How much of that shot was Pure Luck?" But there's no time to recon, both gunshots were heard from every corner or possibly even outside, Mikhail wipes the blood of his face just enough to be able to see, grabs the so called "big gun" and runs towards Manav who was still in the process of melting down from his frozen state. He grabs Manav by the arm and belligerently exclaims, "Come on! RUN"!

CHAPTER FOUR

# TYPHOON

The run for their life paces slowly however more their mind grabs cognizance, faster they go. All they know now is that their lives depend on reaching the only place they could find shelter – The Generator room. There was no need for a discussion; they were fully aware of where they needed to reach and as quickly as possible. Determination to stay alive distracts them completely from the wild conversation that had started taking place on the wireless radio. The remaining five terrorists had started communicating without breaking a single moment of silence, they had started coordinating a plan. When Mikhail and Manav finally stopped pacing themselves, they were shocked but unable to fathom when they found themselves looking into each other's eyes in the same generator room and shockingly they didn't even remember how and when they reached there. Not the digital lock, the server room or the ladder, they remember nothing. They seemed to regain consciousness, but it was still under processing. They held their stomachs as the breathing got harder and harder, there wasn't enough air in the server room for them to breathe. Their tongues were out, breathing heavily like a cheetah after a failed hunt on a fully-grown Impala. They grabbed everything they could put their hands on to balance their senses, they were covered in anxiety like a lamination. If only they could go up into the server room to cool themselves down, unlike the generator room which is blazing hot or perhaps it's just the adrenaline and blood rushing through their veins causing the lava effect. The wireless cannot catch a signal due to all the electronics and the covered basement. Succeeding a few minutes of silence helps them catch some air peacefully, their breathing now was in control. By now Mikhail and Manav are flat down on the floor staring at the ceiling. None of them wanted to speak the first words but Manav could not hold much longer.

Manav – "It's worse than seeing my own blood, it has a different odour. I can feel its taste in my mouth by just looking at it, is this how it feels?"

The taste wanted to get out his body, making him feel like vomiting however nothing got out and the unwelcome taste stayed.

Mikhail – "Every time, it feels the same way but we are taught to hold our emotions. Our duty is to only act, let me save you some time, you will never succeed forgetting about this."

Manav looks at him with eyes filled with tears. He cries and condemns the day that brought him to a point where he had to kill someone. He never could have imagined seeing so much blood spilling everywhere, drops of life completely destroyed. Wherever his eyes turned, he only saw red. Mikhail kept calling Manav's name, however Manav did not respond. His body and mind were still held back in time where he made his kill. Mikhail's voice kept getting louder; he held Manav still and at the top of his voice he called out to him again and delivered a bomb.

Mikhail – “MANAV... Listen to me... I don’t think we have any plans left.”

Manav’s jaw is still open because he cannot fathom there is no possible escape, even after the well played plan.

Manav – “What do you mean? So that’s it? We are stuck here?"

Mikhail – “Until they figure out, we are safe but not for long, no one is ever safe around Hafeez."

Manav didn’t care; he had already come to terms with his death. His one and only hope was to spend time with Mikhail and make memories. His final moments are suddenly his favourite times in his entire life, and all he wants to remember right now is everything Mikhail said or did for him. However, several unanswered facts continue to be a source of curiosity.

Manav – “You called yourself a “Distraction” when we were here last time. What did you mean by that?"

Mikhail sighs, they both know they are not going anywhere for now.

Mikhail – “Better get comfortable, this may take a while. From the day I made the first kill, I thought I was faking enough to show everyone that I am enjoying it but I could not fake it in front of one person – my father. I would see eye to eye with everyone even if I am feeling disgusted from the inside. I would laugh and celebrate our victories but every time I saw my father, I felt ashamed. My father was against sacrifices of innocent men, women or children, but the leaders were not pleased. Only reason they left my father alive was because of his expert intelligence. His plans have always been error proof, the leaders could not afford losing the best expert over their ego. They could not see any such talents in me. I had no choice but to kill or get killed, the worst part was that ‘regret’ and ‘remorse’ are forbidden emotions where I come from. You can only celebrate even if it is the death of one of our own."

Manav – "Sounds like your father is a brave man."

Mikhail – "He is much more than a father to me. He saved me, gave me hope. Taught me how to beat your enemy in their own game."

Manav – "Where is he now?"

Mikhail – "I only have a guess, that too is pretty vague. Nevertheless, I am where I knew one day I would be, but I hoped for more, to make a difference like my father." Mikhail gets a bit more comfortable and like a storyteller with a readable body language he continues. "After my fifth killing, when I got back home, he found me crying and holding my screams, I was not exactly a treat for the eyes. If I had seen someone like that, I would have either shot him or ran away as fast as I could. But my father sat beside me, then he put his hand over my shoulder and as I was beginning to calm down, he wrapped me around with his arms. I cried myself to sleep that day."

Manav – "We are still on the topic of "The Distraction", right.

Mikhail – "It's coming, have patience."

Manav – "Just making sure we are on the same page."

After taking a short pause, Mikhail continues.

"When I woke up in the middle of the night, my father was still with me and was awake. Perhaps making sure I was breathing... Anyway, I finally opened up to him and told him how much I hate myself for killing someone so young. I told him even if he had wronged, he had his whole life in front of him to put things together. I told him I'd rather die but make another killing, but to my surprise he didn't scold, advise or even interrupt my crying. He just sat there listening to me till I stopped and then he said, "I'm going to tell you something that may get us killed if anyone finds out about it, now I leave it up to you, do you want to know?"

Manav was all ears, listening carefully word by word.

Manav – "What did he tell you?"

Mikhail – "I don't remember much; I wasn't in the right mind to hear about some network within some of our organisations who keep records of collaboration with your world and mine."

Manav – "Distractions... Collaborations...my world... Ok!!"

Mikhail – "I know it's like a puzzle, I was on the verge of putting it together, that's when I was sent here. Now it makes sense, I mean not just Government authorities, organisations around the world, large corporate businesses... the untouchables, all using us for their greater purpose. It was hard for me to believe at first but don't tell me it doesn't ring a bell; you never had any questions creeping in your mind? Haven't you ever felt the reality has been orchestrated, designed for a specific outcome. Making you feel like winning even when you are losing."

Manav wass silent and spooked.

Mikhail – "I know you do; I saw that in your eyes. That was the same look I had. This world often conceals hidden motives and agendas, where everything is meticulously orchestrated for the benefit of certain individuals or groups at a specific time. Controlling what becomes popular or unpopular, what is saved or allowed to perish, every act of creation and destruction, all serving a master plan. Our role is to garner attention, ensuring the execution of this grand design encounters minimal resistance."

Manav had no reaction, even after hearing the most chilling information he had ever heard, he kept staring at the dark wall with tears flowing down his cheeks. He did not seem thrilled or puzzled. Mikhail, to his surprise, thought he might have caught Manav off-guard with something so conspiring to hear, a theory like that may have had Manav's brain flooding with questions, however, he was silent as rock. Mikhail didn't know how to respond, he asked Manav, "Are you doing alright?" Manav does not move a muscle, he keeps staring down the wall very calmly but a few seconds later he turns his face towards Mikhail.

Manav – "Do you know how long I have been debating with myself if taking my own life is justified? There are so many anti-suicidal motivations, and I have heard it so many times that taking your own life is somewhat a crime to humanity, especially to your loved ones. I established very early that I am a dead weight and not much of a good use for the people around me, therefore it's not really a crime, probably doing a favour, but I got stuck at one question, is suicide a cowardly act? But you have cleared the path for me Mikhail, I don't see killing myself as a cowardly act anymore but it's my choice."

A dismayed Mikhail looked down at Manav, stunned as one can be.

Mikhail – "From where did you get that inspiration? I don't understand, how did I clear your path to take your own life?"

Talking slow and low, Manav continues.

"I have seen enough of hopelessness and not just for myself. Everyone important lectures on how to make the world a better place while they keep all the power and resources for themselves. A few percent of the entire population own half of the world's wealth but it's still not enough for them. They would not mind firing thousands to add a little more extra to their wealth, and the same men preach that Money is not everything. Like viruses we have destroyed living beings, destroyed nature. So many species are extinct while the homo sapiens keep on expanding exponentially. Ironically, we are the only kind who believe that there is a creator who made all this for us, what a bunch of hypocrites we are. Do you think we will ever get over this, do you think the 'real' good or 'actual' necessity will ever be given importance? They will keep creating illusions for us to make us feel like we are in control. Once there were kings who made us worship them like they were gods, then those kings acted like our protectors and now the illusion of democracy, there is a new form of worship these days, we worship tycoons with power and money, We Ourselves Created The False Deities. Did we really choose the corrupt or was it like one day you woke up and someone had the power to turn your life upside down with least or no affect to themselves. Even if you have solid proof against any or all of them, still it won't change anything. One will fall and will be replaced by someone more systematically corrupt. What you said clarified my doubts Mikhail, I don't feel like a coward anymore for having suicidal thoughts, because I have always been disgusted for belonging to this destructful species. Towards the end, we are the ones who always lose."

He turns himself towards Mikhail, who is so disoriented, and doesn't really know where Manav is going with all this.

Manav - "Does that surprise you?"

Mikhail draws a wide smile looking at Manav, gets himself up and comes closer to Manav.

Mikhail - "This is altogether a different form of yours I am seeing, but all that talk about corruption reminds me of something someone once said, "Corruption is nature's way of restoring our faith in Democracy." Does THAT surprise you?"

It took a few seconds for Manav to realise the paradoxical humour in Mikhail's statement but when he did, they both looked into each other's eyes and an uncontrollable laughter puffs out of their mouth. They sit down on the floor holding their tummy, confident that their voices will not be heard outside the confined basement. Trying to settle down, Mikhail asks.

Mikhail – "What are we going to do, we can't stay here forever."

Manav – "I guess we can stay here as long as we want, it is the safest place in the building, unless your friends have the blueprints, they won't look for us here. Why don't we hold our ground? They are not going to remain in this building forever, even without food or water we should be able to survive at least for a day or two."

Mikhail – "I can but you can't. You have lost too much blood, more than food or water you need a doctor and medical care, you should be on a hospital bed right now, not in this hope we are hiding behind."

Manav – "I am not running anymore my friend, neither have the will to fight. I have already accepted my death, so I don't care much about it now but I hope you survive."

Mikhail – "Fighting alone seems boring, with you at least I had the chance to see the ice sculpture again."

By now they have become comfortable with each other's sarcastic humour.

Manav – "I tell you what. The only thing I was anticipating today was a flashback of my life, the events I don't recall, but that optimism now seems to be in vain. Why don't you share your father's story with me? Consider that as my dying wish, It was pleasant to hear about him."

Mikhail could see the fragility emanating from every aspect of Manav's being. Manav appeared feeble and unsteady, he looked weak and stumbling. His low-pitched voice, the slowing down of movement and painful grunts while making even minor adjustments. Drawing from his own experiences, Mikhail harboured a deep sense of certainty that Manav would not survive the night. He figured "So be it", I could not save him, at least I can make a dying man's wish come true.

Mikhail – "What would you like to know about him?"

Manav – "Anything, what do you always remember about him?"

Mikhail – "What can I say, everyone that I know idolises him. They have a nickname for my Father there, they call him Maktaba. His knowledge and attention to details have kept a lot of our men alive and helped them succeed. For the love towards his family, he kept on doing what he hates. He is someone who can sacrifice the whole world just to keep his own world."

Manav – "What's a Maktaba."

Mikhail – "it means Library."

Manav – "That seems like quite an honour."

Mikhail – "He had a deep desire to utilise his knowledge and skills for a purpose that truly mattered, to be driven by a meaningful mission. However, the weight of external pressures and potential consequences of deviating from prescribed orders loomed over him, there were constant threats towards the safety and well-being of our family. His aspirations and ability became more of a burden than a gift, limiting his ability to freely pursue what he truly believed in. As I reflect on the memories, it seems he had anticipated my forever absence after this mission. It all makes sense now."

Manav – "Why do you say that?"

Mikhail – "I wasn't paying attention then but now it all makes sense. The way he was talking, asking the same question repeatedly. I was ignoring him, I was being rude, but now I see what I could not see at that time, I failed to notice that his eyes were filled. I was angry at him for planning another attack and getting me involved but I am guessing he knew this time the plan won't be successful, he took this chance to keep me alive, but what about him?"

Lost in the depths of introspection, Mikhail retreated into the realm of deep thought. His mind delved into the intricacies of his circumstances, pondering the choices he had made and the path he found himself treading. Immersed in contemplation, he sought answers and clarity that seemed elusive in the complexity of his situation. Manav wanted to come near Mikhail and give him a hug.

"He was also talking about some website he created on the dark web, loading all the information he ever acquired, he gave me the address, but I guess I wasn't paying attention."

Manav – "Looks like he was onto something. What do you think he was planning? It seems too risky to sell out the wolves living amongst you."

Mikhail – "Maybe insurance, for him and his family. Well ... that doesn't seem to have worked out well."

Manav – "I'm sure he tried his best."

Mikhail nods in silence and they dwell in it for a few minutes.

Mikhail – "Doesn't necessarily mean his efforts failed, I probably might be the only one remaining alive from my family. And I am still here and at least we stalled their operations."

Manav – "Yeah! About that ... Something keeps bothering me and I can't help thinking if you and I missed something, something very important."

Mikhail – "Really? What's that?"

Manav – "If your father was so important for your so called 'planning commission', and since your organisation had already decided to take the golden goose out of the equation, don't you think his last plan would be more than just a 'distraction'? Why do I have a feeling that this could be much bigger than what you were informed about?"

Mikhail's jaw nearly dropped in astonishment, but he managed to catch himself, unable to comprehend how Manav had unveiled and grasped what had eluded Mikhail's understanding. A profound sense of disbelief washed over Mikhail as he struggled to accept the fact that Manav had deciphered what had remained an enigma to him. Right from the start, Mikhail had been grappling with unresolved puzzles, the mission details provided to him were vague, and their plans constantly underwent changes. The mysterious looks exchanged between them and their enigmatic conversations repetitively occupied Mikhail's mind, leaving him with the lingering question of what they were truly up to. The urge to unravel their true intentions became a persistent presence, driving his thoughts with curiosity and speculation. He tries to recall if there was anything he missed or overlooked, but it was not quite clear. If their plan was to wipe out his entire family. Is that their ultimate goal? did they come this far just to separate him and his father to execute their plan? All of these facts start to boil Mikhail's blood.

Mikhail – "What kind of a man has no regard for his own people? He does not deserve to live but he does not deserve an honourable death."

Though he did not have a family of his own, Manav could reflect what Mikhail was going through. The state of being in absolute rage and calm, the state of having endless thoughts of ferociousness but at the same time feeling helpless. However, Manav tried to bring Mikhail back to his senses because at the moment only better thoughts could help them get through.

Manav – "From what I understand, even killing them won't make them fall short, there will be more ready to take their place, devoted to the cause."

Mikhail – "You're not wrong, as long as they are backed up, they will keep coming. As long as they know that someone on this side is looking after them, they won't stop. That is what my father intended, pluck out their life support and they won't dare going out in the Sun again."

Manav – "If you're talking about exposing them, I don't think it works. There was a time when everyone hated it, then they started joking about it and now it is a part of life. They get used to it, no matter how big it is, you won't even get a reaction, not even conviction, nothing is going to change."

Mikhail – "Who said anything about exposing?"

Manav – "What else then, What's on your mind?"

Mikhail takes a moment to think and sighs.

Mikhail – "My father always said, "to make a plan work you must have three pillars, a protector, a deviator and a liar", in other words – Someone from the police, a lawyer and a politician. Someone from the police to protect you and keep you informed, the lawyer diverting all the attention from the truth, and a politician for... well... to do what they do best...Lie! All of them working together to create a perfect illusion of control.... Only way you can get rid of an illusion is by destroying it from the root."

Manav – "So more killing? Is there any other solution that does not involve more bloodshed? Shouldn't we let the people decide?"

Mikhail mustered a voice that resonated with conviction, one capable of penetrating the deepest recesses of one's heart, as he responded with a resolute and unwavering statement, "You'd wish."

Mikhail – "People don't fear anything as they fear death. They need to be reminded that they are not invincible."

Manav – "I have to agree with you on that, so coming back to where we are, and regarding the current situation, who is the Protector, deviator and the liar on this mission?"

Mikhail – "We are soldiers, we only get orders. If I must guess, Hafeez might know because he is the only one who has survived, in all the previous operations he is the only one who made it home."

Manav sighs - "just when the story was getting interesting, it reached a dead end."

Mikhail – "Sorry to disappoint."

They chuckle for a bit and then silence takes over, they both look at the floor and keep their eyes there.

Manav – "In any case, what if we kill the, so called "The three." Would it make any difference?"

Mikhail – "Like I said, death is the only thing people fear, that's the most common dread. They feel they are invincible until they are not. Make them face their vulnerabilities, once they know they are not gods anymore. Wealth and life is the only thing they fear of losing. Unless it is someone like you who has nothing to lose."

Manav – "That's not a compliment for me."

Mikhail – "One man's curse is another man's gift."

Manav – "I swear to you, if I ever make it out alive, I won't stop until I find those three."

Mikhail – "And ... what are you going to do about it?"

Manav – "I'm not a fan of killing people but like you said, they don't deserve an honourable death either, at least not a natural one. I can think of many ways right now to make them suffer but what's the point, if I become like them in front of them, they will have the last laugh, while welcoming into their world, not me."

It was a deep thought, but in bits and pieces Mikhail figured out what Manav was trying to convey.

Mikhail – "I'm glad you agree but when it comes to it, one has to be ready and act with whatever he has got."

There was a cloud of judgmental opinions swirling within their mind. While they yearned to be brave and stand firmly by their beliefs, they began to doubt their accuracy in the face of recent revelations. Uncertain if they possessed the confidence and courage to take a firm stand, both Manav and Mikhail found themselves lost in their own profound thoughts, contemplating the paths that lay before them. Hoping several possibilities - maybe the rest of the terrorists might get killed in a crossfire, maybe they will be found and rescued. Amidst the conundrum of their current situation, Manav and Mikhail acknowledged the limitations of their hidden location in the basement, cut off from any form of coverage or communication. The resounding question echoed: how could they make their way to the surface? The apprehensions of potential adversaries waiting for them intensified the perceived risk. Nevertheless, driven by an underlying need, Mikhail harboured a pressing inquiry to pose to Manav, adding another layer to their complex predicament.

Mikhail – "About your aiming skills, as good of a shot that it was, I noticed you froze before you shot Anees, we were lucky he was directly in your line, else things could have turned in any direction."

Manav was a little embarrassed, all this time he was under the impression that Mikhail did not notice.

Manav – “I was hoping you wouldn’t notice."

Mikhail – “It was tough to disregard but I am not your teacher to give you feedback, just sharing something that I learnt during my training, it might help you face your fears next time. If there is a next time."

Out of the blue an interesting topic, after all everyone is one way or another scared of something and constantly on the lookout for a solution even if they are not permanent. Manav was no different. He got so interested that he got into a sitting position like a little pupil, and his eyes and ears all towards Mikhail.

Mikhail – “When you see something that scares you, it’s better you face it than trying to convince yourself that somehow you can avoid it, you may be able to avoid it any number of times, but you have to get rid of it just once. Let it come to you, face it, do not look away even if you are scared. If their job is to scare you, it’s up to you whether you make their job tougher or easier."

Manav – “Face your irrational fear? easier to say but a really thoughtful idea; I’ll bear it in mind."

Mikhail – “I know it is easier said than done but I surely know it can be done. Facing your fear is a one time solution – work it, and keep working till you stop thinking about it, because even though you’re avoiding it, it never leaves you. Just as you can’t stop thinking about Anees, can you? Fathom, that part is over."

Manav’s gaze lowered as he shook his head, a mixture of a smile and embarrassment gracing his face. Little did they know, their situation was about to take an unexpected turn. Unforeseen disaster loomed on the horizon, descending upon them far sooner than both Manav and Mikhail had anticipated. In an instant, Mikhail's training kicks in, honing his instincts and sharpening his senses. A series of metallic noises from above jolt his attention, triggering an immediate realisation of the source. His eyes widened, a surge of adrenaline coursing through his veins. With swift urgency, he lunges towards Manav, his voice piercing the air as he lets out a piercing scream, a desperate warning of imminent danger- "Get Down"!!! Confusion engulfs Manav as Mikhail forcefully wrestles him to the ground, the intensity of the situation was overwhelming. They crash onto the floor, with Mikhail selflessly shielding Manav with his own body. In an instant, a deafening blast shatters their senses, obliterating their perceptions and sending shockwaves through their bodies. In the minuscule fraction of a nanosecond, time seems to stretch agonisingly slow for Manav. Amidst the chaos and the chaotic explosion, he catches sight of Mikhail urgently signalling to him about an imminent threat looming above them. Despite the distorted perception of time, this crucial moment unfolds quickly, leading Manav to comprehend the gravity of the situation at hand. Manav's gaze is drawn upwards towards the source, but before his mind can fully process the unfolding events, he is met with a terrifying sight—a billowing cloud of fire that erupts from the centre was rapidly expanding in all directions, in a circle. The impact of the shockwave, though invisible, is immense, akin to an overpowering force pressing them down onto the floor as if a gigantic hand were bullying and subduing them. As the deafening explosion continues to reverberate through the air, an ongoing, high-pitched ultrasonic whistle pierces Manav and Mikhail's ears, drowning out all other sounds. This relentless whirling noise renders them unable to hear even the faintest words uttered inches away from each other.

They find themselves enveloped in a disorienting world of overwhelming sensory chaos. Amidst the haze of dust and debris that engulfs their surroundings, Manav and Mikhail's vision was obscured, rendering them unable to discern any distinguishable shapes or objects. They found themselves covered in a chaotic mix of broken and unbroken bricks, along with powdered metal, struggling to free themselves from the entanglement. The sheer force of the explosion had left their minds reeling, enveloped in a state of shock that makes coherent thought difficult to grasp. As the dust begins to settle, the faint sound of approaching footsteps reaches Manav and Mikhail's ears. Their senses heightened by the imminent danger, they are acutely aware of the impending events about to unfold. A deep sense of trepidation grips them, as they brace themselves for what lies ahead, their minds attuned to every minute detail in the surrounding silence. Despite their exhaustion and disorientation, Manav and Mikhail muster their remaining strength and scramble through the dust-filled air, desperately searching for anything that might serve as a means of defence. Their hands anxiously sweep through the debris, grasping for anything that could potentially aid their survival. In this dire situation, their instincts drive them to find even the faintest glimmer of hope amidst the chaos. Through the hazy aftermath, Mikhail's keen eyes discern his guns strewn in a corner, calling out to him as a potential source of defence. Summoning every ounce of strength left in his weary body, he drags himself towards the weapons, determination fuelling his desperate crawl. However, despite his resolve, exhaustion takes its toll, leaving him just short of reaching his coveted firearms. The limits of his physical capabilities become painfully apparent, presenting a formidable obstacle in his path to obtain the means of protection they desperately need. Despite the sluggish pace of his movements, Hafeez manages to reach the guns before Mikhail can cover even half the distance. With a cruel and mocking entrance, the spectre of death looms ominously before the two desperate souls clinging to a flicker of hope for survival. The presence of mortality, in all its chilling certainty, casts a shadow over their determined yet faltering spirits. Mikhail's outstretched hand, mere inches away from his goal, is abruptly halted and forcefully pressed into the ground by the weight of Hafeez's boot. The excruciating pain surges through Mikhail's body.

"It was just a matter of time, revelation of traitor's blood."

As the figure responsible for the turmoil before them made himself known, it became apparent that it was the same voice that had shattered Manav's once-proud demeanour. Its tone held a wicked cruelty, yet paradoxically retained an air of unsettling serenity akin to that of a saint. In stark contrast to the other men exuding an air of brutality, Hafeez stood apart. Mikhail's prior warnings about him, the very man they now faced, held weight. While his presence captured attention, it was not due to any savage demeanour. Instead, Hafeez emanated an aura of elegance that drew eyes towards him instinctively. It was a magnetism born of refinement and sophistication, setting him apart amidst the chaos and unleashing an undeniable allure that commanded attention. Hafeez possessed a perfectly measured stride that had a sense of balance and poise, distinguishing him from the other terrorists present. Despite his attire consisting of inexpensive garments, every fold and crease was meticulously ironed, lending an air of care and attention to detail. His refined elegance against a backdrop of chaos further accentuated his enigmatic presence, leaving an indelible impression on those who laid eyes upon him. As the man introduced as Tabib, Hafeez maintained his unwavering tone while speaking, adding a layer of unsettling intrigue to his already mysterious aura. His smile, simultaneously alluring and disconcerting, possessed the ability to mesmerise and unnerve in equal measure. During their earlier encounter, Hafeez had successfully exposed a vulnerability in Manav's confidence. However, now, after hearing his stories, that vulnerability seemed even more evident, Hafeez's demeanour amplified to appear even scarier and more menacing. The realisation of the extent of Hafeez's power and ruthlessness added an extra layer of fear and unease to the already tense atmosphere.

As he strolls through the room, checking all the machinery, the others join Hafeez in a conversation about what to do with Manav and Mikhail. He gently orders to drag them both above because he has plans for them. The remaining terrorists grab their hands and drag them obstinately across the stairs, metal, and bricks, disregarding their injuries. With only a few ounces of life left in them, Manav and Mikhail were unable to sit straight even with the support of a wall behind their backs, they fell over so many times drifting blood stains on the wall. At last, the terrorists got frustrated and left them lying down on their back. Hafeez who was missing for a few minutes comes back with a medium size suitcase in his hand, keeps it on a desk, opens it up. The bag was full of tools that an average person does not see every day. He begins to rub those tools with a delicate, clean piece of cloth, their surfaces glittered like crystal. Only Hafeez knew what plans were convoluted in his mind, he took instructions only from within himself. His facial expressions occasionally change as he talks to himself and expresses dissatisfaction as well as agreement. The changes are so frequent, that within a matter of minutes he can mimic all the emotions known to man, not once he took his eyes from Mikhail and Manav.

Hafeez – “"Somebody say something please, this silence is killing me," Hafeez remarks with a sly smile. "Indeed, I had intended for a private encounter, but it seems our dear Mikhail had different plans. However, as fate would have it, we are all here now." Hafeez’s voice carries a hint of anticipation, his eyes gleaming with an undeniable excitement. "I must admit, I have never felt this exhilarated before. The presence of such interesting individuals like yourselves has ignited a fire within me. Now, let us proceed and make this encounter truly unforgettable.”

With a cruel and confident smile yet with eyes that can see through a man. Manav and even Mikhail were terrified, Mikhail had seen him like this before, however always in the line of sight, not when Mikhail had to look up to make an eye contact, which enhanced the fear. They wanted to look away but the fear of uncertainty of what was going on Hafeez’s wicked mind, kept their focus on him. Unable to move, not only their eyes but any part of their body they finally give up and realise there is no going back, there is no escape when facing the odds of two against six determined and trained murderers.

Hafeez takes out a sharp tool, which obviously wasn’t bought from a shop. They say Hafeez has his tools specially forged according to his barbaric needs. He brings the scalpel closer to Mikhail’s face.

Hafeez - “I want you to know how I had imagined this day, I expected to see your father lying beside you, not this aper. But his time will come."

Using the scalpel he slashes Mikhail's face from forehead through his cheeks to his chin.

Hafeez - "I will tell him everything that I am going to do to you. I will tell him how you squealed and how you begged for a quick death, and the same will happen to him, I can assure you of that. By the way, I wanted to ask you both, how does it feel to be finally caught for your treason?"

Mikhail takes a deep breath, adjusts his almost lifeless body and replies.

Mikhail - "I don't know, you tell me."

Ferociously but controlled, Hafeez pushes the scalpel under Mikhail's chin and says.

Hafeez – "Let's not play this game anymore, let's face the state of affairs as they are. I know you and your father have been up to something, I know his plan was to have you surrendered and have us killed. What I do not know is what that coward planned for himself."

Mikhail with heightened ferocity– "Don't you dare speak his name, six against one? You wouldn't stand a chance against him all alone without your dogs guarding you, maybe then we will see who the coward is."

Hafeez's eyes narrow, a flicker of curiosity and amusement dancing within them as he listens to Mikhail's words. A smirk plays on his lips, contrasting against the intensity of his gaze.

Hafeez – ""Well, well, Mikhail, You have quite the confidence to challenge me from where I see you," Hafeez's responding voice was laced with a mix of admiration and defiance. "I have an ego devoid of boundaries, Impressive isn't it? That's the trait I like the most about myself. But let me assure you, I am not one to be easily fooled or manipulated. But your challenge did not go in vain, it indeed ignited a spark within me, urging me to adapt and improvise. The thrill is intensifying now, isn't it?"

Mikhail – "Why don't you let your actions speak for itself and Shut Up! Listening to your crooked and if I may, predictable plan is a torture in itself, chances are I might die listening to them."

Hafeez making an annoyed face.

Hafeez - "I am unable to assert if it was the first time I heard that, but it always gives me a tingling sensation, especially when the victim makes me detest them even more with phoney bravery and arrogance. Although their remarks induce a small amount of pain, frustration, and uncontrollable rage, the key is to maintain composure. These emotions are all like wild animals; the longer you cage them, the more bizarre they become. When someone's hunger for blood grows intolerable and unquenched, it transforms into much more than just a desire; it becomes a dream."

Hafeez depicts and narrates himself as a legend. Prouder he gets while swaggering boastfully all about him, he licks the air as if the environment just got tastier with his aura. He looked like he went on a journey within his consciousness, recollecting from his past leading on to endeavours to create something new. The remaining terrorists went to an adjoining space for some refreshments and to calibrate their communication devices with a sense of accomplishment at a job well done. The goal was to continue using random frequencies as much as possible to prevent interception.

Recognizing the significance of clarity and trust, the participants in each mission are intentionally separated from the rest of the group. This separation serves multiple purposes, with the primary aim being to ensure a thorough understanding between the individuals involved and the overall plan. Nobody except the leader of the mission would be aware of the details, that too at the very last minute. Team members, even the whole team may be replaced at a moment's notice. Mikhail was deemed non-essential but he was a last-minute addition. One acquires the habit of not being shocked in this trade because surprises are meant exclusively for your target. But when Mikhail's father unexpectedly detected something strange, he had to put in measures. His years of expertise taught him that, while safeguards may only increase the probability of success by a single digit in this specific field of business, they nevertheless give us a real chance.

As Mikhail's father packed his bag for the upcoming operation, a subtle yet significant indication revealed itself to him. It was a clear sign that this mission held greater risks and uncertainties than usual. The carefully prepared bag served as a tangible reminder that he needed to be prepared for the unexpected, anticipating twists and turns along the way. Mikhail understood that this operation would not only be fraught with danger but would also demand heightened vigilance and adaptability. Aban, who usually was a silent and strong personality, started indulging in conversation, insisting on certain things that he may very well order him to do. He insisted Mikhail use his shoes, the old high heel boots, not as easy to wear compared to the modern style but they still had their own looks, rugged and all terrain wear. While Hafeez and the other terrorists basked in the glory of their perceived victory, their attention consumed by self-praise and celebration, Mikhail seized the opportunity to discreetly engage in subtle movements. With every slight bend of his knees, he made calculated progress, gingerly inching his hands closer to the heel of his shoe. His actions were purposeful and deliberate, executed with patience and precision, all the while remaining undetected by his oblivious captors. In the midst of their distraction, Mikhail covertly prepared himself for the unexpected, Hafeez was more interested in Manav than Mikhail. All of his attention was captivated by Manav, whose boldness and unyielding gaze had left a lasting impression. The audacity displayed by Manav, even in the midst of captivity, had piqued Hafeez's interest. Now, his focus was solely fixed upon the individual who had thrown him a formidable challenge, determined to understand and potentially dismantle the source of Manav's unwavering confidence. Hafeez searched for any sign of vulnerability or weakness in Manav's unwavering demeanour, driven by a fervent desire to assert his dominance and prove himself superior. The battle of wills between Hafeez and Manav had become the primary focal point, overshadowing the presence of others, including Mikhail, who remained in the periphery of Hafeez's attention for the time being. Hafeez, his eyes simmering with a fiery intensity, didn't need to vocalise his desire to witness the sight of blood drawn from Manav. The thirst for violence and dominance was etched on his face, manifesting in subtle convulsions and twisted expressions that spoke volumes about the depths of tyranny lurking inside him. Manav wasn't completely over his shock yet. Hafeez, the one person Manav was unable to enrage, carrying the instruments that can hack through bone and flesh, was advancing towards him. The predator is measuring its prey, He approaches Manav, places the scalpel exactly at his thorax, holds it like a pen, and softly pushes in. He reveals his next move with pride, brutality, and a malicious thrill in his eyes.

Hafeez – "I think I am going to do you a favour, after all, you are the new best friend of my best friend's son. I'm going to match my speed with yours, this knife will go in just as slow as you are right now, but don't worry it won't be that close to your heart , just missing it by THAT far. I won't let you die of blood loss either, that's too easy a way to die for a special candidate like you. I am in the process of discovering a new way of torture. You see, this cut will fill your lungs with blood, less and less you will breathe, very slowly you will suffocate. Which gives me enough time to savour the moments, So I can witness your helplessness and powerlessness on display, exclusively for the Tabib. I am going to re-introduce you to all your pain and suffering, all at once, to say goodbye to your worthless life. My advice is to keep quiet, save your strength for your final words."

Any moves Manav made with his hands or legs were overpowered by Hafeez. He tried to raise his head but Hafeez violently pushed him down. Mikhail was watching in despair; he knows he cannot fight. Time and again Hafeez looks at Mikhail, enjoying his helplessness and gets back to his own amusement park of barbarity. Under the influence of his own conviction, he entirely disregarded Mikhail's movement, little did he know Mikhail had a few moves up his sleeve, he had one more trump card hidden in his heels. With every second he brought his right heel closer to his left hand, and when his shoe was just at his reach, he called out Hafeez.

Mikhail - "You are right about yourself, even my father agrees that you do not have an ego."

Astounded by what he had just heard, Hafeez abruptly turns to face Mikhail, his gaze fixated at him who dared to interrupt his actions. The momentum in the room freezes as Hafeez commands an immediate halt to what he was about to do. A mix of surprise and curiosity flickers in his eyes..

Hafeez – “Is that so? What else did he tell you about me?"

Mikhail – “That you have something even worse... Pride."

In a swift and calculated move, Mikhail detaches the heel from his shoe, taking advantage of the distraction caused by Hafeez’s pause. In one fluid motion, he throws the heel into the pantry where the other Terrorists were gathered, revelling in their celebration. The heel bounces a few times before reaching its final fate. Suddenly, with a deafening blast, the heel explodes, shattering the tranquillity of the room and leaving the unsuspecting terrorists frozen in shock. The force of the explosion was so overwhelming that the room itself trembles, unable to contain the sheer power, unleashed heat and numbing gases within its confines. The scene transforms from one of jubilation to one of chaos and confusion in an instant. Glasses and debris flew everywhere, the shockwave and the smell was extremely discomforting. Hafeez, being the only healthy one outside the blast radius, knows that he has been outsmarted and instinctively reaches out for his gun, however his gun holder was empty.

Mikhail – “He also told me; as good as you are with your tools, but you’re sloppy with your guns."

Hafeez’s eyes widen in disbelief as he gazes upon his own signature gun, now firmly clutched in Mikhail’s hands. A wave of confusion washes over Hafeez as he struggles to recall the precise moment when Mikhail had managed to snatch the weapon from its holster. The shock is so profound that his eyebrows shoot up to the highest point on his forehead, nearly touching his hairline. In that split second, Hafeez's sense of control is shattered, replaced by a mix of astonishment and a gnawing realisation that he may have underestimated his captive adversaries. In the moment of desperation, realising that his options are dwindling, Hafeez makes a desperate decision to use Manav as a shield in a bid to escape. The once confident and composed Hafeez now resembles a cornered rat, his worry and fear etched across his face. The power dynamic has shifted drastically, leaving him vulnerable and uncertain of his next move. In a sudden reversal of fortunes, Hafeez is now at the mercy of his captive adversaries, the weight of his actions and the consequences of his choices bearing down upon him. He grabs his hold on Manav's throat and points his scalpel right at it, ready to slash.

Hafeez – "You shoot me, but my fall will still slit your friend's throat."

As the situation intensifies and the risks escalate, Hafeez's once calm and composed demeanour crumbles. The noticeable quivering in his voice betrays the fear and uncertainty that now grips him. The drastic change in his circumstances has stripped away his previous confidence and adventurous spirit, replaced by a palpable desperation to simply survive. Hafeez's shouts lack the calmness and control they previously possessed, reflecting his current state of unease and the overwhelming desire for self-preservation. In this moment, his focus shifts entirely to finding a way out and ensuring his own safety, highlighting his diminished sense of adventure and highlighting his newfound instinct for survival. On the other hand, Manav and Mikhail were not in any hurry at all. Manav was proud of his friend, lest matters now whether he survives or not, but now his friend Mikahil has the upper hand, he will not be killed by the beastly Tabib. They both look at each other's twinkling eyes with an acknowledgement that this moment belongs to them now. But the job was not done yet. Mikhail, rather being worried about Manav's safety, completely ignores Hafeez's threat, But the job was not done yet. Mikhail, rather being worried about Manav's safety, completely ignores Hafeez's threat, glares at him with a ferocious, 'I-got-you-now look', then he turns around and walks away. Hafeez looked surprised but not for long, he realised why Mikhail walked away to the pantry. With Hafeez's own gun, Mikhail, without even blinking, shoots down all the injured and unconscious terrorists right on the head and heart, double-tapping them just like he was trained to, ensuring no more surprises, then he turns back.

He returns in a calm manner, amid the smoke the fulminated mercury released. He occupies the seat next to the table where Hafeez had kept all of his torture equipments on display. picks them out one by one and inspects them. It appeared as if he completely ignored Manav's current predicament. He takes a few cleansing breaths, enjoys and gives himself a momentary break from all the unexplainable events, once he had his lungs filled, he says.

"Take your time, you don't need my help to kill him.

There were two souls shocked to their core hearing the words of Mikhail. Manav could not believe how Mikhail turned on him after all that they went through and Hafeez was surprised for two reasons, first "Why switch sides after going through all of that trouble? and second, does he really think I need any help to kill Manav? who probably is the easiest prey he got hold of." Offended and anxious, Hafeez violently throws Manav down on the floor and shouts at Mikhail.

"You think a lion needs help to kill a gazelle? You fool, you really thought bootlicking is going to help you now after all that you did today?"

He laughed with the caustic glee of a witch prepared to conjure the most evil spell. His face and clothes were covered in Manav's blood, and he was so excited that his eyes were spilling with ideas that would have been unimaginable to a reasonable mind, brutal and agonising plans. As his body dripped with sweat, his blood pressure must have been through the roof. The beads of perspiration glistened under the faint red lights, casting an eerie glow upon his figure, Hafeez seemed transformed, almost demonic in appearance. The combination of his sweat-soaked body and the red lighting lent an otherworldly air to his presence. His features, contorted with rage and desperation, took on an unsettling appearance, evoking images of a malevolent entity from the depths of darkness. The sight of Hafeez, in his sweat-drenched state, exuded a chilling aura. He walked towards Mikhail with cruelty deliberating from his expression. His forehead, his lips, his eyes, every energy released from his existence poured sinisterness, he pauses looking down at Manav and says, "I don't need any help to kill a traitor and an infidel, don't' you know I am the Tabib of ... "before he could utter one more syllable, he was bluntly and disrespectfully, interrupted by Mikhail.

"I wasn't talking to you." Says Mikhail.

The room fell into a profound silence, unable to fully comprehend what they heard. Both Manav and Hafeez turned their gaze towards Mikhail, their expressions twisted with confusion and disorientation. In this suspended silence, the three figures remained locked in a bewildered exchange, each grappling with their own emotions and attempting to make sense of the shifting dynamics. The room pulsated with an indescribable tension, amplifying the sense of uncertainty that enveloped them all. Manav who can barely even stand on his all four, blood gushing out of his mouth and wounds, he could only cry but do anything else. Hafeez, a trained, determined and ready killer, is confused but calms himself believing that both Manav and Mikhail have lost their mind. He mockingly chuckles for a few minutes and says,

Hafeez – “Wait a minute, so you think there’s still hope left for you, and this Kafir has what it takes to kill a soldier of Allah? Hmm, I do not know if I should laugh or get angry at this derision. You both really have hit your head hard this time."

In all the craziness, it was Mikhail who remained remarkably composed and focused. Despite his exhaustion and the gravity of the situation, he maintained a steady presence, slanted against the table with a calm determination. Even with Hafeez’s attempts to provoke and insult him, Mikhail saw through the fear that was thinly veiled behind Hafeez’s laughter. His keen perception allowed him to recognize the true nature of Hafeez’s actions and intentions, refusing to be swayed by the theatrics and intimidation. Hafeez wondered if he failed to notice any important fact. Ignoring Hafeez’s reaction he addresses Manav in a serene and untroubled voice.

Mikhail – “You have a few breaths left in you and a countable drop of blood, a few minutes from now nothing else will matter. What do you want to do with it? Cry on it or pay back the person who put you through all this."

Mikhail’s words captivated Manav’s undivided attention, drawing him in with a magnetic force. Despite his weakened state and the pain he endured, Manav’s focus remained fixed on ·Mikhail, hanging onto every word uttered. Meanwhile, Hafeez, feeling threatened by Mikhail's words, began to retreat towards Manav, his face contorted into scornful expressions, attempting to undermine the impact of Mikhail's speech. However, undeterred by Hafeez's attempts at ridicule, Mikhail's voice grew louder and more resolute with each word he spoke.

Mikhail - "Every emotion has its own time. Forget all but anger and rage. Mourning over what you haven't lost just yet, won't bring you justice . He is right in front of you, use whatever you have left in you - and kill him."

Hafeez reached out to Manav, he grabbed his hair and pulled him up effortlessly, while ridiculing every sentence Mikhail addressed to Manav. He seemed eager to witness just how much resistance the feeble 'Ant' could muster against the might of his own boots. Manav, struggling to maintain his balance and barely able to stand, had been drained of all strength. Helplessly, he found himself at the mercy of Hafeez's grip on his hair, relying on that tenuous hold to remain on his feet. It was an unbalanced and vulnerable position for Manav, teetering on the edge of collapse, his fate precariously balanced on Hafeez's whim. In that charged moment, Hafeez's gaze became fixated on Manav's bloodied face and Mikhail's seemingly arrogant expressions. In a dominating way , Hafeez forcefully coerced Manav to move closer towards him until their eyes locked. Sensing the urgency of the situation, Mikhail, driven by a fierce determination, raised the pitch of his voice to its greatest level. With each phrase he uttered, he modulated his voice, aiming to reanimate and reinvigorate Manav, injecting a surge of energy into his weary and battered body. The resounding sound of Mikhail's voice reverberated throughout the room.

Mikhail - "Look at him, look right into his eyes. Doesn't he look familiar? Doesn't he remind you of Someone ... or Everyone? Everyone who betrayed you, Everyone who mocked you, Everyone who used you, Everyone who hurt you, Everyone who kept you away from what you rightfully deserved, Everyone who lied to you. Everyone!! Everyone who deserved to die but you could not kill them. Look at him, look right into his eyes, you will find them all there, in him, all together. He is the one AND THIS is the One opportunity you have been praying for. What are you going to do? Let them live or give them what they always deserved? With the last ounce of life left in you, are you going to die or will you try?"

In the intricate tapestry of the natural world, a profound contrast exists between humans and animals. While animals are bound by their innate instincts, unable to operate outside their natural boundaries, unable to consciously choose their roles as predator or prey. However, at times, an extraordinary phenomenon occurs when a prey finds itself in an absolute situation of powerlessness, and the predator who was once assured of victory faces a savage force that surpasses their wildest expectations. A phenomenon such as this was transpiring right there.

As all hope slips away and fear reaches its crescendo, a remarkable transformation takes place. The prey, stripped of all illusions and robbed of any escape, transcends the limits of fear itself. This primal rage, untamed and untethered, becomes a force beyond comprehension. It surges through every fibre of the prey's being, fueled by a sense of injustice and an unquenchable thirst for vengeance. With every ounce of strength, they summon an unstoppable madness, defying the laws of nature and shattering the fragile balance of power. In this surreal twilight between desperation and surrender, fear recedes like a morning mist, giving way to an insurmountable rage. The same sort of transition was taking place, ironically not in the jungle but in a civilization.

As a new strength coursed through his veins, Manav underwent a remarkable transformation. The flicker of life ignited within him, fueling his muscles to straighten up in preparation to face his predator head-on, the jaws that were once marked by fear and vulnerability now morphed into a formidable weapon. The grunt before the leap of death, the lethal claw of a predator ready to clench. In this pivotal moment, a rush of memories flooded his mind, each one a painful reminder of his earlier plea for death. But now, as he re-lived those moments of despair, a new understanding dawned upon him.

Every word Mikhail spoke reminded him of every moment of anguish that carried a deeper meaning. The pieces of the puzzle began to align, revealing a hidden purpose behind his capture and his presence in that very moment. It was then that Manav realised he had been brought to this point in time for a reason, and his destiny awaited him. As a surge of power coursed through his transformed form, Manav's mind became consumed by an overwhelming desire for vengeance. His thoughts turned dark, fueled by the magnitude of his suffering and the conviction that his adversary was the sole obstacle in his path towards freedom. In the depths of his imagination, he concocted the most horrifying and torturous scenarios imaginable, envisioning the excruciating pain he could inflict upon his enemy. With each grinding of his teeth, he visualised the torment and suffering that he believed his adversary deserved.

As Manav's rage and vengeful thoughts reached their zenith, he felt a sharp sense of frustration and despair. The adrenaline that had fueled his transformation began to fade, leaving his body weakened and fatigued. His once-mighty limbs, now burdened with numbness, betrayed his desires for retaliation.

With each passing moment, Manav's ability to physically act upon his violent imaginings dwindled. The harsh reality settled in, reminding him of his limitations and the growing impossibility of overpowering Hafeez. The vivid options that had consumed his thoughts slowly faded away, slipping through his grasp like elusive wisps of smoke.

In this sombre realisation, Manav's rage began to subside, giving way to a creeping sense of powerlessness. His once-vibrant spirit dampened, and the shadows of fear and helplessness gradually returned to the forefront of his mind.

Like a flickering flame extinguished by a gust of wind, the fervour that had driven him to envision acts of vengeance waned. Bit by bit, Manav succumbed to the weight of his circumstances, slowly reverting back to his original state of fear and silence.

In a cruel display of power, he does what he does best, Hafeez revels in his dominance over the defenceless Manav. With a sadistic grin, he unleashed his fury upon him, violently mauling and shaking him. Each brutal strike left a haunting trail of blood, staining the surroundings as a chilling testament to Hafeez's ruthless authority.

Throughout the assault, Hafeez's gaze would periodically flaunt towards Mikhail, ensuring that he remained subdued and posed no threat. Mikhail, however, remained a silent observer, his arms crossed in a stance of unwavering composure. His steady demeanour seemed to unsettle Hafeez, further fueling his sadistic desire to assert control.

Hafeez refused to let go from relishing in the helpless struggle of his prey. The words that had escaped Hafeez's lips so far were laced with cruel taunts and a twisted amusement. His actions and words served to emphasise his dominance, in order to further instil fear and submission within Manav, with a tight grip on Manav's hair, Hafeez mockingly pulled him closer, In the most gruesome way he says.

Hafeez – "You've been quietly staring at me for a while now, open your mouth boy, humour me."

That proved to be his last Mistake.

As Hafeez pulled Manav closer, his eyes sparkled with a glimmer of hope and determination. In that fleeting moment, he saw a potential opening, a slim chance to turn the tables on his tormentor. The adrenaline surged through his veins, electrified his senses, sharpening his focus.

Realising the fabric of his opportunity, Manav's heart pounded in his chest, but the sheer exhilaration coursed through his being, overpowered his doubts and hesitations, fueling his desire for liberation. Manav surpassed the intensity of a parched person stumbling upon a life-giving river in a desert, a starving individual discovering a feast after days of hunger. In that crucial moment, Manav's hesitation transformed into an unwavering determination.

The strong position, Hafeez had held, probably had the lowest risk margin. He was flying high in the sky until he was brought down, without wasting any time Manav grabbed the opportunity with perfect timing, Hafeez did not have a second to react. By the time he realised his mistake, Manav's jaws had clenched on Hafeez's throat, it was far too late for Hafeez to react, he dropped his knife in the panic and started using his hands to hurt Manav and force his hold loose of Hafeez's throat, but Manav had endured it all, his pain sensors had given up a long time ago and now there was nothing Hafeez could do to hurt him. Once he had a hold on Hafeez's throat, Manav did not spare any energy for other bodily activities, with all the strength left in him, Manav pulled his teeth together, grinding the larynx. Hafeez, Unable to breathe or make a sound, he began to realise the danger he was sinking in. His eyes started ballooning up, he was shocked to his core, Manav's move was so horrific even Mikhail was taken aback, he almost stepped up to stop him, but pulled back right away as Manav's stare was a defiant dagger, no one could steal a meal from a Lion.

Hafeez attempted to wield the scalpel to harm Manav and free himself, but with Manav fueled by his drive of instinctual ferocity, lunged at Hafeez like a lion mid-pounce. Fear gripped him like a vice, overwhelming his senses and causing his body to react in shock. Every part of him, from his trembling limbs to his racing heart, was paralyzed with terror. He could not hold anything on to him, not the scalpel, not even hope. Hafeez's mind became clouded, and his thoughts tangled in a web of panic. One could argue that Hafeez realised that he has been served with what he has been delivering. His attempts to resist or retaliate seemed feeble and futile in comparison to the unleashed rage of Manav, who now held him in a grip not only physically but also emotionally. As fear took hold and Hafeez grappled with the harrowing realisation of his ultimate vulnerability, the balance of power shifted in a way that neither of them could have foreseen.

Hafeez struggled to maintain his composure and Manav didn't want to, he kept Hafeez's upper arms restrained, debilitating him from making any attempt to free himself. Manav, almost seems to have started enjoying himself, he grunts his way into Hafeez's throat, any move he makes just creates more space for Manav to grind his teeth in. Manav was grunting so wildly and his sound became so animalistic that it hunted down the remaining hope or courage left in Hafeez. By now his face was tomato red, the veins could be clearly seen as they bulged all over his forehead, his oesophagus was crushed. His last breath and his last sound was trapped between Manav's jaws and it was clear that he wouldn't release it until he pulled Hafeez's soul out.

At the precipice of crossing over, Hafeez teetered on the edge of despair, his eyes turned towards Mikhail, filled with a desperate plea for mercy, since the other man who could spare his life was all out of mercy. His gaze bled with unspoken remorse and a yearning, begging for his life from the men he was about to creatively kill.

As time was rapidly dwindling for Hafeez, Mikhail stepped forward and leaned on to him, his hands were held firmly behind his back. Face to face with Hafeez, he locked his eyes on to his, took a moment to savour the fear he saw in his eyes and says,

"Now you will know how all of them felt. It's time.... You are almost ripe enough for HELL."

Those words behaved like the final nail in the coffin, devouring the remaining hope and ultimately his life. Hafeez was gone, his soul finally left his lifeless and hopeless body. His head was bent from the neck and resting on Manav's shoulders. The one who was most feared is now nothing but a lifeless rubber doll. His legs had gone wobbly, hands were in the motion of pendulum, but eyes were still open in amazement, perhaps his body was still in the state of shock. Not realising that Hafeez is dead, Manav looked to be annoyed with Hafeez's head resting on him. In the midst of Manav's barrage of ruthlessness, his fury intensified as his actions mirrored the ferocious death roll of a crocodile. With each violent shake, Hafeez's lifeless form twisted and contorted under Manav's unyielding grip, his grunts blending into an almost primal roar of pain and terror.

As this scene unfolded, Mikhail's presence served as a silent witness, with a sense of detached calmness. He chose not to intervene in the unleashed fury before him. Mikhail understood the transformation that had taken place within Manav, he reminisced on the person Manav once was, their shared memories of gentleness and compassion and recognized the depth of his journey from a peaceful, pacifistic soul to a vengeful and ruthless beast

## CHAPTER FIVE

# FIRE

Manav could no longer carry the dead weight anymore, unable to even stand straight he tends to fall down often. Trying his best to keep the balance, Manav puts Hafeez down on the floor with his jaws still wrapped around his throat. He started to realise that his kill was not resisting anymore, he shuddered Hafeez a few times to see if there was any movement, but there wasn't. Unable to fathom that the beast is dead, slowly but cautiously he lets him go. His teeth were gouged into Hafeez's throat and it took a bit of struggle to get them out. Finally, after freeing all his teeth, he kept staring down at Hafeez's popped-out eyes emotionlessly. Looking at his dead face he caught sight of evident fear personified all over him, it gave him a sense of pride that during his final moments, the merciless maniac was scared for his life, he did not die an honourable or natural death, just as Manav had imagined. Manav was though a bit worried about how easy he was feeling right now, he imagined he should be shivering with uneasiness, on the contrary he was breathing easily. He pushed Hafeez's dead weight off his legs and kept pushing himself back until he found a wall to rest his back. As Manav's transformation reached its peak, he resembled a battle-hardened warrior, his once peaceful visage now completely obscured by a mask of blood, rendering him almost unrecognisable. With his arms and legs confidently crossed, he sat poised, his gaze unwaveringly fixed upon his conquered foe, he forgot all the struggle he went through. Both men, Mikhail and Manav, did not speak a word to each other. A few moments later, Mikhail joined Manav and sat right beside him, after a few minutes of silence.

Mikhail – "When did you realise he died?"

Manav thinks for a moment – "I think I stopped feeling his pulse minutes ago, but it took me a while to notice that there was no more struggle. Right before he died, I felt an air pocket in his throat that was struggling to get out of my jaws. I wanted to hold on to it as long as I could."

Mikhail – "You confirmed your kill, that's a trait of a predator."

Manav – "Don't mind if I 'Thank you' for that."

As Manav and Mikhail turned their gaze back to Hafeez, their faces adorned with a subtle, almost sinister smile, it became evident that they took pleasure in the sight of their conquered antagonist. The serenity that enveloped the room belied the intense struggle that had just taken place. Yet, beneath the superficial calm, the toll of their physical exertion began to surface. The fading rush of adrenaline gave way to a heightened awareness of the pain that coursed through their bodies. With each passing moment, the mind no longer shielded itself from the distressing sensations, revealing the various spots of discomfort etched across their forms. The tranquillity they now shared came with a small but unavoidable cost. The battle had left its mark upon them, both physically and mentally. Every breath sent reminders of strained muscles, every twitch served as a testament to the lingering ache.

Despite the emergence of this discomfort, a resilient determination flickered within their eyes. They remained resolute, unwilling to let the pain extinguish the ember of victory that burned within them. The physical reminders only served to solidify the reality of their triumph and the arduous journey that had led them to this moment.

In this temporary lull, Manav and Mikhail contemplated their next course of action. The silence hanging in the air carried unspoken questions, a quiet invitation to explore the uncertain terrain that lay ahead. But for now, they allowed themselves a moment of respite, fully aware of the challenges that awaited them and the hurdles they would need to conquer.. Even a minor scratch ached, and Manav was covered in swellings, severe cuts, and other injuries that could have rendered a man crippled. Mikhail excuses himself and asks Manav to wait for him as Manav was struggling to move due to excruciating pain. A few minutes later Mikhail raced back with a first aid kit in his hand and began applying bandages, though it was extremely painful for Manav with all the antiseptics and tightly applied bandages, but he had no choice anyway, he was bleeding dangerously. Looking at a deep wound above his chest, Mikhail got worried.

Mikhail – “The bandages won’t be able to stop bleeding from this one. I’ll have to do something to prevent the spread of infection, here bite on this piece of cloth, it’s going to be excruciating."

Mikhail inserted a piece of cotton soaked in antiseptic inside the cut wound, Manav’s eyes initially erupted and he began to writhe in agonising pain, he nearly passed out. Mikhail then swiftly wrapped a bandage as firmly as he could. Mikhail asks in a rush.

Mikhail – "Is there anything I can get you to eat or drink, is there a cafeteria in this building."

Out of breath Manav replies.

Manav – "Yes there was, before you blew it up, hopefully there is still some water I can drink, what the hell was that anyway, a shoe-bomb?'

Manav was completely puzzled but Mikhail was amused with Manav's question.

Mikhail – "That my friend, was Mercury Fulminate, extremely explosive and unstable when highly purified. My father had been working on it for a while now. As far as your pantry is concerned, I don't recommend eating or drinking anything from that room for now."

Manav – "As if you left us with any choice?"

Manav was still perplexed; the only aspect that provided him with any sense of security was Mikhail, who made every effort to maintain Manav's health. He got up and grabbed a thermos from one of the Terrorists and handed it over to Manav. Water worked like black magic for him, making him yearn for more with every sip. He has come to appreciate several values that he had previously disregarded, and one of them was water. As the weariness in their bodies slightly subsided and a renewed energy flickered within their beings, Manav and Mikhail found themselves in a stalemate of unspoken thoughts. They both understood the burning question that lingered in the air, yet neither of them dared to broach the topic. The weight of uncertainty hung heavy, knowing that once they stepped back into the outside world, their identities would be perceived as sharply distinct. In the quiet of the room, they lingered, feeling a strange sense of comfort in their current state of refuge. The sunlight, finally breaking through the darkness after a long night, cast gentle shadows that danced upon the walls. Both Manav and Mikhail hesitated to leave this safe haven, reluctant to face the inevitable changes that awaited them beyond the now-familiar confines.

But amidst the calm, it was Manav who took the initiative to break the ice, to breach the barrier of uncomfortable silence that surrounded them.

Manav – “You sure there aren’t anymore? I am in no position for another round. A part of me says, even if there are, let them win, I don’t care anymore." Manav chuckles.

Mikhail – “Nope, you counted correctly. We are done but the question is what’s next. I am not sure I’ll be getting the same courtesy as you, when we get out."

Manav – “Don’t worry, I got your back. I will tell them what you did for me, and we have CCTV to prove it."

Mikhail – “We had taken care of them when we hijacked the building, cameras have nothing. We made sure of that."

Manav – “You still have me, so you better make sure I get out of here alive."

Mikhail looks at Manav with amusement as says,

Mikhail - “I’ll do my best... Now we need to decide if we are going out or wait for the forces to come find us."

Manav – “How long do you think I can hold up?"

Mikhail – “It depends, but I think your wounds need better care."

Manav – “Alright then, help me up, let’s get away from all these dead bodies."

Mikhail – “Sounds good, let’s get going. We have a long way to go, by the way we disabled the lifts as well, so stairs are the only way. You better buckle up."

Amusingly Manav shows a little frustration.

Manav – “Can’t buy a break."

Mikhail lifts Manav up, then takes his arm on his shoulder, supports his waist with another hand and they move very carefully making sure every step taken by Manav is balanced and cautious, irrespective how time consuming it was. Manav started to get bored, to keep his mind occupied, he asks several questions to Mikhail,

Manav – “Why don’t you entertain us meanwhile with some of your father’s stories, he seems like a great man."

Mikhail chuckles but remembering about his father made him look a bit relaxed and cheerful. Mikhail starts to think.

Mikhail – “Hmm, what kind of stories?"

Manav – “I don’t know, anything you prefer, anything that might be relative to our current circumstances."

Mikhail – “‘Never hesitate’ was one of them but that is quite common. His words largely rely on how he is feeling and the type of day he is taking. One recollection that stands out in particular is one where we were awake and spent the night outside in the chilly weather. That was a day he resolved a major contradiction of authority and power within our group. It really struck him how people with the same cause in mind were fighting for superiority, anyway, once he took care of everything to the best of his abilities, he came back home but did not enter. He stood outside for hours and I was watching him from the window wondering what was going on in his mind. Now, that house is far outside from even the outskirts, it’s a cold desert, a barren land, but we liked the quiet and peace."

Manav – “It does sound peaceful though."

Mikhail – “It is, when the weather is clear, at nights you can see so many stars so clearly that you wouldn’t want to be anywhere else. Almost as if the stars are so close that an imagining mind would want to pluck them like flowers. It’s a crazy idea but it does cross your mind, and my father without bowing down his head kept on looking at them."

Manav listened intently to a fantastic story without even batting an eyelid as his eyes sparkled with pleasure with each statement from Mikhail as he continued...

"After a while I could no longer keep myself inside, I was compelled to join him and try and understand what's happening in his brain at that moment. I grabbed all my courage, walked and stood right beside him. I waited for him to say something, but he just looked at me with a smile and continued with his contemplation."

Manav was listening to him with great attention and interest as this was the first time he had encountered someone whose consciousness and level of observation matched his own. He could feel where this story was going, and for a moment he fantasised Mikhail's father as his own. He could not wait to hear what happened next, his imagination was being fed with the right ingredients and he felt like daydreaming without daydreaming. Pain was not felt anymore, he was being energised like nothing else before, and his mind was going into a frenzy which he did not want to control. This overpowering of his ecstatic emotions was incredible, with all these he wonders, is this how happiness feels like? Is this how you smile without having to force it?

Mikhail – "Are you ok? You seem like you're going to faint."

Manav – "I'm fine, please continue, I'm just anxious to know what he said, out of all, I want to know why is that memory so special for you, because it is becoming a special memory for me as well."

Mikhail laughs inwardly, "It was a disappointing thought that was going through his mind, he told me that he met a few people that day, best in their class and of higher ranks, and ironically best of academics too, who were fighting for a piece of land on this granule rock that we call planet, when there are worlds unexplored in our own world. So narrow their vision is, they can't even picture what lies past their greed. Sometimes I wonder, the choices they make, is the reason why people like us are not allowed to choose."

"I never could clearly understand what he meant, maybe he just wanted to vent out some unexplainable thoughts in his mind, I don't even know why I remember that so prominently, maybe it was the beauty of that night."

They both stopped for a moment in between the staircase landing for a quick break. Deep in their own thoughts, they were attempting to decipher what Mikhail's father really meant.

Manav – "That was beautiful, I wish I could have been there."

Mikhail – "We both know that's unachievable. Once we are outside, the possibility is that we will never see each other again. You may walk free, but I have incarceration waiting for me, likely a death penalty."

Manav – "I can't let that happen, if a confirmed terrorist can get a highly ranked lawyer, someone who surrenders should get one too, you will surrender right?"

Mikhail – "Of course, I don't have a gun and neither the will to fight. I want to rest."

Manav – "And I will tell everyone how you helped me, how you saved my life so many times in just a day, whatever you go through I promise I will be there with whatever help I have to offer."

Mikhail – "Thank you my friend."

With a smile adorning their faces, Manav and Mikhail set off on their journey, their steps guided by a newfound sense of purpose and shared understanding. As they walked, they engaged in lighthearted conversation, swapping small stories and anecdotes in an effort to pass the time and keep at bay any lingering nervous thoughts. Laughter echoed between them, serving as a shield against the nagging uncertainties and doubts that occasionally crept into their minds. They knew that, despite their attempts to dismiss these thoughts, one cannot deceive oneself completely. Beneath the surface, a quiet recognition remained - an awareness that challenges and uncertainties would inevitably arise along their path.

Yet, rather than let these uncertainties overpower them, they chose to walk forward together, finding solace in the bond they had forged. As they shared their stories, their laughter created a tapestry of shared moments, weaving together threads of joy and resilience. In the midst of their journey, they continuously reminded themselves to hold onto this camaraderie, to draw strength from one another as they confronted the unknown. Nervous thoughts may have lingered, but they were met with courage and determination. Together, they would face the challenges that lay ahead, knowing that they had each other's unwavering support.

CHAPTER SIX

# AVALANCHE

The moment of truth arrives and is right in front of them. The front entrance was locked, and the reception area's lights were turned off. Even though it was pitch-black outside, dawn was soon to break. Manav advised it will be a good idea to turn on the lights so that the police unit can see them. He held his company ID card in his hand, in case there was a need. Manav sat on a chair while Mikhail looked for the switches, as soon as he switched on the first, the enforcement units were alerted, they could hear the boots marching from everywhere. With the ID card in his hand, Manav raises his arms and advises Mikhail to walk slowly beside him.

Manav – "Stand with me, let's not make any sudden movement. Let us walk as slowly as possible, we can't afford to surprise them."

As Mikhail's nervousness became apparent, Manav recognized the need to provide reassurance and support. Understanding the weight of his companion's unease, Manav gently met Mikhail's gaze, offering a silent understanding that transcended words. They kept their arms raised in surrender as they proceeded slowly to approach the main door. They could see outside through the glass walls, but all they could see in the darkness were bright torches rushing frantically towards all directions. They were unable to determine where the men on the outside were. Suddenly they saw torch lights brightening up the dark reception. Manav and Mikhail continued to walk across the reflective floor when suddenly they heard a shrieking, loud, and harsh voice telling them to stop right away. Alarmed, they both stop and turn to face each other. It was one of the leading commanders, he continued his instruction which sounded no less than a threat.

"STOP! Keep your hands straight. No sudden movement and Do Not Run!"

They couldn't, even if they wanted to, they were frozen. Commander continues.

"Stay where you are, sit down if you want to but very slowly. Do not move until ask, nod your head if you understand."

Like a scared child they nod their head abruptly.

Commander – "Is any of you hurt, is anyone bleeding?"

They look at each other wondering if that's the level of ignorant stupidity they're dealing with, however, Manav raises his hand and says, "Yeah! Me." Commander goes silent for a few seconds.

Commander – "Identify yourself."

Now it became tricky, in their mind they were hoping this situation might come after their wounds were dealt with. However, with his brains working much lower than its capacity, the only intelligent strategy Manav thought was to answer them as quickly as possible, taking longer might build suspicion. Wasting no time Manav replies as calmly as possible. "I am Manav, this is Mikhail, and we are both wounded. I have lost a lot of blood and need immediate medical attention."

Commander – “Is there anyone else in the building?”

Manav – “Not that we know of, why don’t you let us out and check it yourself."

Commander – “Standby!!”

Manav’s nerves start to play. He turns to Mikhail.

Manav – “They are making us wait? Can you believe that?”

Mikhail was silent but also calm, he replied.

Mikhail – “Anyway, it will all be over soon, just a routine check I believe. But we are not in danger anymore, all that is left to do is wait. I would suggest you sit down. Do not take too much stress, you’ll be fine soon enough."

Manav found solace in the comforting presence of Mikhail, his worries momentarily eased by the enchanting warmth of his companion’s smile. As they took a seat on the ground, it became apparent that their wait would extend beyond a mere few minutes. The authorities seemed to be conducting thorough checks, ensuring the validity of their affiliations with one of the offices in the building.

With annoyance brewing inside him, Manav couldn’t resist expressing his frustration towards the authorities. He unleashed a string of complaints, his words carrying a tinge of bitterness and impatience. But in contrast to Manav’s aggravated disposition, Mikhail remained a pillar of tranquillity, responding to each comment with a bright and radiant smile.

Mikhail’s unwavering calmness worked as a counterbalance to Manav’s agitation. With every smile reflected back at him, Manav found himself inexplicably drawn to Mikhail’s positive energy. It almost seemed as if Manav purposefully played the fool, relishing in the joy that bloomed within him whenever he elicited one of Mikhail’s radiant smiles.

This dance between Manav's complaints and Mikhail's beaming responses continued, captivating them both in its own peculiar way. The passing time seemed to fade into insignificance as they became lost in this unique interaction. Laughter intermittently punctuated their conversations, their light-hearted banter transforming the wait into a shared whimsical experience. As minutes turned into hours, the atmosphere remained filled with the paradoxical blend of Manav's frustrations and Mikhail's unwavering smiles. They found themselves momentarily disconnected from the weight of their circumstances, momentarily transported to a shared space of silliness and amusement.

And so, this delightful interplay continued, their laughter mingling with the passing time, as they found solace in one another's company amidst the unexpected wait.

Manav – "I am glad my misery is pleasing you."

Without responding, Mikhail occasionally cast his gaze outside before returning to Manav. A little while later, the megaphone's voice resumes.

Commander – "You are clear to exit, keep your hands behind your head, walk slowly and no sudden movement."

Manav – "Oh finally! And can you stop with your nervous smiles, the worst is over."

Mikhail comes over to Manav, out of nowhere hugs him. Kisses on his cheeks and with the same nourishing smile he says.

Mikhail – "I am not nervous. I am glad to have met you. I will always remember you as a blessing."

Manav returns the smile, takes his hand, and moves towards the door. He is cautioned to keep his hands behind the head by Mikhail. Two commandos open the exit door and leave immediately, the voice over the megaphone continues his step by step instructions. A little distance later, they arrived at the exit and were surrounded by flashlights. Outside, it was so bright that they could not even make out a person's outline. They gather further instructions.

Commander – "Spread out and walk towards the opposite direction."

As they exchanged glances filled with unspoken understanding, Manav and Mikhail conveyed a sense of completion. Their eyes became the vessels for a multitude of emotions: farewell, well wishes, and the anticipation of meeting once more. They wordlessly communicated their sentiments, hoping that their unspoken messages reached the depths of each other's souls. Walking towards the light that beckoned them forward, they acknowledged the instructions provided by their commander with a nod of agreement. Realising a barrage of possible outcomes, Mikhail turns towards Manav..

Mikhail – "Manav, tell my father...."

Before the sentence was added with another syllable, a sudden and unexpected turn of events shook Manav to his core. First, he heard a sharp and abrupt pop like a tiny blast, akin to a fleeting explosion, which caught his attention in an instant. Something darted right past him with such swiftness that he could barely register its presence. It vanished before his eyes, leaving him bewildered and unable to discern its nature or purpose. Turning towards Mikhail for reassurance or explanation, Manav found himself confronted by a sight that defied all logic and reason. A bizarre occurrence unfolded before him, rendering him speechless and struggling to come to terms with what he was witnessing. As much as he desired to dismiss it as mere imagination or a trick of the mind, the evidence before him was undeniable, impossible to unsee: a furious stream of blood gushed out from the left side of Mikhail's skull. When Manav's awareness increased, he realised It wasn't just blood. Mikhail disappeared from Manav's line of sight, he fell on to the ground as his body and blood followed earth's gravity. Similar to a series of dominos, he hits his head first then his body bounces a little before remaining motionless for the rest of the moment, the moment that will last forever in Manav's conscience.

Manav's mind grappled with the harsh reality that unfolded before him however his heart stubbornly refused to accept it. A paralysing sensation clutched his body as he stood rooted to the spot, unable to comprehend the devastating scene that lay before him. The person who had been his pillar of support, his companion through the darkest day, now lay lifeless on the ground. It was as if the world had suddenly shifted, plunging him into a state of numbing disbelief. His mind acknowledged the truth, but his heart resisted it with every fibre of his being. Time seemed to slow down as Manav's attention became fixated on the lifeless form of Mikhail. His gaze remained locked on his fallen friend, unable to tear his eyes away. The once clear and commanding instructions from the commander now morphed into unintelligible murmurs, their meaning lost in the overwhelming grief that washed over him.

The world around him seemed to fade into a blur of sounds and images, as his senses dulled in the face of this devastating loss.

As Manav redirected his attention towards the source of sound, from where the shot came from, a peculiar transformation seemed to take place within him. The blinding brightness of the flood lights no longer affected his corneas as he stared directly onto them, as if attempting to look beyond and find out who did that. His gaze held an intensity, a longing to find the finger that triggered the bullet, who destroyed his newly built world. Whenever his eyes shifted back to Mikhail's lifeless form, the struggle between his mind and heart reached an agonising pain. Despite the horrors they had survived, the imminent threat of death they narrowly escaped, none of it mattered anymore, his world was devastated to its core.

In that moment of surrender, the scales tipped decisively in favour of his mind, his heart still didn't want to believe. The relentless battle between acceptance and denial subsided as Manav recognized the inescapable truth before him. The pain of losing someone dear transcended any other hardship that had come before. With a heavy heart, Manav allowed himself to fully feel the weight of his grief. The world around him faded into insignificance as he focused solely on the magnitude of this personal loss. The enormity of the void leads to absence of emotions.

A primal, animalistic cry erupted from Manav's depths, reverberating through the air like a wounded creature. In his inconsolable anguish, Manav's sorrow manifested itself in a chaotic display of grief. His tear-streaked face contorted with an intensity that bordered on the edge of madness, rendering him unrecognisable in his pain and despair. The cruel reality that he had lost his sole friend, the very person he had bonded with the day before, seemed to crush his sanity. Desperate for even the slightest sign, Manav attempted to sit down beside Mikhail's lifeless body, hoping against hope that he would witness a miracle, a sign that his friend would look at him one last time. But before he could touch the ground, two commandos abruptly approached him, forcefully dragging him away from his fallen comrade. Transfixed by the sight of Mikhail being carried away, only intensified the scene. Manav could not approve how inappropriately they carried and threw Mikhail's body.

Manav was then carried into an ambulance and put down on a gurney. There were authorities, police and doctors who were talking and asking him questions, he could not understand a word, he looked like a terrified baby in the middle of Hyenas. Any movement they make near him startled him and soprano his crying goes. The EMT's had a hard time controlling Manav, they were unable to use the stethoscope or inject him. They seek help from the commandos to hold him down and tie him up the gurney to restrain him, but every attempt was futile. He wasn't loud, though, ferocious and stared right back at the enemies who murdered his friend. He kept his mouth shut while aggressively holding his cries. Similar to how he responded to his earlier tortures, he screams and grumbles within, not making any sound. One might even argue that his pain had intensified a thousand-fold by now. He wanted to protest for what they were doing to him but it was pointless, he could only lament for his wretched loss. Everyone around him was baffled by his behaviour, their best hypothesis was probably because of the predicament he was in for the last 24 hours, alternate theories included even 'Stockholm syndrome'. They expressed sympathy but not for Manav's grieving. If one could accurately describe the circumstances: Manav was surrounded by the same people who killed the only person he ever cared about, and the worst part was that those people did not even know what they had done, Manav couldn't care less for their sympathies and care, he didn't just lose a friend, but also his life. In his mind he had already established a future and planned everything, but with Mikhail's presence at every turn. He had plans to write a blog about the events that night, everything that a stranger did for him, risking own life to rescue him. Nevertheless, whether Mikhail was imprisoned or not, he really intended to visit him, he would hire the best attorney for him, he would wait for him. Thinking about what is left for him to live for, he felt empty, even emptier than before. He feels like a dead weight on this world or the world was a dead weight on him, leading a life devoid of meaning.

Manav was thus provided with adequate medication and the medical personnel applied bandages wherever necessary. While some of his injuries required hospital care, they had to wait for everything to clear out for the reason there were news agency vehicles and an enormous crowd gathered in the vicinity. They were additionally obligated to perform a search for any survivors before dismissing the ambulance. Manav wasn't fully at ease, but he was beginning to do so. He could feel anaesthetised as they gave him painkillers, but the medical personnel was oblivious that the pain was not bodily. It was only a matter of time before Manav went unconscious. He was unaware of what was happening outside with Mikhail's body. One by one the commandos were inspecting their trophy and making comments. It turned out that another ambulance was not available, and since there were many other bodies to carry as well, the authorities decided to put Mikhail in the same ambulance with Manav, they were all being taken to the same hospital. Discourteously they throw Mikhail into the ambulance, Manav was about to lose his consciousness. He notices some movement and recognizes something has just been placed on the ambulance floor. He turned his head and saw lifeless Mikhail; Mikhail's eyes were still slightly open.

Just when he started to settle down, the sorrow engulfed Manav once again, the intensity of his grief rendered him almost incapacitated. Tears flowed uncontrollably from his eyes, his weeping echoed the helplessness of a lost child. Every fibre of his being yearned for someone to show even the slightest reverence and close Mikhail's lifeless eyes, but the effects of the drugs administered were leading him into a state of numbness. His senses dulled, leaving him unable to even feel the sensation of his own lips. With the limited grasp of his fading consciousness, Manav longed to lock eyes with Mikhail one last time, to connect with the essence of his departed friend's spirit. However, the ambulance had already started its journey, propelled forward at full speed as all obstacles were cleared. The movements of the ambulance, though necessary, felt disconcerting to Manav. The jolting and swaying only served to further unsettle his fragile emotional state, as if adding another layer of unease to an already overwhelming experience.

With tears streaming down his face, Manav mustered the last remnants of his strength, his heart throbbing with anguish. The drug effect had started, the world around him began to fade, peripheral view was blurring out, as his focus narrowed towards the centre. Time seemed to slow as he embraced the inevitable moment to bid farewell. Summoning all the energy within him, he whispered through the pain, "Goodbye Brother...". His voice trembled with a mixture of sadness, longing, and newfound acceptance. It was a solemn acknowledgment of the finality of the situation, a quiet release of the connection that had once thrived. His farewell hung in the air, a delicate thread linking past and present, friendship and loss. Every ounce of his being poured into those simple words, carrying with them the weight of love and the ache of separation.

He repeatedly says, "Goodbye Brother"! Till he could keep his eyes open and gave in to the dark unconsciousness, with a desire to never wake up.

Manav remained unconscious for two days. Little did he know that he had become a centre of attention everywhere. He was "The Talk" of the town, be it an office conversation or the arguments on News channels. There were huge gatherings and prayers for his quick recovery, marches, and public admiration of his courage. Manav was a headliner for almost a week.

The authorities, however, were impatient and sought an explanation for the events that arose that evening. How he prevailed the explosions and metal-piercing weapons under the hands of skilled terrorists, it was a tremendous mystery. Most importantly, how did they all die? Some conspiracy theorists held nebulous beliefs about Manav, but even their most absurd theories were far from the truth. When he opened his eyes two days later, he was immediately demoralised by the fact that he was still alive. He was irate, but he didn't show it; he simply kept staring up at the ceiling until a nurse arrived, she asked him if he was okay, how he was feeling. Manav just nods his head and says "Yes" and "Okay" to everything. He asked when he will be discharged, to which the nurse replied that the Doctor will decide the next day. As the news spread that Manav had risen, everyone who was curious couldn't contain their excitement. The police didn't waste any time and arrived at Manav's ICU within an hour. They begin with their drab as usual, insincere sympathies and queries, and then they go about their business. Three representatives, each from a different age group, were present. They repeatedly question him for three hours while trying to make it look like 'not' an interrogation, the same questions asked in a different voice, style, and vocabulary. Manav answered all of their queries with just a few prepared sentences, without even twitching a muscle or nerve, he repeated the same answer, just as their questions were. "I don't know what happened, a bomb exploded, and I got free. On the way to the exit, I spotted Mikhail, and I believed he was attempting to escape too. I remember very little, but they had tied me up and locked me up under the server room.." They questioned him in every manner, but Manav's answers never changed, they could not break anything out of him.

According to a recent study, humans can indeed experience a wide array of emotions, approximately 27, each with its unique flavour and intensity. However, for Manav, that fateful night took him on an emotional journey unlike any other. As the hours unfolded, Manav found himself immersed in a torrent of emotions, as if the floodgates of his innermost being had been flung wide open. Each experience he encountered seemed to tap into a new facet of his emotional spectrum, and he was swept away by the intensity of it all. He delved into the depths of joy, feeling the warmth of laughter resonating in his chest, his heart overflowing with happiness. But alongside it came a tidal wave of sorrow, and he found himself consumed by grief, his tears flowing uncontrollably. Fear gripped his racing heart, tightening its hold on him like a vice. Anxiety knotted in his stomach, twisting and turning as if to devour him whole. Anguish and anguish writhed within him, their presence both tormenting and unavoidable. Surges of anger surged through his veins, fueled by the injustices he witnessed and the pain he felt. And in a rare moment of respite, he experienced tranquillity, a subtle calmness that came like a gentle breeze on a summer's eve. And yet, as the night wore on, Manav found himself drained, each emotion wrung out of him like a wrung-out cloth. He had explored the depths and heights of his emotional existence, tapping into reserves he never knew he possessed. Now, as he stood at the precipice of emotional emptiness, a profound stillness settled within him. It was as if he had exhausted his entire inventory of emotional-possessions in a single night, leaving him in a state of temporary emotional numbness.

The authorities, hoping for some breakthrough, expected Manav to provide them with answers and insights during their relentless questioning. However, they soon realised that Manav was unyielding in his silence. No amount of pressure or coaxing could draw out the heartfelt response they sought.

As a result, Manav was kept under observation in the hospital for a week, where doctors and professionals sought to understand the depths of his emotional state. They observed him closely, monitoring his behaviour and interactions, but the solitude he had chosen for himself remained unbroken.

Throughout his stay, Manav remained withdrawn, uttering only the bare minimum when necessary. He responded to inquiries with succinct and direct answers, focusing solely on what truly mattered to him. The walls he had built around himself seemed impenetrable, protecting his thoughts and emotions from prying eyes. In his self-imposed isolation, Manav found solace, seeking comfort within the confines of his own company. Perhaps it was within the depths of silence that he could truly process the whirlwind of emotions he had experienced, allowing himself the necessary space to heal and find his own sense of understanding. While the authorities might have yearned for a confession or explanation, it became evident that Manav's healing process required time and introspection. He chose to prioritise his own well-being and mental stability, resisting the pressure to provide immediate answers. And so, Manav remained shrouded in silence, his thoughts and feelings protected from the outside world as he embarked on the endlessly difficult journey of pi.

As Manav stepped foot back into his neighbourhood after his release from the hospital, he was greeted with an unexpected display of enthusiasm from his neighbours. Their warm welcomes and offers of support echoed in the air around him, but Manav couldn't help but feel a tinge of scepticism. Having recently learned his name, the sudden attention and concern from his neighbours felt disingenuous to him. Where were these gestures of kindness when he felt lost and alone? The world had turned a blind eye to his struggles, deeming him unworthy of their attention before the events that unfolded. Now, their efforts felt hollow, tainted by a sense of superficiality. Manav's transformation had made him resilient, unyielding in his perception of the world. He had seen the darkness that lay beneath the surface, the flaws and deceptions that others seemed blind to. The world, once deemed as the judge of his worthiness, now fell short in his eyes. The offers of help and support, though well-intended, carried a shadow of doubt for Manav. He couldn't help but question the sincerity behind their gestures, wondering if they were just prescribed acts. He simply accepted everything they offered with his own sincere acknowledgment of gratitude, and disappeared into his apartment. When he entered his apartment, he expected it to be dusty and that he ought to clean it, yet, was astonished to find everything in its proper place, it seemed as though it had been years since he had been home. His entire lifetime's worth of experiences were assembled for him in a single day, all at once. His head could barely carry the weight of emotions, he walks around his room, settles on the couch, and falls asleep with his utterly blank thoughts. After taking a brief rest, he completes all of his chores, sets everything ready to go for the following day's work, and finally goes to bed. Cannot say that he slept peacefully since serenity is also an emotion.

He showed up for work the following day with the same people beguiling him in different ways, or so it appeared. Even after working together for years, individuals who did not even know his name were hugging him, shaking his hand, and attempting to strike up a conversation. 'Offering support and willingness to assist whenever necessary' was a common statement that almost everyone used, at the mere cost of a selfie. There must have been thousands alike, but ironically there wasn't a single call or a message on his phone.

The events Manav had experienced seemed to have granted him a unique superpower. He found himself able to see through people, discerning their true motivations and intentions with a keen clarity. It was as if a veil had been lifted, revealing the hidden layers of human nature that often remained concealed. Armed with this newfound perception, Manav became acutely aware of the true nature of those around him. Their hidden agendas and ulterior motives were no match for his ability to pierce through the façades they presented to the world. As a result, the number of strangers seeking his acquaintance drastically declined. This newfound superpower also brought with it the bliss of ignorance. Manav was no longer swayed by the trivialities and superficialities of everyday life. He saw beyond the masks people wore, and this knowledge freed him from the need to engage in shallow encounters. Time, once perceived as a relentless force, became pacific in his eyes. Months passed by in a serene rhythm, almost unnoticed by Manav. He remained grounded in his newfound perspective, navigating life's intricacies with a sense of calm detachment. The burdens and distractions that once plagued him seemed to dissipate, leaving him with a clarity of purpose and an appreciation for the simple joys of existence.

Authorities never stopped questioning him, at times he was even called to the station but Manav made no changes to his statement, his background check proved to be very helpful, as everyone had the same opinion about him - 'Calm and Quite'. Since the cameras were already destroyed by Hafeez's men, and no other living soul to verify, Authorities had to finally assert and ultimately conclude their report based on the statement provided by Manav. Finally Manav was let go.

All those thousands of caring and curious souls who cared and shared their 'relatable experience' with Manav to make him feel better, failed to notice something significant that had changed about Manav, and amazingly, he was too damn clever at disguising it; he exhibited no indications of an anomaly from what he was in the past. Before the events that unfolded, Manav had been adrift, lacking a clear objective or purpose in his life. Like a motionless body in the vast expanse of the ocean, he felt trapped in a state of stagnancy. However, everything changed after he acquired his superpower – a newfound ability to see through people. With this ability came a newfound sense of purpose. Manav became determined to pursue a specific target known as 'The Three'. It was a puzzle, a mystery that consumed his thoughts. Even in the solitude of his home, when no one was around, the concept of 'The Three', shared with him by Mikhail, swirled incessantly in his mind, dominating his thoughts and curiosities. Every waking moment became an exploration, a search for answers. Manav delved deep into his thoughts, analysing every detail, every interaction, and every possible lead that could bring him closer to unravelling the enigma of 'The Three'. As he connected the dots and pieced together fragments of information, his wits became sharper. 'The Three' became his obsession, driving his every action and decision. He immersed himself in research, seeking clues and connections that could lead him closer to his target, so far the leads have been leading to the next lead. Who was The protector, The deviator, and The liar? and who ordered Mikhail's killing? He was not even given a chance to surrender, he was unarmed, and nobody even talked about it, his death was rather celebrated. Manav's once-consumed work at the office and mundane chores at home now took a backseat to his primary objective: unravelling the events of that fateful morning. The gravity of the mystery he sought to solve overshadowed his previous priorities. His focus became laser-sharp, dedicating every spare moment to investigating, questioning, and uncovering the truth.

Manav's investigation led him to uncover the identities of the police officers and security personnel he believed to be responsible for the events of that morning. With tenacity and persistence, he followed their trails, observing their actions and seeking to understand their roles in the larger puzzle. Although his investigation skills were still in their infancy, Manav refused to be deterred by his initial limitations. He recognized that he had much to learn and improve upon, but this did not discourage him. Instead, he saw it as an opportunity for growth and honing his investigative abilities. The information he collected was often incomplete or left him feeling unsatisfied. But Manav understood that true understanding and pinpointing 'The Three' required patience, diligence, and perseverance. He was willing to dedicate a lifetime to unravelling the truth, aware that the path to finding answers was rarely straightforward or immediate. With each piece of information gathered, he added to his arsenal of knowledge and skills. He studied different investigative techniques, sought guidance wherever necessary.

As Manav delved deeper into his pursuit, his approach became methodical and calculated, akin to a cold-blooded nocturnal reptile waiting patiently for the perfect opportunity to strike. Days turned into nights as he tirelessly dedicated himself to his mission. Utilising the resources at his disposal, Manav strategically utilised the office servers to download vast amounts of information. With each piece of data, he meticulously cross-referenced it against the events that took place, searching for connections and patterns that could guide him towards the truth. In his relentless quest for answers, Manav even learned ethical hacking. He learned and practised the art of breaching digital barriers, using his newly acquired skills to gain access to elusive information from secured databases. It was a means to an end, a necessary tool in his pursuit of 'The Three'. He collated whatever was needed, came back home and probed everything, arranged all the information in an order according to the work the information required;

1)'Further probe needed - Information that seemed relevant but still lacked certain details or was unconfirmed.

2)'Confirmed' - were the ones that he was sure had to do something with Mikhail's killing, and 3)'Long term' - He did not have the resources to research the 'long term' options, but they are unquestionably worth considering.

Tonight wasn't indifferent from other nights. He completed his work as usual and went to bed, but was awakened by an abnormally pleasant smell that at first seemed to be coming from the outside. However, his brain quickly detected the danger because he started to feel funny at first then slowly felt his body getting incapacitated. The smell wasn't good news, he got up from his bed and every movement was becoming tougher and slower, he could only take a few steps, could not even reach the switches before falling down, there was still some reactivity left in him. He looked everywhere but with lights switched off he could not see much; he had the option to shout and alert the neighbours but decided to give in and see what comes out of it. A few minutes later, just like falling asleep, he blacked out.

As Manav slowly regained consciousness, he became aware of his restrained state, tied up to a chair. A dryness pervaded his mouth as it was filled with cotton, rendering him unable to speak or make any sound. Panic welled up within him, but his attention was suddenly drawn to a peculiar sight. There, right in front of the window, sat a figurine in the shape of a human form. It appeared motionless, yet its presence emanated an intense aura that Manav couldn't ignore. Its eyes seemed fixed on him, piercing through the very core of his being. Questions swirled in his mind, attempting to unravel the mystery that sat before him.

In the dimly lit room, the mysterious figure concealed himself in the shadows, his presence shrouded in secrecy.

The figurine remained silent, seemingly anticipating a reaction or response from Manav. Yet, Manav remained resolute and motionless, refusing to give even the slightest hint of acknowledgement. A tense stillness hung in the air, resembling a high-stakes poker game or a prolonged contest of wills. Neither party seemed willing to break the standoff, their gazes locked in a silent battle of determination. Time stretched on, the passing minutes blending into an indiscernible haze. Eventually, the figurine rose from its stationary position and boldly stepped closer to where Manav was seated. Despite the proximity, Manav maintained his unwavering focus, refusing to raise his head to meet the gaze of the approaching figure. His resolve remained unbroken, and he remained motionless, waiting to see what would unfold. Without a word, the figure reached out and removed the cotton from Manav's mouth, granting him the ability to speak once more. Though now freed from the restriction, Manav chose to keep his head lowered, his nonchalant demeanour remaining unchanged. He no longer felt the need to actively engage, preferring to let the figure make the next move. It was a tense moment, an unspoken exchange of power and control. The act of removing the gag was a veiled indication that the figure desired a dialogue, but the silence persisted between them, each waiting for the other to make the next move.

Manav - "I was beginning to think you have fallen asleep."

The man comes back from the kitchen and brings a bottle of water, gives some to Manav, and while Manav takes relishings sips, The man says, "Sorry about the cotton, I was told you had a big mouth."

Manav – "Oh really! So, what changed your mind?"

The man – "You don't have to show any act of bravery, I am not here to hurt you, with what I have seen you are good at doing that on your own."

Manav was puzzled, in his mind he went through all the information he had obtained, trying to figure out what exposed him, and which department could be on to him, not to find an escape. Even tied up, he was thinking about his hunt for "The three."

The man – "Give your mind a break, I will tell you who I am, you do not have to associate any of your information with me, but first I have some questions for you, are you ready to answer?"

As Manav observed the man before him, his attention shifted from the physical details to the man's manner of speaking. The man's words flowed with a deliberate slowness, each syllable pronounced in a distinct and measured manner. The serenity in his speech had a soothing effect, yet it also held a perplexing aura. Although the man did not push or demand a response, his crystal-clear words held an undeniable power. It was as if his discourse had the ability to compel a response, even against one's own will. Manav acknowledged this influential quality and recognized the importance of maintaining his own agency and discernment. Learning from his past experiences during his relentless pursuit, Manav understood the value of gathering more information requires strategic silence. With a nod that signalled his agreement, he chose to answer the man's questions, cautiously navigating the delicate balance between providing information and safeguarding his own objectives.

The Man – "Good, I am grateful. So, what are those documents in your cupboard?"

Being open and honest right away didn't seem like a good idea. He needed to know what the man knew, but Manav responded with snarky remarks.

Manav – "Office stationery, possible clientele. We study them for future presentations."

The Man – "Ok! and what were you hoping to achieve after gathering information about the commands, the police force, the minister and there was one lawyer you followed till his house, was all that to seize a clientele?"

Manav made the decision to stop circling in the bushes; his intent was evident in his comments. He had no regrets about what he did.

Manav – "I did what was necessary; I am at a crossroads for explanations. You carry out what you have to do. I truly don't care anymore."

The Man gets agitated, he straightens up and raises his voice.

The Man – "You are a fool who thought will never get caught looking for secrets. It was just a matter of time."

Manav – "Since you got the answers to your questions, now allow me, who are you? And how do you know about me?"

The Man pauses, turns his back to the window, gazing outside he says,

"The day my son died, there was one more person I saw broken, just as I was".

As the man flicked the switch, flooding the room with light, Manav's eyes adjusted to the sudden brightness. His earlier assumptions were confirmed-the figure before him was indeed an elderly person, with hair tinted with shades of grey. The revelation sparked a surge of anticipation within Manav. With every shred of information he had gathered, Manav's mind raced to calculate the probabilities, searching for patterns and connections. The pieces of the puzzle started to fit together, and a glimpse of understanding began to take shape. A mix of hope and trepidation filled his heart as he prayed that his deductions were accurate. At that moment, Manav sought guidance from a higher power. He turned to prayer, submitting his hopes and wishes to God that he was right about who this man was.

*The Man continued, "Perhaps you've heard of me. My name is Aban, but I go by the moniker "Maktaba."*

## CHAPTER SEVEN

# WIND

"I'm facing the man who inspired my adoration. My nerves are shattering like glass at breakneck speed. I can only hope that my enthusiasm and nervousness aren't obvious. God! How do I get rid of these goosebumps? If only I could see myself, which I don't want to do. This is Mikhail's father - Aban. I've been fantasising to meet him ever since I heard his praises. Can't remember when I was this nervous, not even at my first interview." The moment froze in time as the man that Manav dreamt to meet stood right before him. It was a convergence of admiration and awe, a collision of dreams and reality. The gravity of the situation sank deep into Manav's being, leaving him momentarily speechless. In the presence of his idol's idol, Manav's heart pounded with a mixture of reverence and disbelief. The full weight of his own idolatry seemed to bear down upon him, intensifying the significance of this encounter. Thoughts and emotions surged through his mind like a hurricane, each one fighting for attention. Aban's presence seemed larger-than-life, radiating an undeniable aura of charisma and accomplishment. Manav could not help but be captivated by every nuance of his idol's idol—his posture, his confidence, his mastery of his craft. It was as if time stood still, allowing Manav to absorb every detail, every gesture, with utmost clarity. In this extraordinary encounter, Manav felt the fusion of two worlds colliding. The man he idolised and the idol of his idol converged in this single, extraordinary moment. It was a humbling yet exhilarating experience, as Manav became acutely aware of the layers of inspiration and influence that intertwined between Mikhail and his Father - Aban.

The void between their little conversations was causing a rise in his anxiety. Aban, as usual, stayed clear of unnecessary formalities, kept his questions direct and straight to the point. The awkward introductory moment had already been lost. Self-consciousness gnawed at him, tormenting him with doubts about his ability to make a good impression. Every word he considered felt heavy with potential judgement, causing him to second-guess himself at every turn. The pressure to impress and live up to his idol's idol was mounting, threatening to suffocate his ability to confidently communicate. Amidst the whirlwind of emotions, one question loomed large in Manav's mind—an unspoken inquiry that he was hesitant to voice, even to himself. "What is he doing in my apartment?" The very thought sent shivers down his spine, mingling curiosity with trepidation. The reason behind this unexpected encounter remained a mystery, and Manav's inner monologue wrestled with the implications of this enigmatic presence. A part of him yearned for answers, urgently craving an explanation for this welcome intrusion.

"I will look like a fool if I introduce myself now. Should I smile? On second thought and considering the fact that I am the reason behind his son's death, smiling doesn't seem to be a good idea. However, if there is one man who deserves to know the truth, it's him; I must tell him everything his son did to save my life and who knows how many others." Without discounting the probability that a stranger broke into his house, and tied him up, most probably to redress his son's death, the thought of being killed - did cross Manav's mind several times. His introverted neuroticism was at overtime. Since it was too late to offer a positive response, staying quiet looked to be the most intelligent move, but in his defence, Aban was restless in his own way. As Manav struggled to regain his focus and gather his thoughts, Aban's intermittent movement disrupted his concentration. Each time Manav felt a spark of clarity or a train of thought forming, Aban would disrupt it with his controlled and deliberate strolls around the room. Despite the late hour, Aban moved with a practised grace, mindful of not disturbing the silence that enveloped the space. His field of vision was vast and penetrative. Manav found it difficult to keep his chin up whenever Aban made eye contact. Aban would wander from window to window, trying to hear every little sound while he searched every inch of the apartment. It seemed as if Aban's presence itself carried a weight of significance, demanding attention and respect. However, the asynchronous rhythm between their dialogues and Aban's wandering path only added to Manav's bewilderment. The controlled movements were not arbitrary but served a purpose, perhaps to create an atmosphere or maintain an air of secrecy. As Manav observed Aban's careful navigation of the room, he couldn't help but wonder what hidden clues these movements might hold or what hidden intention they sought to conceal.

Finally, he spoke, "You don't have much food in the kitchen, crockery is almost nonexistent. Did you just move in here?"

Ever since Aban introduced himself, Manav had been stuttering at every word. Surprisingly, the conversation with his dead friend's Dad was going way better than he expected. "At least I am not dead yet? I'll take that as a good sign, I got to say something now, it's been awkwardly quiet for a while."

With a little bit of stumble and pause, Manav answered, "I live alone and usually order something or eat out. If you're hungry I have some eggs, perhaps you would like some?"

Giving no regard whatsoever to Manav's response, Aban grabs a chair and sits right in front of him, gets a bit closer and begins to untie Manav. "I am not hungry, just curious, there is so little information about you, almost like you are not in this world and yet, there you are. Either all of this is real, or it is the best-kept secret. You must forgive me for my intrusion, I am a calculative person by nature."

After being released, Manav stands up, rubs his wrists, takes a glass of water and replies, "I'm not either, you should go out more often, see the world. I'm sure you could find thousands like me."

Manav starts to walk towards the bathroom when Aban interjects. "Your reaction when I introduced myself was a bit peculiar, perhaps you have indeed heard of me, question is, from whom?" With the exception of a few stumbles here and there in his phrases, Manav did well overall but fell short of his own expectations. He did his best to hide his nerves and breathed normally. He looked at Aban very strangely with his chin down and eyes directed at him.

Manav - "Your son was the most honourable man I have known; you were in his thoughts till his last moment."

Quickly absorbing the information, Aban calmly says "I am surprised to hear that, because reports tell me that my son was also amongst the men who put you in harm's way, and held you hostage at gunpoint, wasn't that the reason he got shot?"

He was overcome with a range of emotions when he heard what Aban had to say, but this time Manav responded loudly and clearly without a single stutter.

Manav - "Mikhail saved me from those men, he was unarmed when they shot him. Evidence was falsified according to everyone's convenience, and I just added to their story, as you can see there was too little a man of my stature could do." Manav continued, "I was right in front of him when they shot him. I do not know why YOU are here but if you think I am the one responsible for your son's death then you are right, I am the reason why Mikahil's dead, and I will not hold it against you if you are here to take my life in return."

Aban like a good listener nodded his head all along and acknowledged everything Manav had to say, he stood up and continued walking around the house, which again caused an unbalancing effect on Manav's thoughts and expectations, his eyes kept following Aban's movement, assuming he will get a response any moment now, and little later he did.

Aban -"I am going to be here for a while Manav, just for a few days so we get acquainted with each other, I hope I am not trespassing, and I do apologise for the lack of notice."

Manav was at a loss of words and simply stood there staring at Aban with his hands crossed. For a brief period, he believed his eyes were the only parts in his body that could move. He took a while to comprehend everything. After repeating it again and again in his head he was finally able to acknowledge the reality. "This is not what I was expecting, what is he up to?" Sensing his discomfort, Aban speaks, “Do you seem to have a problem with that? It’s just for a few days, I am expecting to meet a few friends here, after that I’ll be gone but while I am here, I can help get the prattles out, the ones you have been desiring to talk to about. But If your answer is ‘NO’, I won’t hold it against you."

Mannerly Manav has hardly ever said ‘No’ to anyone, only this time he felt welcoming to say a ‘Yes’. “Of course, Sir, I will be very happy too, just embarrassed by the mess in the house." To which Aban replies, “Do not worry about that we will think of something, however, we do need to have a backup story; you see you are a famous orphan now and a sudden intrusion of a stranger might look bizarre. If anyone asks about me, tell them I am your adoptive father, I was away and couldn’t track you. Now that I have finally found you, we are trying to get to know each other." Perhaps after recent events in his life, Manav’s reaction to an offbeat situation had become considerably calmer than before. With a gentle smile, he responds, “I do not think that will be necessary, I hardly interact with anyone but if you say so. Let me arrange the bedroom for you, you must be tired." Walking away towards the door, Aban takes a moment’s pause, “There is no need for that. I am not staying, people do not know you, yet they notice everything. I will come back in the daylight; it will give us an edge for our cover story. And... Take a couple of days leave from work, we are going to need you."

Curiosity kicks in. “WE!? who’s we?“ asks Manav. Aban with a smile and inconclusively, says, “Have a good rest”, Then he leaves without further clarification, whatsoever.

There was still some night left. Manav sat on the edge of his bed and spent the rest of the night staring at the blank wall. A part of him wanted to jump and dance and part of him was asking the question, "What just happened?" A puzzled Manav stares at the blank wall and starts painting an imaginary picture of Aban's facial expressions with whatever he could remember, he was astounded to recall only one. His soul-penetrating eyes that can make you feel naked even when they are not looking at you. His smile looked like it was overcompensating for some sort of notorious, mysterious scheme going on in his mind. "Why did he have to be so virile with me? I am mindful of his extensive knowledge and emotions following the death of his son. but acting in that manner towards a new acquaintance is inappropriate. However, it is pointless weighing it because, based on what I know about him, if he had desired it, I would already be dead. I suppose he was acting appropriately after all. Now that I think about it, he probably has no true knowledge of what truly transpired that day. I can only hope that he will allow me to talk about Mikhail, as I truly need to." He sat like this for a few hours before growing weary of it. He was now at ease with the thought of his potential escape from death or impending demise. Manav laid on the bed remembering a few glimpses that he had saved from his meeting. His eyes were heavy from bearing too much weight for too long, and he quickly dozed off with an empty mind, or so he believed.

As Manav stirred from his sleep, his mind awash with dreams and remnants of the night's subconscious wanderings, he was abruptly yanked back to reality by a loud and unfamiliar noise. At first disoriented, he struggled to identify the source. Gradually, he recognized it as the unmistakable sound of a door knock. However, rather than immediately attending to the interruption, Manav found himself fixated on the remnants of a vivid dream that still lingered in his mind. The dream held a certain significance, its content begging to be unravelled and understood. Curiosity tugged at him, urging him to delve into the depths of his subconscious and uncover the message trapped within. Intrigued by the dream's potential significance, Manav momentarily ignored the persistent knocking, opting instead to sink back onto the edge of his bed. Determined to recall the elusive details, he closed his eyes, allowing his mind to navigate the fragments of the dream. Apparently, something about the dream was making him smile and he was piqued to find out what it was "What was it? What am I smirking about?' He occasionally glanced at the door in the hopes that the pounding would cease so he could pay closer attention to the hazy visions of the unmet people and unvisited places he saw in the dream, somehow everything in the dream was as familiar as reality, sadly there wasn't much he could recall to complete his jigsaw puzzle. He eventually gave up as he figured it would be 'donkey work' trying to recall something that was stored in his subconscious. With his half-rested mind, a grumpy Manav walks towards the door, loathing every knock. In his defence It wasn't a gentle knock either, more like someone hammering the door. Manav, at the peak of his annoyance, opened the door with such force that it created a gust of wind powerful enough to knock down trees, so to speak. Opening the door revealed what needed a large entry nonetheless, and it was difficult for him to make sense of what or who was in front of him. For all he knows his mind went chaotic trying to figure out the person he saw. Even after determining it was Aban, he still rubbed his eyes to make sure they were working.

Aban was entirely different from the previous evening; he appeared more like an eccentric twin on a protracted pilgrimage. He was dressed very differently, with pyjamas and leather sandals at the bottom and a baggy Indian tunic with a Nehru-Jacket on top, all of which gave him an authentic look of a character from a family feature film. Manav must have had several indescribable thoughts however the most provoking was. "Well he does look much more like a human now, but this is so weird, he is smiling at me, I may have never pictured him a smiling type and I think I have been staring at him for far too long." The biggest surprise was the smile. Aban portrayed an adorable little smile on those wrinkled pink cheeks, only if he could grow a long beard with the same colour as his hair, he could compete with the real Santa for a lookalike contest and probably even win. "There you are, I thought you were not at home, May I come in son?" Manav was still stunned, he peeked around his neighbourhood, anxious to see if someone was noticing an orphan being visited for the first time. Indeed, there were some women running around with their children and men having their usual political discussions in groups, however not one paying direct attention to Manav. Manav welcomes Aban into his apartment, only this time it was a regular visit. Aban had a different look this time, he did not look eery or dangerous as he was in the night before, he was rather jumbled. He took a seat and asked Manav to join him.

Aban - "All my efforts to blend in appear to have gone in vain, not a single person paid attention to me, nobody asked me where I was going? Or whom am I meeting? Or if I needed any help? I must say that was peculiar. However, In some way I think that will work perfectly for us."

In his half-awake state, Manav could only manage a nod in response to whatever Aban was saying or doing. His face remained blank, concealing the anticipation and anxiety that coursed through him. Every movement, every word from Aban felt like a hidden clue, a piece of a puzzle that Manav was desperate to solve. As Manav watched Aban wander around the apartment, taking careful measures as if it were his first visit, he couldn't help but feel a mix of unease and fascination. Aban remained perfectly in character, maintaining an air of mystery and intrigue. Each action seemed calculated, intentional, and meticulously planned while Manav remained in his own thoughts. "My first guest in a long time, and it had to be him. What is the conventional method of attending a 'World's-Most-Wanted?" It was an awkward rotation of the heads for a seemingly-long-time. They would stare at the wall then the ceiling then the floor, like a cycle running in succession. "Would you do me a favour? May I watch your TV Please?" A 'Yes' appeared to be an appropriate answer but more importantly, favourable. Manav said, "Yes, Of course." He hands over the remote, and after a small pause Manav says, "May I go back to sleep If you don't mind?" Aban turns towards him, leaning his head down as he stares out of his petite specs, "Yes, Of course... rest well." Tired, Manav could not wait to forget everything and crashed himself on the bed. "Too much to process for one night." He goes back to sleep again.

As the day turns warmer, Manav wakes up frantically. Shell shocked, he looks around while concocting the events that took place before he slept. As he sees no movement and hears no sound in his apartment, he thought "Was all that real? Where is he, were last night's events just a dream?" He walks around a bit while his senses calculate and register the specifics of his surroundings. Alas, without warning, Aban casually walks out of the kitchen with a cup in his hand, momentarily startling Manav and probably giving him a mild stroke. "Oh, dear me! You frightened me there", Taking a deep breath, Manav says, "So that was not a dream, after all, you were here last night and now in the morning as well." To which Aban responds very casually and makes himself like he is home, he sits on the couch, treats himself with snacks, smilingly he says "And I am still here. I hope you don't mind. I used some of the items in your kitchen to prepare tea. Please have some, it is a recipe I learnt from a very good cook. Not as good as I hoped for though." Manav walks into the kitchen, pours himself some tea and takes a sip, It was nothing like he ever tasted. It made him ask "Is this what heaven tastes like?"

As the hot tea touched Manav's lips, an extraordinary sensation swept through him. It was as if the tea defied the boundaries of physical contact, floating over his tongue and releasing its delightful flavour to all his taste buds simultaneously. His eyes widened with delight as he felt a sense of illumination wash over him. The tea, surprisingly, didn't generate a typical warmth; instead, it provided a cool and refreshing sensation. Manav reveled in the harmony of flavours that danced on his palate – the essence of cardamom, the subtle hint of clove, and the invigorating freshness of spearmint. The sweetness and quantity of honey, just beneath perfection, heightened his craving with every sip. Manav relished each moment, taking his time to savour every drop of the delectable tea. His entire being became engrossed in this experience, blocking out everything else in the world. The taste, aroma, and sensation of the tea enveloped him completely. Almost spellbound by the pleasure of the tea and the craftsmanship of its preparation, Manav found himself gazing at the person responsible. His appreciation for this new-favourite cook overflowed, evident in the gleam in his eyes. With a sense of pure contentment, he settled into a chair, finally allowing himself to fully immerse in the moment of pure indulgence.

Watching him closely and with curiosity-filled up to the highest level, Aban asks Manav, “How do you like it?" With a twinkle all over his face, he replies, “I'll tell you, I do not want to finish this tea”, and smiles. Manav's response encourages Aban, with pride he says “Good that is good, I am glad you liked it. I could have done better if we had some saffron." For a moment Manav stares at Aban and looks back at the tea cup, “How can anything like this be improvised?" Aban found it funny, as he laughed and said, “Why not? Just because something is good doesn't mean it cannot surpass where it is right now, even if something is at its absolute best, there will always be room for improvement, if not, then a better way to achieve it." Manav was more than impressed, he was already a fan now he became a desperate and hopeless follower. He could not present a sentence as appreciative of what Aban said, therefore he simply replies, “That is well said sir” and tries not to say anything else in an attempt to not-look-like a fool in front of the wisest man he knows.

After a few minutes of silence and several sips, Manav notices Aban working on something on his laptop and there were different types of documents spread across the table, including some Manav had acquired which caught Manav's attention, “You seem to have been busy, mind if I ask what are you doing with those documents?" Aban, almost ignoring Manav, just looks at him for a fraction of a second and continues typing on his laptop, while he does that he asks “Are you happy here? I mean living in this one-bedroom apartment. Seems very small and discouraging, it could be extremely tough to raise a family here." A bit surprised by his question, Manav replies, “I have no complaints, I find myself content here and family is out of the question." Holding his empty cup, Aban stands up, as he walks towards the kitchen he says, "We are going to need a bigger Apartment." He says that with such ease, which was the exact reverse of how Manav responded to it: squealing with alarm as it engulfed him, Manav asks, "What do you mean 'We'?"

All he could hear was the water splash and plates rattling from the kitchen. A few minutes later Aban walks out, wiping his hands and sits down. "Do you remember when we spoke the first time, I said that I am expecting some friends, how on earth can we accommodate them here." Manav gets a little irritated feeling that Aban is being extremely intrusive, however, controlling his anxiety, he takes a few calming breaths,

Manav - "First - I am not sure why you keep referring as 'We', second – you never told me that your friends are going to live here and third – and most importantly, I am a technician, this is all I can afford, I can only wish to own a big place to accommodate as many as possible but I can't. I do regret the inconvenience."

As Aban continued to listen attentively to Manav's words, he simultaneously fiddled with the keyboard, seemingly engaged in his own thoughts. Suddenly, he broke the silence and directed Manav's attention towards his carry bag, instructing him to bring it over and open it. Manav's mild surprise at receiving another enigmatic request was quickly replaced by a sense of cautious acceptance. Recent events had taught him the importance of adapting and pushing past the boundaries of his comfort zone. With newfound resilience, he chose to embrace the unknown and fulfil Aban's request without hesitation. As Manav retrieved the bag, he immediately noticed its weight and sensed that its contents were composed of some sort of paper. Conflicting emotions surged within him, as his senses and logic engaged in a silent battle against the context of the materials enclosed within the bag. On one hand, his logical mind pondered the possibilities of what kind of papers could be hidden within. Were they documents, letters, or something entirely different? The weight of the bag hinted at the volume of papers it held, leaving him to wonder about the significance and purpose behind them.

As Manav placed the bag on the table, he began to carefully unzip it, his anticipation mounting with each passing second. As he opened the bag, he was initially greeted by a neat stack of clothes occupying the top half. With a determined resolve, he swiftly removes the clothes and sets them aside, revealing the true nature and contents of the bag beneath. A strange mixture of curiosity and exhilaration surged through Manav's veins as he beheld the hidden treasures concealed within the bag. It was as if a dark fantasy was gradually being brought to life before his very eyes. In this moment, his senses appeared to triumph over his logic. Though his logical mind had initially invalidated the notion of the bag being filled with money or extraordinary riches, the estimations he made earlier still echoed in the back of his mind. However, Manav understood the need to approach the situation cautiously. The too-good-to-be-true nature of his estimations tempered his expectations, reminding him to remain grounded in reality. With a blend of apprehension and intrigue, he prepared himself to uncover the true nature of the contents that awaited him within the bag. All of this was being fuelled by Aban's indecent-little-smile, he was watching and waiting to see how Manav's reaction would be. Manav himself could not help anymore and was beyond anxious to see what was inside.

He unties the drawstring of the khaki bag, holds it upside down, and lets gravity do the rest. Aban was watching very closely how Manav was reacting and he wasn't disappointed when finally the materials were put out in the open. The bag was filled with different currencies. He may have seen the pound, yen, and dollar, yet so many notes he could not recognize. He picks every pack of notes and notices that every note has a big number on it. The dollar was in the hundreds, the pound was in the fifties, and so on. All notes were so fresh as if recently printed-out in high definition. There were also a bunch of documents with Promissory notes and bonds on them. He puts them all aside in a very organised manner. The spectacle was compelling and intriguing, not something Manav would call comfortable, unlike Aban who had planted himself pleasantly on the sofa with his hand resting on the back support waiting for a verbal response from him. Manav's observations seem to be giving him correct answers thus he sensed something was wrong or something was going on beyond his comprehension, and was compelled to ask, "You haven't told me the purpose of your visit."

Aban – "I was informed that you are not a person who gets unsettled in discomforting situations, yet you seem undeniably perilous by a view that most people find fascinating."

With a relaxing smile on his face, Manav responds, "Clearly you have not met everyone."

Aban – "Agreed! but what makes you so different from others, that is the question."

Manav – “I am not different, I do daydream about easy luxury, but worry about the cost too."

Aban – “It’s just money Manav, let us not get ahead of ourselves. I have no one or should I say nothing to spend on, these are the earnings of my life. Consider the next few days as a gift from me, you gave peace to my son at a time when I could not, compared to that, this is nothing."

Manav was unresponsive for over a minute, as he could not assimilate a reaction to a father who lost his son, all of a sudden, the excitement of acquiring the largest sum of money he ever saw was dwarfed by guilt, grief and a tremendous loss. The silence in the room was rather comforting as both men could see into each other’s eyes and recognize the mourning of Mikhail. Glimpses of understanding passed between their eyes, their smiles now tinged with a bittersweet sadness. Words hung on the tip of Manav’s tongue, With a deep breath, Manav finally found the strength to speak, his voice laced with trepidation and empathy. The words struggled to escape his lips, but at last, he managed to say, “We never spoke about Mikhail since we met, I want to know everything about him, but I guess first and foremost you need to know what happened that day. So here it is...He saved me from Hafeez and his men on several occasions, I wouldn’t be alive if it wasn’t for him." Manav describes all the details, reciting the events like a poem, characterising Mikhail as The Protagonist.

Manav – “The bomb you made for Mikhail proved to be very useful, and he picked an absolute moment to use it."

Aban – “Everything went well I suppose."

Manav – “Except that he did not make it."

The room grew still again, both men understanding the significance of the moment and the tremendous loss that had unfolded before them. In this shared moment of silence, they found solace in their unspoken connection. Aban had a smile on his face, but not a happy smile. His eyes were filled and looking down, imagining Mikhail's thoughts they adjoin in a reverie of reminiscence. They remained silent for several minutes however at times they looked at each other and exchanged pleasant smiles. Perhaps one can do that too when hugging seems way too soon and way too awkward.

Aban (in a very gentle voice) – "He spoke about you, you know. Not just him, Hafeez too. They told me your behaviour was aggravating them so much that they were least interested in letting you keep your life. It was against the plan though, however when Hafeez decides something, I do not know anyone who has ever succeeded in opposing him or changed his mind. I believe that is what influenced my son to rebel against him, against arguably the most feared one. You say you are the reason he died, it may be true because I remember when they were relaying the mission report, Hafeez and his men had clearly stated their plan to execute you, but Mikhail, as turbulent as always, must have seen something in you that must be saved, that must be given hope. He never gave his All at anything, except trying to save you. None of us could believe it when we heard that Hafeez and his hyenas were killed. The conclusion may be that having developed a likeness towards you got my son determined enough to even to make the ultimate sacrifice. For that much certainty, there must be something that he recognized in you and I am here to find out. So... how long do you think I am going to need?"

Manav – "Sir, you are welcome to stay as long as you want to. (Pointing towards the money bag he says) Considering the expenses Are not my concern now. I don't have a second thing to worry about, other than you and your friends' comfort."

This time, Aban had more than a smile on his face. Though Manav meant it in a very methodical way, Aban found it amusing, he had a feeling Manav might be a bit apprehensive about all this. With an effervescence of excitement, the conversation between Aban and Manav flowed effortlessly for the rest of the day. The topic of discussion centred on Mikhail, as memories and stories were shared, each recalling their own unique experiences with him. Aban held the role of a storyteller, offering anecdotes and narratives that allowed Manav to delve into the depths of his introverted nature and gradually open up. Together, they remembered the parts of their lives where Mikhail had once been present, weaving a tapestry of shared experiences.

In the evening Aban decided to go for a walk and invited Manav, he was a bit sceptical but then thought it over, "I must be seen with my 'father' at some point in time, what the hell, let's do this." There was a certain captivating quality to the reflection, an indescribable sense of unfamiliarity. It was as if he were seeing himself through a different lens, with a veil of mystery draped over his features. However, as the intensity of his gaze heightened, Manav suddenly felt a need to avert his eyes. The overwhelming fascination stirred feelings of discomfort, compelling him to seek a distraction elsewhere. Moments later Aban from the living room loudly asks, "Are you almost ready to go?", to which Manav replies, "I am." Manav comes out of the bedroom wearing active-wear clothes while Aban wears the same outfit he was wearing earlier. They both head out, "How about you give me a tour of your locality?"

Manav - "A tour? Not sure if anything will interest you here, it's a very ordinary and a very busy neighbourhood, we can take my bike, go to a park maybe ."

Aban - "Hold on! There was a sweet shop somewhere if I remember it correctly, I want to see what happened to that place."

Manav - "You've been here before?"!!

Aban - "I have, a long time ago, spent some of my childhood years here, with Uncle Fawaz and his wonderful family."

Manav - "Wow, I could have never guessed, let's see if that sweet shop is still open, what was its name?"

Aban - "I cannot recall, let us take a stroll, I might be able to gather the memories once I get acquainted."

They wander around the market for hours with in-between snacks and rests. Even though Manav had been living in the same neighbourhood for years, it was like a new experience for him as well. All this time, not once Manav had looked outside his own window. The exhilaration was the same for both as they saw the colourful but crowded market, overly decorated shops and to top that, the mouth watering snacks. Aban insists on buying a lot of things for Manav, dresses, shoes, mobile phones. It was like Christmas came early this year for him. He was being showered with all these gifts, as if finally getting compensated for his lonely past. All they did was take the next "left" or "right" whichever they found convenient, that's how much they were enjoying their walk.

Manav - "We still have a lot to cover, if your plan is to shop at every store, then i must tell you, your bag might not be enough."

Aban - "Don't you worry about it, that's not my only bag. Please, you have been so kind to me, you must allow me to return the favour."

Manav - "Really!? For some people that bag is their life's work, and by the way this is more than enough. We have already shopped for years for me."

Aban - "If you say so but where are we heading to now? it seems we have left the market behind."

Manav - "I was going to take you to the place I like the most here, it's a bit illegal but totally worth it. I have a feeling you will like that too."

Aban - "Is that so? Then what are we waiting for, I'm almost intrigued by the surprise. Just don't understand what is so illegal about it?"

Manav (With a delicate but indecent smile) - "We are going on the roof of a tall apartment building where we don't live, so that is what's illegal about it."

Aban (Puffing air out of his mouth) - "Okay, to tell you the truth, that is a relief, since I had no recognition of your concept of ''Illegal."

With a smirk exchanged between them, Manav took the lead, leading Aban towards a posh locality. As they made their way through the streets, they couldn't help but notice the air of opulence that emanated from every house and apartment they passed. Each dwelling seemed to exude an aura of elegance, style, and luxury. Manav and Aban found themselves surrounded by an abundance of affluence, where extravagant displays seemed to be the norm. Every building boasted cars with prestigious names like BMW or Mercedes, and even other vehicles with names that were difficult to pronounce. The extravagant array of automobiles emphasised the wealth and stature of the neighbourhood, leaving Aban feeling somewhat anxious in this sea of ostentation, he walked closely and whispered to Manav.

Aban - “Seems like it is a very important part of this locality, are you sure you’ve done this before? One thing I know about “The Rich”, they are very serious about their privacy."

Manav - “Just play the part, act like you belong here. They will only pay attention when they see someone suspiciously nervous."

Aban had no other option but to follow his lead.

They arrive in front of an apartment building with a gate that rises to the first floor and is decorated with a massive metal lion. Aban attempted to count the stories but gave up at fourteen because there were still many more to go. In order to enter, one has to pass through a boom barrier which was to be lifted by the guards placed there. Manav walking in front of Aban, just waves and smiles towards the guard, the Guard with a look of validation on his face, smiles back and opens the boom barrier. Aban does exactly what Manav did, following in his steps. They entered through the main door of the building where there was a reception area that was grimly functional and deserted, except for another guard behind the desk. The guard takes a few seconds to recognize Manav, smiles and then lets them pass. Aban was blankly inscrutable, dazed and confused with all that was going on, he continued to follow Manav, and they approached the lift area. Surprisingly Aban couldn’t see any buttons to press, only a fingerprint panel. Manav confidently presses his thumb on the panel and within a fraction of a second the panel turns green and the lift indicator shows it’s coming down. As the lift approaches and they enter the elevator, Aban finally breaks the silence that he had been holding on for a while now.

Aban - “Aren’t you full of surprises, I could have never imagined you a breaking and entering kind of a person."

Manav - “It’s not breaking and entering if you are in the authorised database. I work for a company that manufactures access controls. When we were installing these locks, some of us had the access to enter, I never deleted mine."

Aban - “Curious, but Why?"

Manav - “Let me show you."

They reach the top floor and take stairs to the roof. Once reached, Manav walks towards a particular direction and reaches the edge at which point he stops and looks down, Aban joins him. While taking cleansing breaths and smiling peacefully, they gaze out to the boundaries of their eyes. It was a lovely silence, with only faint sounds of human activity to be heard.

Aban - “What really is so special about this place, Manav. Don’t misunderstand me, it is a magnificent view, something tells me we are looking at different things."

Manav stays silent and keeps his eyes steady towards the ground. A couple of minutes later he says.

Manav - “Mikhail told me a fascinating story about you two stargazing one night and how you defined this planet could just be a grain of sand, I haven’t forgotten that story, it has been in my mind ever since, I wish I was there to see that view and hear your thoughts." he turns towards Aban.

Aban - It was a beautiful night, but it wasn’t the only...

Aban’s sentence was cut short by Manav. In a whispering voice he continues.

Manav - “You know what I see when I look down, I see everything is so small, same is what I see when I look up. All those gigantic stars as small as a grain of sand. Nothing else confuses me more about my existence and nothing else I question more. It appears to me I am between grains of sand in both directions, I am not even sure what I am talking about."

Very calmly and soothingly, Aban asks, “what is it that you want to talk about?"

Manav - “I am not really sure. I can’t remember a time when I talked so much to anyone. I guess what I am trying to say is that I used to take pride in being different and seeing things in different ways from others and I felt some day I will be at peace when I find the answers I was seeking. I am not sure when ‘being different’ started feeling like a disease and I got quiet, so quiet that it became a habit.”

After a moment of silence, Manav starts to feel awkwardness in the air, he tries to change the topic by cracking a joke, “You and your son have a knack of getting people to talk, does that help when you’re interrogating someone?"

Aban (Replying with a laugh) - “We’ll get to that but If I may, I would like to share a story, it may or may not help but its worth knowing. I told this to Mikhail as well (Aban had Manav’s undivided attention). I was reading a book on Gautam Budha. Obviously you have heard of him and his teachings but this writer mentions Budha’s earlier days of wealth and luxury in a very unique narrative and in a much simpler way for us ordinary minds to understand. He wrote that Budha might have seen all his wealth and family as an obstruction to the answers he was seeking. Perceptibly before being enlightened he might have hated all these obstacles, might have got furious on all his servants, thrown away all the expensive clothes, jewellery and food. He might have at least once hated all his family and all his belongings. But a day came when he decided to run away, not from his assets but his hatred. He decided he'd rather seek answers than being hateful to others. We all know what he finally discovered, the suffering and the pain he found outside his palace attained him with self discovery. In his travels and meditation he found every answer he was looking for, the whole world and beyond, he sighted, was always in him with him. We are obviously not as great as Budha, however the peace he found in days shouldn't be a problem for us simpler minds to find in years, don't you think?"

Manav - "Easier said than done."

Aban - "Spoken like a true believer, but it has to be done, no comfort in burning yourself from within."

As Manav continued his conversation with Aban, a touch of agitation started to creep into his thoughts. Until now, no one had been able to truly understand or penetrate the depths of his thoughts. Friends, acquaintances, and even psychiatrists had provided him with information and insights he already knew, offering no fresh perspectives or approaches. However, with Aban, it was different. The way he described facts and approached conversations seemed to resonate with Manav in an uncomfortable way. It felt as though Aban had an uncanny understanding of him, delving into his innermost thoughts and feelings with an accuracy that made Manav uneasy. The precision with which Aban perceived him made him wonder how much Aban truly knew about him. Manav's discomfort grew, raising questions about the nature of their encounter and Aban's motivations. Manav felt exposed as a sense of vulnerability washed over him, as if the protective walls he had built around himself were being dismantled piece by piece. Manav was wrestling with the conflicting emotions of intrigue and unease.

Manav - “I am sorry but I have to ask, why exactly are you here? I cannot conveniently accept the fact that a man of your reputation is having a reunion, without any ‘distractions’ planned."

The phrase "Your reputation precedes you" resonated strongly with the situation at hand. Manav stood with his arms crossed, his body language reflecting his queries within. Every part of him, metaphorically speaking, was focused on Aban, awaiting a response. The tension in the air was palpable. While Manav appeared visibly troubled, Aban seemed to be in stark contrast, seemingly unaffected by the atmosphere. He leaned back, savouring the cool evening breeze and taking in the scenery, his smile and soothing expressions contrasted with Manav’s distress. As the cool breeze continued to sweep through, carrying the weight of the moment, the tension between the two seemed to rise. The wait for the words that would bridge the gap between their perspectives and bring clarity hung heavy.

Aban - “You don’t trust me, I can understand why. Would it be any different if I’d rather invite you to my house?"

Manav - “I’d rather get an honest answer, because I cannot feel the rationale behind your arrival.”

Aban - “If you want an honest answer, I do not know. I Have been in disagreement with my own logic and reasoning since the day I lost my son. At first the facts made me hate you, But my instincts led me to believe in another possibility. If you are trying to understand why you are alive, that is what it is."

Manav - “What possibility?"

Aban - “In peacetime Sons bury their fathers, when fathers bury their sons it’s war and when you are at War, you keep your enemies close, and we have been keeping an eye on you Manav, closer than you can imagine. If it makes you feel any better, I'd like to say that even though we hacked your last six months, none of us were disappointed. We are anxious ONLY to be your friend. We knew exactly what you are from the day we first saw you."

Manav - "And what did you discover?"

Aban - "Exactly what I was hoping for. When I heard the news that the mission was a washout and none of my men survived, I was furious and anxious to see who did that. Then I saw you, I was right there. You were weeping when they were taking you away, everybody thought that you were under a post-traumatic-stress but let me put it this way, nobody can fake mourning, at least not to me, only someone with unfortunate experience in that area will know, that makes two of us, doesn't it Manav? Does that answer your question? I am not sure why someone would grieve over a person he just met. All we want NOW is to mourn together because something tells me that you love him too."

As Aban's words reached Manav's ears, they landed with a weight that shattered him from the inside out. Tears welled up in his eyes, overflowing and streaming down his face, a testament to the overwhelming emotions that engulfed him. The impact of Aban's words was so profound that Manav crumbled, metaphorically resembling a dead tree, unable to stand straight or form a coherent thought. His once composed demeanour now dissolved into chaos, leaving him incapable of articulating his emotions. Jumbled noises and incoherent utterances were the only sounds that escaped his trembling lips. Inside his mind, a storm raged, an onslaught of thoughts and sentiments bombarded him relentlessly. Like a tumultuous sea, his thoughts churned and twisted, but the words to express them eluded him. He struggled to form reasonable sentences, as his mind raced, fabricating ideas and emotions faster than he could vocalise them. He was overwhelmed by a flood of emotions that screamed for release, yet he found himself trapped in a realm of incoherence. His inner turmoil and inability to express his thoughts only intensified his anguish, creating an overwhelming sense of frustration and isolation. As tears continued to stream down his face, Manav yearned for solace and understanding, desperate to find a way to convey the complexities of his emotions that were trapped within his conflicted mind.

Like an overflooded dam, the weight of Manav's emotions became too much to bear. His legs could no longer support him, consumed by the weight of his despair, he crumbled to his knees. Tears flowed freely, mingling with his gasps for breath. The pain in his head intensified, throbbing as if it were on the verge of exploding. All efforts to control his emotions proved futile. With a moment of understanding, Aban allowed Manav his space to grieve. He stood back, observing with empathy, before gradually approaching. As he neared, Aban gently ruffled his fingers through Manav's hair, his touch conveying a sense of care and compassion. Slowly, he began caressing Manav's head with his toughened palms, offering a surprising comfort that eased the turmoil within him.

Aban then positioned himself to be eye to eye with Manav, holding his face in both hands. Their eyes locked in a profound connection, filled with unspoken understanding. With a soothing tone, Aban began to speak, his voice gentle yet resolute. "Manav," Aban whispered, his words carrying a sense of support and empathy, "It's okay to feel overwhelmed. Grief has a way of overpowering us, tearing us apart. Your pain is valid, and you don't have to feel alone."

Aban - "Don't hold anything back, let them all out. you are not alone anymore, everything is going to be just fine."

As Manav's emotions overwhelmed him, he found solace in Aban's touch. Without uttering a single word, he expressed his need for comfort by pulling Aban closer and embracing him tightly, seeking refuge in his arms. Resting his head on Aban's shoulder, he surrendered to his grief, without any hesitations or reservations allowing his tears to flow freely. The sound of Manav's cries echoed through the air, drowning out any other noise around them. Both remained motionless and locked in their embrace as Manav's wails reverberated through the space. Aban continued to caress Manav's hair with unwavering tenderness, offering a comforting touch as a steady source of support. Time came and went, and slowly, Manav's cries began to soften. As he gradually found moments of respite from his overwhelming emotions, his cries would occasionally resurface, like an injured puppy whimpering in pain. Throughout it all, Aban remained steadfast, never showing any embarrassment or impatience, providing a safe space for Manav to grieve without judgement.

Unaware of how long it had been, they became so comfortable in each other's arms that time became irrelevant. A while later Aban felt Manav was nodding off, he taps gently on Manav's head and calls out to him a few times. Though Manav was well awake, it was too awkward for him to look into Aban's eyes after his breakdown. Avoiding embarrassment he tried to keep it locked but the crying tired him out. It was less than a child's play for Aban to take him off his shoulders. He held Manav's face and asked to look him in the eye. It was effortful at first but eventually Manav looked down at Aban with his tearfilled eyes.

Aban - “Listen Manav, I wish I was there with him during his last moments, But I’m glad it was you who gave him farewell. I wish I had loved him as much as you do, I truly do because he deserved it. You and I are probably going to mourn him forever so save your energy, there are many more stories to be told. Now let’s get out of this building before they catch us. Don’t forget we are illegal occupants my friend."

Manav - “You’re right, you’re right. It’s late, let’s scoot."

They got up and gave a last glance at the closing lights of the city, but not before Aban gave him another hug and assured him that everything will be fine. They leave the terrace and head towards the lobby. In the lift Aban expresses his likeness towards the apartment and how much he liked the view and style.

Aban - “What would you say about buying the penthouse in this apartment?"

Manav - “Only that it is too expensive and not sure if that is a good investment."

Aban - “Investments? Nothing in life is an investment Manav, even the ‘returns’ will fade away someday. Besides,I have enough of the said ‘investments’ at my ancestral home in Lucknow, seems a good time to invest in other kinds of properties."

Manav - “Lucknow? That’s interesting. I’d like to visit someday."

Aban - “Of course you will, We do have a visit in the itinerary, just waiting for everyone’s arrival."

Manav - “I’ve been meaning to ask, who are these people that you are expecting?"

Aban - “Some close relatives of mine, Sana, my daughter, Abbu and my son Khalid."

Manav - “Really, that baffles me a little but I’m happy to know that you’ve got family, can’t wait to meet them."

Aban - “Well Sana seems to be running late, she should have been here by now, Khalid is a hard man to reach and Abbu is in Lucknow waiting for all of us to join him there."

As the waves of emotions gradually subsided, Manav felt a newfound sense of calm washing over him. A fresh smile tugged at the corners of his lips as he allowed his mind to wander into the realm of possibilities. Thoughts of meeting Aban’s family and, more importantly, Mikhail’s relatives filled his imagination, igniting a spark of anticipation within him. The turmoil that had consumed him just moments ago slowly transformed into a sense of excitement. With each passing moment, Manav’s mind began to predetermine what his family vacation could potentially hold. Images of shared laughter, warm embraces, and cherished memories danced in his thoughts. Imagining the prospect of getting to know Aban’s loved ones and connecting with individuals who had also shared a piece of Mikhail’s life brought a mix of emotions. Alongside the excitement, there was a sense of reverence and a yearning to honour Mikhail’s memory in the presence of his family.

Aban - “It looks like it’s about to rain, your young legs must be faster than mine, don’t hold back because of me. I will take shelter till some cloud clears off, I do not want to experiment with the new weather. It may take me down under, Wouldn’t want that to happen on a vacation, would we?"

Manav - “Are you sure you want to wait?"

Aban - “Yes, I will be fine, besides I would like to investigate in the neighbourhood if any of my old mates are around. It will be a great surprise for them, and don’t order anything, I’m cooking today."

As Manav parted ways with Aban at the gate, he briskly walked back to his apartment, a sense of urgency guiding his steps. The sky above grew darker, and the light rain that had initially started began to intensify into a raging storm. Realising that the rain was not going to let up anytime soon, Manav made a quick decision that it would be more efficient to equip himself with an umbrella from his apartment and then go back to Aban.

However, something unusual went unnoticed, there was something serene about him, for the first time in a long time Manav was so comforted and relieved that he couldn’t care less about getting wet and dirty. He walks over the shin-deep water logged roads, unstirred and uncaring while everyone else were sheltering themselves under the shop awnings. Stress was not agreeing with him today. The relief after shedding long-held tears left him with a smile he could not draw off his face. Trying to hide the smile was making it even harder to control, but he was enjoying these silly moments. While ruffling his hair, he turns his face upwards to the downpour and closes his eyes. He lets the rain drops fall on his face and relishes the chilling sensation, not to hide his tears but to express his joy. Maybe his winner’s-walk was so graceful or was it the ecstasy of incalculable happiness, everything appeared to be slowing down on him. He walked against the rain like he was in no hurry, he felt every gust of wind and endured its chill, his body was so relaxed that the racingly-heavy raindrops did not bounce off him rather they became a part of him. If one were to observe closely, they would notice that Manav was not merely walking past or against the water, wind, and rain. Rather, it seemed as though he was walking through them, as if he had achieved a state of harmonious unity with his surroundings. In that moment, he embodied the essence of a hero who had discovered a sense of fulfilment beyond his wildest dreams.

## CHAPTER EIGHT

# RIVER

His cold-blooded walk continued till his apartment, as he reached the premises, he vaguely noticed that people walking around him had suddenly started to observe him. Unlike earlier times when he felt invisible and non-part, but today he felt like he existed, something he could not describe. His eyes could not have opened more, he could see people and people could see him. The woman living opposite to his flat has great hair, the old man on the first floor has a beautiful mole by his chin, the kids he kept distance from have an infectious laughter, and the neighbour he always hated! Well there wasn't much difference there, that neighbour was an ignorant mess. Everywhere he turned, he saw brilliant colours and shiny things. Even the frowning faces were adorable. His focus seemed enhanced by many levels, the excitement he carried was as if he was born again and was seeing everything for the first time. "What a day?" He chats with himself while greeting and smiling at everyone he passes by, unaware of how dirty his clothes or even how messy his hair was.

A few doors before his flat he noticed that someone was sitting by his door wearing a black hoodie and some trolley bags around. Strangely enough, another stranger sought Manav for the second time that day despite the neighbours' apparent lack of interest. Some just couldn't let it go, the focus of their eyes and ears were at Manav's doorsteps. Manav gets close enough for the person in the hoodie to see Manav's feet. "Hello" said Manav, but there was no reply or reaction, this person seemed to be wearing headphones and completely zoned into the music. As Manav turned to leave, unsure if it would be impolite to disturb the person in the hoodie, he suddenly felt a soft yet penetrating grip on his knee. The touch sent a wave of goosebumps racing across his skin, a sensation unlike anything he had ever experienced. Despite the rain, storm, and strong winds that had failed to make him shiver, this touch managed to reach deep within him, stirring a profound response. The stimuli, almost like a mild electric shock, triggered a mini trance-like state within Manav. He longed to keep feeling that touch, to experience that unique sensation over and over again. Although his response seemed absent in that brief moment, the internal shivers resonated throughout his body. Finally, the mystery was solved. The person in the hoodie was none other than Sana, Aban's daughter. With this realisation, a combination of surprise, excitement, and a renewed sense of connection surged through Manav. He was now face-to-face with a significant figure in Aban's life, someone who probably held a high importance in his new family.

Sana - "Hi Manav, glad you finally made it. I am Sana. Where is Abbu? I thought he was with you?"

As Sana removed her hoodie and took out her headphones, Manav's initial surprise transformed into awe. Her appearance deviated significantly from his expectations, causing his mouth to involuntarily form a slight O-shape. Sana's body was adorned with intricate and captivating tattoos, spanning from her shoulders to her neck and covering her hands with mythical imagery. Adding to her unconventional and mesmerising appearance, there were piercings on her lips and a pair of other-worldly earrings, only if you want to call them "rings" they looked like spears going in from the lobe to the top of her ear. Despite her petite frame, Sana exuded a commanding presence. Her voice carried hints of masculinity, yet it possessed a softness that brought a charming contrast to her overall demeanour. Manav found himself wondering about the genetics that creates such marvellous and striking beings. All of them are so beautiful. Manav, though still slightly unfocused due to the unexpected encounter, shaking off his temporary lapse in focus, he finally took charge as the host. He carried her bag inside and extended an invitation for her to make herself comfortable. She seemed relaxed and at ease, making herself at home as she crashed onto the sofa and became engrossed in her phone. Her nonchalant behaviour suggested a familiarity with the surroundings, as if it were not her first visit.

Manav - "Can I get you something?"

Sana - "Why not, what do you have to drink?"

Manav - "Your Abbu has made some tea, let me warm it up for you."

Sana - "That would be great, been a while since I had his tea, May I use your bathroom?"

Manav directed Sana to the bathroom, ensuring she knew the way, before busying himself in the kitchen. As Sana returned from freshening up, she found a pot of freshly brewed tea waiting for her on the living room table. Appreciating the gesture, she changed into comfortable baggy sweat clothes, her towel wrapped around her hair like a turban. Making herself at home, Sana settled onto the sofa and turned on the TV. The familiarity in her actions conveyed a sense of ease and comfortability, as if she had been in this space many times before. Manav observed her natural ease and felt a sense of contentment, realising that Sana had truly made herself at home without him even needing to ask. With the tea steaming on the table, the room filled with a warm and inviting ambiance. Manav joined Sana on the couch.

Sana - “mmm.. Saffron is missing, you should have this with saffron, that really is a secret ingredient, completely changes how it feels on your tongue."

Manav - “Your father said the same thing."

Sana - “Where is he by the way?"

Manav - “He should be here any minute."

After observing the surroundings of his apartment, Sana starts the conversation.

Sana - “So Manav, how are you liking the overnight fame, you went into the night as someone else and got back as someone else."

Taken aback by an odd question, Manav thinks for a moment and replies.

Manav - “Like a dream you want to wake up from but somehow stuck."

Sana - “You are not at all like I imagined you'd be."

Manav - “You are the third person from your family to imply that, and you are the third person I met."

Sana - “I'm sorry, we all are freakishly similar at some things."

Manav - “I won't use the word “freakish” but it's adorable that you have something in common. The genetics were really kind to all of you."

"Manav, I have a question for you," Sana says, her expression slightly intense yet reserved. Manav, intrigued by her sudden shift in demeanour and the directness of her tone, responded with curiosity, "Of course, Sana. What would you like to ask?" Sana paused for a moment, gathering her thoughts before she continued, her eyes locked with his.

Sana - "The following question might have been asked many times in many forms and you must have answered it in all sorts, But tell me as you want to tell, How are you doing Manav?"

As Manav processed Sana's question, he couldn't help but be captivated by her presence. It was as if she possessed an innate understanding of his innermost thoughts and feelings. She exuded a sense of confidence and control, her poised posture and enigmatic gaze holding him in a state of anticipation. Time seemed to stand still as Manav gathered his thoughts, feeling the weight of Sana's piercing gaze upon him. Her unwavering stillness added to the intensity of the moment, amplifying the significance of his response.

Choosing his words carefully, Manav finally broke the silence, his voice carrying a mix of vulnerability and determination.

Manav - "Like I don't want to speak about it until I can remember it on my own. All the questions, no matter how someone asks, bring only bad memories of that day."

Sana - "No, I did not mean just 'That' day, I have been watching you Manav, and truly I have never seen someone so quiet. At times I have walked beside you with dearly expensive perfumes, strong enough that can be smelt across the street. You can sense 'Smells' right? Everybody else turns around to me but not you. Why do you have to always look down, it's an extremely depressing posture."

Manav portrayed an adorable smile with a hint of blush in it, taking his time to fabricate a response, alas, they heard a knock on the door, momentarily pausing, he turned towards the door. As he swung the door open, he was greeted by the sight of Aban, fully drenched and covered in dirt just like Manav and Sana. But before Manav could even react, Sana's excitement got the better of her. With a burst of energy, she rushed towards Aban, her genuine joy radiating from every pore. Jumping up like a kid, she wrapped her arms tightly around Aban, engulfing him in a bear hug. The room filled with laughter and warmth as Sana's exuberance echoed through the air. It was a moment of pure happiness and reunion, bringing together the three in a shared connection that surpassed the boundaries of time and circumstance. Manav, still wearing his smile, watched the heartwarming scene unfold before him. The bond between Sana and Aban was undeniable, their love for each other shining through even in this simple embrace.

As the laughter subsided, and the room filled with a sense of comfort and familiarity, Manav couldn't help but feel grateful for this serendipitous encounter. Little did he know that this meeting would alter the trajectory of all their lives.

Sana - "Abbu!", She screams and swarms him with questions. "When are we going to meet Aljadu? When is Khalid arriving?"

Aban cherishes the meeting with his daughter for a moment and smilingly addresses Manav.

Aban - "I hope this little one didn't give you much trouble."

Manav responds with laughter.

Manav - “Not at all Sir, My pleasure. Let us clean ourselves now. Bathroom is yours.”

Aban - “By the way, I checked a few penthouses from the building we were in earlier. They are really good, I was impressed. Sana, My dear, would you accompany me tomorrow to finalise it?

Sana nods in agreement and Aban excuses himself to go for a shower. Meanwhile Manav could not wrap his mind around the fact that Aban is taking Sana tomorrow to finalise the most expensive house in the most expensive apartment situated in one of the most expensive localities. He had his doubts if it was all too-much-too-soon that may grab unwanted attention but the sudden profusion of happiness just couldn’t make him worry about anything. He was indulged in a fantasy that became truer than he could have fantasised. He felt protected but at the same time felt responsible towards his protector. His hair would erect every now and then just thinking about what happened in the last 18 hours and what may lie ahead. Noticing his hardly-hidden smiles, Sana interjects his daydreaming.

Sana - “ "Hey there, Mr. Dreamer. What’s got you lost in your thoughts? I’m bored, wanna share what’s making you giggle inside? I may find it funny too.”

Manav - “I won’t be too sure, people usually creep out knowing what I find funny or serious. That’s what made me minimise my interaction with people.”

Sana - “That’s right isn’t it, you were smiling alone imaging things when tied up, you were laughing at those men when they tortured you. An Evil-Incarnate like Hafeez who was good at nothing but petrifying people, even he failed.”

Manav’s eyes widened in surprise as Sana mentioned the events of the day when he was held captive. Her awareness of that day left him wondering how much she knew and how she had come to possess that information, however Sana continued.

Sana - "Don't be shocked, Hafeez and Mikhail shared their mission reports with us during the operation, and Abbu told me. They had the complete opposite description about you, but Hafeez, he tried as much as possible to hide his fumes that you raged in him. You should be proud to be the-one-and-only who made a man furious known for driving people mad."

Manav - "I .... Wanted to be afraid but I wasn't terrified. I wanted to silently die without complaints, without worry, without holding anything against anyone. I don't know why I wasn't scared, something was driving me against my will. I had lost my soul already, my body didn't seem to be important after that. Enraging them energised me, losing blood made me feel stronger, pain was like an adrenaline rush. I couldn't wait to leave my consciousness and dive into uncertainty."

Sana - "Most people do their best when they feel they have nothing to lose. You are peculiar though, you wanted to lose and somehow it worked in your favour. I can't help but mention that it was really idiotic of you."

Manav - "It was a miracle that I came out alive, and that 'Miracle' was your brother."

Sana - "In many ways the comparison is very similar between you two, he wasn't much of a talker just as you aren't and that might be the most I know about him. In my defence I kept travelling around for studies to stay out of my people's reach. He may have even forgotten that he had a sister. I should have been in touch with him, it was years ago when we spoke. I hope I can remember more of him."

Manav - “I wouldn’t mind having a family, if you would grant that honour.”

Sana - “That’s an ‘Idea’, but seems too soon to throw around relationship-tags for now, Let us feel it and see where it takes us."

Manav gently smiled and acknowledged Sana’s idea with a nod. In the meantime Aban comes back from his shower, rubbing a towel on his silver hair.

Aban - “You kids talk, I have some cooking to do.”

Aban gets busy in the kitchen preparing for supper, Manav went inside the bathroom to clean himself. With all the privacy, he did not compromise on his smiles, with nobody watching he celebrated his new life like a conqueror, he spent some time looking at his “New Me." By the time he was back Aban had prepared an authentic arabic mutton curry. Just the smell of it made Manav’s and Sana’s mouths drain water, their tummies started burning with craving and hunger.

Aban - “Yoghurt wasn’t fermented enough, Next time it will be better."

As they started eating that delicious curry, both didn’t even bother to compliment or critique. They wanted to but none of them could stop their hands or jaws from munching away the salty and spicy however tremendously appetising Mansaf. Even when the hot spices scorched their taste buds, so much that they started sweating, however, the delicacy never stopped, they continued chomping with thankfulness in their eyes for Aban. A time came when they were both full and were in no state to speak. With a mouthful of food, Manav says.

Manav - If you could better this up, you will underrate ‘The Heavens."

Aban laughs with almost tears in his eyes.

Aban - “That’s an honouring compliment Manav, I’m glad you liked it."

Sana just as Manav was struggling to stop too.

Sana - “I must have had my share of food for a week, but I still don’t want to stop. Abbu, I can’t believe you can still cook.”

It was a proud moment for Aban, he gestures his gratification. After Sana had her fill, she got up.

Sana - “I need to walk, digest some of it. I won’t sleep with a bloated tummy. Manav, get up. Walk me through your neighbourhood."

Aban - “Leave him be, dear. He must be very tired after our walk."

Sana - “Alright...

Manav interjects.

Manav - “That’s okay, I can use a walk myself. Aban, your cooking is admirable at the same time I’m hating it. Please keep cooking like this."

Manav’s humour wasn’t at it’s best but the sentence he said in seriousness was taken as a matter of laughter. The room was filled with chuckles and giggles, but Manav was clueless. Aban pats Manav’s back.

Aban - “You kids go ahead with your walk, by the time your digestion is complete, I’ll see if I can prepare some sweet delicacies."

As Manav and Sana stepped out of the apartment, a sense of excitement bubbled within them, discussing the delicious treats Aban had prepared for his kids in the past back at thome. Their conversation flowed effortlessly as they strolled along, savouring the anticipation of dessert.

However, as they made their way through the premises, Manav’s heightened senses detected the gaze of neighbours and even strangers; it felt uncomfortably intense. The scrutiny, the close proximity of the observers, triggered a wave of anxiety within him. The sudden attention unnerved him after being accustomed to blending into the background and virtually invisible all thus far.

Sana, ever observant, quickly noticed Manav's unease, what she did next was completely unexpected. Without hesitation, she reached out and firmly grasped his arm, a gesture of both support and protection. In that moment, an electric sensation coursed through Manav's body, but it eventually settled into a calming reassurance. Sana's grip transmitted her unwavering confidence, as if she had passed on a portion of her own strength to him.

With newfound courage, Manav casts a defiant glance back at those scrutinising eyes, each stare was met with an unwavering gaze. He no longer felt invisible or small. Sana's presence and support had transformed his mindset, rekindling his self-assuredness. As they continued their walk, Manav's steps grew more relaxed, his breath steadying. The nervousness that once consumed him dissipated, replaced by a newfound sense of calm and confidence. Sana's simple act of solidarity had been a powerful reminder that he didn't need to shrink away or fear the scrutiny of others.

After passing the crowded area, they reach a park. It was a beautiful night. As Manav and Sana strolled through the park, the ambiance became enchanting. The full moon cast a gentle glow over the surrounding greenery, turning the grass into a mesmerising shade of purple. They couldn't help but pause and admire the beauty that surrounded them. With each step they took, they turned their gaze upwards, peering through the leaves of the trees as if they were looking at the moon through a natural filter. The moonlight seeped through the foliage, creating a whimsical and ethereal display.

At that moment, time seemed to stand still. They were wholly present, mesmerised by the moonlit scene and the enchanting atmosphere it created. The rustling of leaves accompanied their footsteps, creating a peaceful soundtrack to their journey. As they continued to walk, their hearts synchronised with the rhythmic beauty of the night, immersed in the tranquillity and awe-inspiring nature surrounding them. It was a moment of shared wonderment, a testament to the power of nature to captivate and bring people together.

They decided to sit on a bench for a few minutes to admire the view, as they started talking their breath was visible in the chilly January air. The cold breeze tickled their noses, turning them a rosy shade, and with each exhale, a puff of "cloud smoke" formed in front of them. It was a familiar sight, but one that never failed to amuse them.

Giggling uncontrollably, their conversation turned into a string of senseless jokes and lighthearted banter. The pressure of communication and the need for deep conversation seemed to fade into the background as they embraced the simplicity of playful moments together.

The echoes of laughter enveloped them, filling the air with their shared joy. But as their silly jokes began to ebb, a moment of silence settled between them. They felt the weight of unspoken expectations, an unspoken pressure to continue the conversation. There was a brief lull, an awkward pause that left them both momentarily at a loss for words.

Manav, feeling the weight of that silent pressure, mustered the courage to speak. His expression grew perplexed, searching for something meaningful to say.

Sana's gaze wandered momentarily, but as she recognized Manav's intention to speak, her attention shifted entirely to him, her eyes fixed on his every word.

In that moment, Manav took a deep breath, his voice thoughtful yet unsure, "You know, Sana, sometimes the gaps in conversation allow us to appreciate the depth and comfort of just being in each other's presence. It's not always about having something profound to say; sometimes it's the quiet moments that we share, hold the most meaning. I learnt that from your brother and your father."

Sana's eyes softened, a gentle smile gracing her lips as she nodded in agreement.

Manav - "I want to talk to you but I don't know where to begin. It all sounded so viable in my head but it's all jumbled up now. I can't find the origin of what I want to say."

Sana, sensing his bafflement, delivered a cute smile and calmingly looked deep in his eyes. She holds his hands and says.

Sana - "Start from wherever you want, we have 3 days to figure it out, we don't have to stop talking. I too want to know everything about you, Manav."

Manav - "It doesn't seem wise to start from anywhere but from the beginning, It has to come exactly as I thought otherwise the message won't be delivered as intended. Even a perfect message becomes harder and harder as time passess by. All I wanted to tell you is how amazing and one-of-a-kind I think you are. You have this magnetism in your aura that it's impossible not to get enchanted by your charm. Your youth and appeal might be the first thing everyone else notices but that's the least of all. I know it sounds ridiculous but I'm being forced to believe by my-own-self that you might have the power of healing through alchemy. You are like a character that came out of a fantasy book."

When a payload is delivered, a silent but deadly suspense follows, leaving everyone anticipating the impact of the explosion. Sometimes people wish to take back what they said right after they said it, just like some trigger fingers, unfortunately both are impossible to undo. Manav regretted the bomb he just delivered, though it hasn't been more than a few seconds; however, the 'Wait' to see the impact was unearthly. A part of him wanted to get over with it, a part of him didn't want the wait to ever be over.

Sana was not very different from Manav either. She took her sweet time to recognize what just happened, but the suspense was finally coming to an end. She initially appeared to be in need of medical assistance as her face transformed into what seemed like an inflated balloon and her radiant complexion turning red, painted a comedic picture. Sana barely managed to hold on, but a few seconds later she broke free with a contagious laughter. Manav was shocked but wasn't actually offended, ordinarily people would, when they get laughter as a response on a serious topic, However, Manav's eyes were rather lit up and targeted at Sana as though utterly bewitched. Sana's enthralling laughter did not stop and Manav succumbed to the infection she was spreading. The seriousness of the moment dissolved into pure mirth as they laughed without inhibitions. Oblivious to their surroundings, they created their own space of happiness, the sounds of their laughter echoing through the park.

Time seemed to stand still as they relished in the moments of shared joy. With each glance exchanged between them, their laughter erupted anew, intensifying the merriment. It was a rare and precious experience to be completely present in a moment that felt so right, so aligned with their true selves.

Lost in their laughter, they were blissfully unaware of the passing time and the attention they may have attracted. They let go of any self-consciousness, surrendering to the sheer delight of the moment. In these precious instances, they found themselves exactly where they were meant to be, embracing the pure essence of joy.

However, their joy of a relishable laughter dialled down when they sensed some kind of movement behind the trees that some may call predatorial. Crunching of dry leaves and a couple of shadowy figures in the dark, striked to be watching Manav and Sana. Two strange men directly approach them from the darker part of the park. As those strangers made their way closer to Manav and Sana, they realised the silhouettes were of two policemen patrolling the park. The policemen acted like they were roaming around however, Undeniably of course, their eyes and ears were on Sana and Manav. Keeping their advance towards them noticeable, the policemen approach Manav.

Policeman 1 - “Look who’s here, it’s the Indian Harry Potter. The boy who survived."

He says it while confidently portraying a wicked-smile from his crooked teeth. It never looked genuine before, neither was it today. If anything, it may just be something that can scare little children in an instant. However, the policemen kept smiling proudly, waiting for a response from Manav or Sana. The second policeman, who was not showing any fake friendliness as the first one, came a bit too close for comfort, also rather stiff and demanding. Altogether, it was an awful comedy of poorly-performed conventional good-cop bad-cop routine. His voice was already raised to the maximum volume.

Policeman 2 - "No romance allowed in the park after dark, the park is closed. Why are you still here?"

Manav did not like the yelling in front of his guest at all. He was ferociously getting ready with a response, that's when surprisingly Sana took over. Calmingly and confidently she responded.

Sana - "Oh! We are sorry officers, but if the park is closed then why was the gate still open? That is how we let ourselves in."

Policeman 2 - "Do not argue with me girl, you broke the rules, do you see anyone else in the park, Who is she to you?" He asks Manav but Sana stays in-charge.

Sana - "Oh! We are lovers, you caught us a bit early. We were about to get down to business, a few minutes after you could have caught us in live action."

Manav's eyes went wide, so did the policemen's but they made a naive attempt to hide their discomforted astonishment. Sana's response was filled with so much confidence and determination that their breaths might have stuck in their throats for a second. But a trained policeman knows how to tackle an unforeseen situation, the well-mannered one's use their brains, the ill-mannered use their bullying skills. Unfortunately these policemen weren't so well-mannered. They step up and raise their voice again, demanding identifications.

Policeman 2 - "Show me your ID."

Sana - "Don't have one."

Even though Sana had, she refused to be bullied and decided to confront their arrogance.

Policeman 2 - "Then you will have to come to the police station."

Sana remained cool as a cucumber.

Sana - “Is it so? I was not aware of any such rules passed recently. Let me call my lawyer friend to get some clarity."

She was just about to get her phone out of the pocket, when suddenly the policeman tried to grab her hand almost as if attempting a brawl with her to get her phone. He wasn’t very keen on letting them use their phones when, unanticipatedly like a sound of thunder, Manav roared.

Manav - “DON’T YOU DARE TOUCH HER”!!!

They all froze, even Sana but unlike the policemen she had a mild smirk on her face trying to control the puff of laughter. They stood still and dazed. Unleashing an unexpected force that reverberated through the park. Manav, fueled by a surge of adrenaline and determination, his roar carried a raw intensity that sent shivers down the spines of all who heard.

The sudden roar caught the policemen off guard, freezing them where they stood.

Manav - “Here’s my driver’s licence, and BE respectful."

The policemen, recovering from their initial shock, exchanged a brief glance before realising the importance of de-escalating the situation. Sensing the strength and determination radiating from Manav, they quickly composed themselves, their manner shifting to a more respectful and apologetic tone. Policemen trying to save his day, says.

Policeman 1 - “There’s no need, we were just doing our duty. As you know that Republic day is near, we need to make sure everybody is safe."

Sana - “Safe from what?"

Manav interjects.

Manav - “That’s alright, we were leaving anyway but from next time remember if the park gate is open, anyone can enter after-hours but for sure it won’t be us."

Manav, though still fueled by the adrenaline surging through his veins, nodded slightly, acknowledging the explanation. His intensity softened as he recognized the policemen's duty. They all thank each other for their understanding with a fake smile of approval and all went their way. As soon as the policemen went far enough, Manav and Sana looked back to make sure they were alone, then looked at each other and laughed their lungs out like little kids.

Sana - "That was so bizarre but so much fun! You might have made him piss his pants Manav, How about that?!"

Manav - "What about you little badger! You are like an upgraded and advanced version of Mikhail."

Hearing that compliment, Sana stopped walking and looked at Manav with a smile and with a whispering voice she asked.

Sana - "Is it so?"

Manav - "Of course you are, tackling undesirable situations with grace. That's what he was all about and that's what You did. Now I miss him more."

Sana - "You made my day twice, today, Manav. Protecting my honour, that was really sweet of you."

With sparkly eyes she looked right into his eyes and reached out to him, straightening a lock of his hair, she says.

Sana - "Thank you, Manav."

Manav - "I like the way my name sounds when You say it."

Manav was not overstating, Sana was blessed with an alluring and tempting voice with the added advantage of her impeccable vocabulary and articulation. Every single syllable was music to his ears, he just couldn't have enough of it.

Hearing that welcoming praise lifted Sana's spirits, but also gave a little nudge to her naughtiness. She re-imaged herself in a flirtatious mood, taking Manav for granted for a tiny bit, however with good spirits, she responds in a sultry voice.

Sana - "Oh really! Manav, Would you like me to keep calling your name, Manav."

Responding with a smile, he says.

Manav - "I would, but not in this manner, it seems you don't know what your voice does to others. Let me try and explain. I have no idea what it feels like to soar over an abyss of soft clouds, inhale the aroma of fresh flowers, or experience a light that is not warm but soft and bright, illuminating the path ahead with warmth and clarity. It's difficult to capture the essence of your presence in mere words, for it transcends the limitations of language. So, know that your presence is a gift, one that fills my heart with gratitude and brings a smile to my face. It's a feeling that will forever be etched in my memory, a treasure I will always hold close to my heart."

With crossed hands and thinking posture, Sana's eyes survey Manav for an awkward bit of silence.

Sana - "Whoa! Steady 'Harry Potter' of India, are you really falling for a woman you just met."

Manav - "I don't think so, I am just stating what seems like 'obvious' to me."

Sana - "Well, I must say that was really sweet of you, not to correct you but, 'Abyss' is usually deep in the sea and 'Clouds' are high in the sky."

Manav - "Maybe that's what's wrong about you, you make flying and falling feel the same."

After a short awkward silence, and trying to bring the spirits back to prosperity.

Sana - "No one ever noticed me that way, not even me."

Manav - "Perhaps due to your scary tattoos."

And he promptly laughs at his own joke.

Sana was taken aback initially, shortly after she joined him too.

Sana - "You're a good person, Manav. I am sorry for what you went through, nevertheless I am glad I met you."

The beauty of the situation was that it was creating its own gravity, an unexplainable and unstoppable force pulled them towards each other, resolving into a soothing warm hug. In the grip of their undeniable connection, Manav and Sana found solace in each other's embrace. Their hug was a sanctuary, a comforting haven amidst the chaos of the world Manav was big enough to devour her into his arms, he enveloped Sana, holding her close like a precious pearl within his protective shell.

When they finally broke apart from the hug, their hands remained intertwined, unwilling to let go of the connection they had discovered. Hand in hand, they began their journey back to Manav's apartment, their laughter and senseless jokes filling the night air. The sound of their voices echoed through the stillness and silence of the night, reaching far beyond their immediate surroundings. But neither of them seemed to care.

When they finally reached, they found the door was locked from inside, Manav used his keys to enter. The lights were switched off, and it seemed like Aban had already marked the bedroom as his territory. However there were some changes. There were more bags than before and two sets of loud snoring. Manav switches the lights on and notices there were several laptop bags and one big backpack added to the cumulative luggage. Sana goes into the bedroom to check on Abbu. She comes back with a little aftershock on her face. She whispers.

Sana - "It's Khalid, he might have come in while we were on our walk."

Manav - "Oh, so the bedroom is acquired, you can take the sofa."

Sana - "Floor is fine for me, I like it better."

Manav - "You sure?"

Sana - "Absolutely, I'll be more than fine."

Manav arranges the sofa and floor with some sheets and pillows. Puts all the luggage in an organised way before he crashes on to the sofa. The lights were switched off, however a street lamp's dim light coming through the windows was just enough for them to notice that their eyes were on each other. They communicate using their eyes for a bit.

Manav - "I can't help remembering I was in the exact same position when I said my final goodbye to Mikhail."

Sana, not saying a word, prowls towards him and gently shuts his eyes with her fingers. Whispering and giggling while she does it, she says.

Sana - "You have drained your brain enough for today Mr. Potter, go back to your fluffy-cottony magical-sea-world."

She giggles softly like a child, Manav lifts his head up, Sana immediately covers his eyes and gently pushes his head down back on the pillow. Taking full advantage of her gifted voice she continued.

Sana - "uh uh uh.. Don't you open your eyes or say another word. Time to go adrift in your dreamland, don't have to feel alone anymore, my eyes will watch over you, let me sway you to nothingness. Enjoy your stay, I'll come back to get you at dawn."

She then gently kisses his cheeks and a pleasant smile erupts on Manav's face.

Sana - "Keep that smile... always, don't let it go. Sweet Dreams Manav ".

Mesmerised is a state of mind that some creatures often experience when preyed upon. This state can be observed in certain creatures when they are in the presence of their predator. The combination of suspense and amazement can create an odd attraction towards the very entity that poses a threat to them.

In nature, examples can be seen in the hunting tactics of predators that use mesmerising techniques to lure their prey. They may utilise patterns, movements, or other captivating displays to draw the attention of their unsuspecting victims. This mesmerization can temporarily immobilise the prey, leading them to become more vulnerable to the predator's attack, akin to the flashing colours and waves of lights displayed by a Cuttlefish, creating a sense of wonder and fascination for its prey.

Such a phenomenon can also be observed in human interactions, albeit in a metaphorical sense. There are instances where individuals may find themselves inexplicably drawn to someone or something that has the potential to cause them harm. It may be the enigmatic nature of the predator or the thrill of the unknown that entices the prey, blurring their judgement and promoting an ill-advised attraction.

An unknown feeling takes away the ability of recognition or even to move a muscle, everything becomes so unclear that harder it gets for the sensations to remain Lucid in the state of incertitude caused by the lack of ability to accept the truth, when the truth is astonishing but deadly at the same time. The allure of the predator's presence, the sensation remains the same however the situation wasn't. It is a state of being caught between conflicting emotions of interest and fear, unable to fully comprehend the implications of the situation. The Sheep, seemingly, gets drawn towards the Wolf.

## CHAPTER NINE

# TORNADO

Daybreak - As far as Manav could remember, he never had a dreamless and peaceful sleep or even woke up with hope for a better day, but today He was well-rested. As Manav slowly opened his eyes, he couldn't help but smile, hopeful to see the familiar and beautiful face that had seemingly enchanted his dreams. The sunlight streamed gently through the window, casting a soft glow on the room and illuminating the anticipation in his eyes. With a contented sigh, he inhaled the peaceful surroundings, cherishing the stillness of the morning as he stretched his arms and yawned like a cub. He opened his eyes anticipating to see the pretty face he saw before his consciousness wandered off.

However to his surprise, he soon realised that he was not woken up by the brightness but rather an unfamiliar large foot that kept barging on his sheets. Manav's eyes focused upon the unfamiliar large foot intruding upon his peaceful slumber. Disoriented and startled, he reluctantly turned his head towards the owner of the foot. To his surprise, he found himself facing a stern and imposing figure of Khalid, his presence cast a shadow over the tranquillity of the morning, leaving Manav on edge.

Khalid's expression conveyed a mixture of irritation and displeasure, further intensifying Manav's discomfort.

Although caught off guard, Manav summoned his courage and managed to inquire in a cautious tone, "Um, apologies, for a moment forgot you were here."

Khalid's gaze bore into Manav's, his voice tinged with authority as he replied

Khalid - "Oh! Look, 'Harry Potter' is finally awake. Rise and Shine little Man."

Manav's first impression of Khalid was not a positive one at all. Khalid exuded an air of grumpiness and carried the weight of grudges on his shoulders. Sarcasm practically dripped from his face, creating an uncomfortable atmosphere for Manav. Facing someone with the physical presence of Khalid was certainly not a pleasing scenario.

Despite the slight size similarity between them, Khalid's towering height and imposing weight gave him an intimidating aura. Manav couldn't help but notice Khalid's fully grown beard, which added to his rugged appearance. But what stood out the most was the dark eyeliner adorning Khalid's eyes, serving as a striking visual statement that he had his gaze fixed on everyone around him.

Manav, still groggy from his interrupted sleep, was far from pleased with Khalid's mocking remarks and dismissive body language. Nevertheless, he rose from his bed, mustering the strength to confront Khalid. Murmuring his response to the 'Harry Potter' comment, "Heard that name enough for a lifetime." He moves closer to Khalid, looks eye to eye and offers his hand for a handshake.

Manav - "Nice to have finally met you, Khalid, hope you hadn't much trouble finding the place last night."

Khalid - "Not at all, your fame precedes you and follows you home, If I had known I would have asked where 'Harry

Potter' lives."

As Khalid displayed his enjoyment and indulged in ridiculing chuckles at Manav's comment, a flicker of irritation crossed Manav's face. However, he chose not to let Khalid's behaviour rattle him. In a display of composure, he maintained his gentle demeanour, standing tall and refusing to be swayed by Khalid's attempts to undermine him.

When Manav reached out his hand for a handshake, he made a conscious decision to tighten his grip slightly, subtly asserting his own strength and resolve. It was a silent message that despite Khalid's dismissive attitude, Manav would not be diminished or disregarded.

Their hands met, and as their eyes locked, Manav held Khalid's gaze steadfastly, unyielding in the face of the mockery. His expression conveyed a quiet confidence, a reminder to Khalid that despite any perceived power dynamics, they were equals in this encounter.

Though his grip remained firm, Manav's touch carried an essence of respect and willingness for open communication. It was an offer of understanding, an invitation for Khalid to engage in a more respectful and equitable conversation.

By standing his ground and asserting his presence with grace, Manav aimed to create a space where mutual respect could bridge the initial tension between them, with the hope that their interaction could proceed on a more constructive and genuine level.

Manav - "Fame is complicated and if you ask me it is overrated too. I've had more than enough for my share. So if it is not too much trouble, you can continue calling me with my other famed name - Manav."

Manav maintained his firm but measured grip during the handshake, never once breaking eye contact with Khalid. While he projected an outward sense of calm, like a peaceful millpond, he couldn't deny a hint of enjoyment in sensing Khalid's irascibility permeating the room. Manav seemed to be willingly allowing the elephant to be aware of his own presence.

However, their standoff was abruptly interrupted as Aban emerged from the room, sensing the tension and rising temperature in the atmosphere. The interruption brought an end to the moment that Manav would have liked to prolong, as he had hoped to navigate the situation further on his own terms.

At the sight of Aban, Manav's gaze shifted momentarily, his attention drawn to his friend. Recognizing that Aban's intervention was meant to diffuse the tension, he relinquished his grip on Khalid's hand and redirected his focus towards Aban.

Manav silently acknowledged that perhaps the encounter with Khalid could be revisited at a more opportune time. For now, finding a pathway back to a sense of calmness and understanding took precedence.

"Good Morrow Sir, I hope you are well rested, we have a big day today." Aban tries the cheerful side of himself by using old english words, Manav softens the grip and moves towards the kitchen.

Aban - "I made some new arrangements with the tea, do you take milk with your tea?"

Manav - "I have no other preference but your cooking, I'll drink or eat whatever your hands prepare, and good Morrow to you too Sir."

As Aban took charge of steering the conversation towards more pleasant topics, the smiles returned to the room. However, a lingering sense of awkwardness remained, causing occasional moments of discomfort. Khalid couldn't help but feel unsettled when he caught Manav's gaze away from him, as if his attention was anywhere else but at Khalid. This feeling of being overlooked or not being paid attention to, added to Khalid's discomfort. While Aban continued to try and keep the conversation pleasant and interesting, Khalid couldn't shake off the underlying unease caused by the detachment he observed in Manav's demeanour.

Aban, being the peacemaker, did his best to keep the conversation engaging and enjoyable. He shared his plans for the day, bringing a sense of excitement and anticipation to the air. A visit to a nearby orphanage, followed by a series of shopping quests, lunch, and culminating in a 3D movie experience with special effects. The evening would be topped off with a fine-dining experience at an exclusive hotel, reserved for the wealthiest patrons.

Just as the plans were discussed, Sana entered the apartment in her running activewear, clearly exhausted and covered in sweat. Instead of joining in the conversation, she simply collapsed onto the floor, trying to catch her breath after a challenging workout.

Aban - "Get up from the floor dear and have some tea, you'll be relished."

Sana - Gasping for breath "Why is everyone so quiet, did I miss something?"

Aban - "Nothing to be concerned about dear, remember we have to go to some places today, better start getting ready."

Even though she hadn't been in the flat until just a short while ago, Sana could feel something wasn't right. She didn't give it much attention, though, and began savouring her Abbu's tea. Around 9 in the morning they all leave the apartment for their first item in their itinerary, the Orphanage.

The taxi dropped them in front of an old, unmaintained building with damp walls. Confusion and hesitation filled Manav's mind. He couldn't fathom why Aban had chosen that particular place for them to visit. The atmosphere seemed eerie, as if the building itself could be the setting for a horror movie. Despite their uncertainty, they enter through the gate. Anticipation mixed with a hint of trepidation consumed their thoughts as they ventured further inside, while their eyes scanned the surroundings.

Aban, seemingly unperturbed by the unsettling ambiance, led the way. While the others remained uncertain. Each step they took unravelled a new facet of the environment—creaky floorboards, shadowy corners, and the lingering scent of age and neglect.

As Manav's eyes swept across the premises of the old building, his presumptions became reality - it was home to a multitude of unwanted and ignored orphan children. Their ages ranged from infancy to the teenage years, though the exact number remained unknown. To the children, Manav and his friends seemed like aliens, foreign beings stepping into their world. Their faces lit up with a mixture of surprise, intrigue, and a hint of hope. These little ones, who had experienced neglect and rejection, saw a glimmer of something different in the visitors that stood before them. Without hesitation, the children approached Manav and his companions, their welcoming nature shining through their gaze. It was as if they had found a source of newness and possibilities in the presence of these "aliens."

As the children sprinted towards Aban, Sana, and Manav, Khalid made a conscious decision to remain a distant spectator. Meanwhile, the kids greeted Manav and his companions with warmth and excitement, in return they too received positive responses.

However, Manav found himself pausing, unsure and uncertain, with a blank expression on his face. His eyes roamed over the group of enthusiastic children, observing their curiosity and intrigue. He couldn't help but feel slightly overwhelmed as he became the centre of attention, especially for those with television exposure who recognized him from news reports and interviews. Surrounded by a sea of twinkling eyes, Manav sensed that the children were attempting to recall where they had seen him before. In hushed whispers that gradually grew louder, the children exchanged their speculations and memories, trying to piece together the puzzle of this unexpected celebrity guest in their midst.

Manav's insecurity grew, and he frequently sought solace in glancing towards Sana and Aban.

"What is the protocol in this situation?" He thought.

Manav had always struggled with his discomfort in social gatherings, the prospect of interacting with the children left him feeling a mix of thrill, excitement, and chills. While he was intrigued by their presence and curious about their stories, he felt unsure of how to approach and greet them.

In contrast, Sana seemed to effortlessly exude warmth and openness. With her relaxed demeanour and genuine enthusiasm, she stepped in to introduce not only herself but also Aban and Manav to the children. As Sana shared their names with excitement, the children became eager to introduce themselves to her, one by one. They took pride in sharing their names, basking in the attention and validation that Sana's interest brought. Sana's ability to connect with the children and create an inviting atmosphere allowed Manav to witness firsthand the power of her empathy and genuine engagement. He admired her ease in navigating social interactions, and he found himself grateful for her presence at that moment, else he would have been clueless. With Sana's lead, Manav began to feel a glimmer of confidence and gradually started opening up with smiles and short conversations.

As the hours passed, Khalid decided to stay out of sight, perhaps feeling like an outsider in the midst of the interaction with the children. Meanwhile, Manav, Aban, and Sana found a spot to sit together with the children, creating a naturally beautiful space for conversations. In this intimate setting, Manav's transformation from uncertainty to a confident man began to unfold, observed by those around him. As he engaged with the children, he discovered a newfound tranquillity and ease in their company. The children, mirroring aspects of his own image, exhibited a sense of wonder, curiosity, and with a slightly diminished confidence.

The hesitation and uncertainty in the children's approach to Manav were evident as they took a step forward and then retreated, unsure of how to interact with this seemingly unresponsive individual. But in a moment of eureka, their hesitation turned into awe as Manav took the initiative to extend his hand for a formal handshake to one of the orphans. The atmosphere was filled with anticipation as everyone watched the interaction unfold. The little orphan, though nervous, mustered a shy smile that melted the hearts of everyone present. She looked around, seeking validation through people's reactions, and found it in the form of curious smiles and anticipation. Manav, too, eagerly awaited the little girl's response. And in a simple yet profound gesture he bestowed upon her what she longed for – a genuine smile. The little girl, touched by this act of kindness, gently placed her hand over Manav's and blushed, before running away. Her innocence and bravery brought laughter and joy to the group.

Inspired by the little girl's courage, the other children took it as a "trendsetter" and lined up to shake hands with Manav, their eyes filled with curiosity and excitement. Manav reciprocated their innocence with his own, maintaining a mild smile on his face. In the midst of these interactions, a few children recognized him, they started throwing their innocence filled questions at Manav,

"are you the one from the TV, did you kill all those bad men?"

As Manav continued to engage with the children, he found himself fully present in that moment, not dwelling on the past or any event from six months ago. Each handshake and interaction brought a new kind of smile to his face, as he maintained eye contact with every child he connected with. Despite Sana's gentle encouragement, suggesting that the children were looking up to Manav and perhaps expecting him to say something, he remained in his own trance, seemingly undisturbed. His focus was on the genuine connection he was making with the kids on an individual level, rather than feeling compelled to address them as a group.

Sana comes close to him and says, "You should say something Manav, they are looking up to you." He remained in his trance, undisturbed.

As the tour of the orphanage commenced, the warden guided Manav, Aban, and Sana through the various sections of the facility. Along the way, the warden took the opportunity to share both the immediate and long-term needs of the orphanage, highlighting the challenges they faced and the support they required.

During this time, Aban seized the opportunity to have a private conversation with the warden, discussing their observations and listening attentively to his insights and concerns. Meanwhile, Sana silently accompanied Manav, providing him with quiet support as he absorbed and processed the multitude of faces and interactions from earlier. As the conversation between Aban and the warden concluded, a noticeable change in the warden's demeanour was evident - there was a newfound sense of happiness and contentment on his face. With a genuine smile, the warden extended an invitation for them to stay for lunch.

Manav, though initially feeling reluctant, found himself unable to decline the invitation. His desire to respect his guests and the gracious host overruled his personal reservations. With a nod, he silently conveyed his acceptance, recognizing.

Together, Manav, Aban, Sana, and the warden proceeded towards the dining area

"I need to prepare for a few things, Please make yourself at home, you can use my office to rest your feet If you'd like", says the warden and leaves.

As the tour of the orphanage continued, Aban paused and excused himself, leaving Sana and Manav just a few steps behind. Sensing Manav's inner struggle and the seemingly challenging nature of his smile, Sana approached him with care and compassion. Taking hold of his hand, Sana gently expressed her observation, acknowledging the effort it took for him to put on that smile for the children. Curiosity was evident in her voice, she gently asked if he would be willing to share what had transpired within him during that moment.

Sana - “That was a tough smile Manav, it looked very challenging but you pulled it off and the children seemed to have liked it, care to share what happened back there?"

With a mixture of vulnerability and sincerity, Manav began to reveal his thoughts. He shared how being in the presence of the children and witnessing their innocence and resilience had touched him deeply. The memories of his own struggles and his own journey resurfaced, and he recognized a shared connection with the children, as if looking into a mirror of his past self.

Manav - “Most of these kids are too old to be adopted, People used to come here all the time just like today, the warden would try and persuade the visitors to adopt one, like a salesman, and just like people browsing online and sorting options from ‘low to high’, visitors would prioritise adopting the youngest children, but they hardly found what they were looking for."

Manav reflected on the disparity between the desires of the prospective adoptive parents and the reality of the orphanage. The children, who had already endured so much, struggled to find the love and stability of a permanent family due to their age. The knowledge of these challenges made Manav’s smile in the presence of the children all the more significant. It represented his understanding of the depth and impact of their experiences.

He points out towards a broken water fountain.

Manav - “That was my place, where I felt unalone, where I felt something or someone speaking to me, that’s where I used to sit down and witness all that selection process. People trying to choose the best looking healthy kid. No one wanted someone unpresentable like me or many other kids. You start to inculcate hatred towards the people better than you when you realise the unfairness, but it was fine with us, we were happy just seeing a new face, something different than the usuals, and all we ever wanted was an honest greeting, not their sympathy. Just a genuine smile from their heart would have made our days. It took me a while there to bring out that smile that they deserved. Could have done better."

Sana - "I don't believe anyone could have done better, you are not a good observer, you didn't just smile, you saw them from heart to heart. They saw someone who understood their journey, someone who had started from the same place of uncertainty and vulnerability. Now they see you not as a visitor, but as a mentor, don't you see that."

Manav paused for a moment, reflecting on Sana's words. He realised that perhaps he had been too focused on his own reservations and self-doubt, failing to fully acknowledge the impact his presence had on the children. Sana's reminder made him see beyond his own insecurities and recognize the hope that shone through the children's eyes after meeting him. However, he still felt he was not fully prepared for today's encounter.

Manav - "When are we leaving?"

Sana - "Are you in a hurry?"

Manav - "No, just asking."

Sana - "I am not sure, Abbu said something about staying for their assembly, warden has some plans."

Manav - "Ok, no worries, It's a beautiful day, I can use some good company while I take a trip down my memory lane."

Sana - "Alright, but keep it interesting. I find mute philosophers extremely annoying."

Manav - "Well then, keep asking interesting questions, but you already know a lot, don't you?"

Sana - “Not this part, I did not find any quarrels or misbehavioural incidents when you were here. Your previous warden stated and I quote ‘Least Maintenance’. I guess most of your work was done by your mind but it also remained there, no actions or reactions. Until you met my brother and all of sudden hell broke loose."

Manav, undisturbed, stares at the ground with his big round eyes and speaks.

Manav - “I’ve been wanting to die, Sana. That laughter wasn’t just to annoy them, I was rejoicing that finally the end is near. Sometimes I wonder If I had refused to go with Mikhail, I would have been the ONLY dead person that day, and you still would have had your brother."

Sana - “I still have my brother, death doesn’t discount the fact that Mikhail, even dead, is still my brother, and we all love you not because you got him killed, but because you brought him peace. We know what he was like but None of us knew him like you did. He wouldn’t have given his life happily for anyone, but for you he did. Manav, never forget that, it would be an insult to his ever-living soul that lives with you now."

About to be bursting out with tears, Manav stops himself and says.

Manav - “Say that to me again when we get home, Please."

Sana - “So that you can cry? No Mister."

Manav looks at her with his puppy-eyes like pleading for a treat.

Sana - “I am just trying to lighten the mood, I will try not to make you cry, I promise."

Sana tried to come close to give him a hug.

Manav - “Let’s not hug it out in front of the kids, they won’t know how to react to public display.”

Sana - “They'll learn."

As Sana moved forward, looking Manav in the eyes, he was both stunned and puzzled, unsure of what she was about to do. His mind raced with various possibilities, trying to anticipate her next move. To his surprise, Sana, with a mischievous smile on her face, acted as if she was about to hug him but instead pranked him by swiftly grabbing his hand for a handshake. It was a playful gesture, catching Manav off guard, but also bringing a moment of laughter and lightness to the atmosphere.

Sana - “You need to learn too, so many things and fast."

As Sana excuses herself from Manav's company, giving him the space to be with his thoughts, Manav finds solace in sitting on the bricks of the broken fountain, watching the children play. Despite their limited knowledge of his specific fame, the children approach him with the enthusiasm and curiosity of encountering a celebrity they had seen on TV. Amidst a flurry of questions, ranging from inquiries about his wealth, living situation, and the size of his house. “How rich are you?" “Where do you live?" “Is your house bigger than mine?" “Are you here to fix our building?" One question that stood out among the rest: "Do you have parents?" Though the question hinted at their own experiences as orphans, Manav responds with a cheerful and genuine spirit, answering all their inquiries with kindness and understanding. Gradually, the crowd around Manav grows, and the children start requesting him to play with them. Manav, embracing the contagious joy and energy in the air, joins in their games wholeheartedly and finds himself truly enjoying every moment.

In this whirlwind of playfulness and connection, Aban approaches Manav,

Aban - "My apologies to break this exciting moment, I've been watching your cheerfulness, what a pleasant sight Manav but we have arranged something at the assembly area, would you be so kind to follow me?"

As Manav bid farewell to the children, he followed Aban, assuming that they would be heading towards the lunch that had been mentioned earlier. Meanwhile, the warden instructed the children to gather and make their way to the assembly area. When Manav reached the stage, he saw that Sana and Khalid were already seated, along with a few additional chairs that had been set up. Curiosity filled the air as the children lined up and took their seats on the ground in an orderly and neat manner. Manav and Aban found themselves sitting on the vacant chairs, still uncertain about what was planned for this momentous gathering. It wasn't Republic Day or any other special occasion, so the purpose of the assembly remained a mystery.

Then, at that moment, the warden stepped onto the stage and addressed the children, drawing their attention. He made an announcement about the visitors, his words shedding light on Aban's generous act of donating a significant sum of money on Manav's behalf.

As Manav's mind buzzed with questions and mixed emotions, Aban sensed his inner turmoil, offering support and comfort with a gentle touch, he rubbed Manav's shoulders and locked eyes with him, communicating a silent understanding and reassurance. After a few moments of gratitude and praise from the warden towards Manav and Aban's generous donation, the stage was turned over to Manav. There was an expectation for him to say a few words, to address the gathered children and express his thoughts and sentiments.

Indeed, the awkwardness and tension in the atmosphere were palpable as Manav found himself unexpectedly thrust into the spotlight. His face flushed, and he could feel the heat rising within him. Public speaking was never something he excelled at, and the thought of addressing a crowd made it even more challenging. As Manav scanned the crowd, he felt his confidence wavering. The weight of the moment seemed almost too heavy to bear, causing him to hesitate and struggle to find the right words. His mind raced, and his breath grew shallow, barely able to muster more than a barely audible "NO" in response to the request.

Sana and Aban, sensing his unease, stepped in to offer their support and encouragement. They knew that Manav had important thoughts and feelings to share, even if he didn't realise it himself. With gentle reassurances and understanding glances, they urged him to gather his courage and take those few minutes to address the crowd.

Those quick events annoy Khalid, he whispers, "If he can't even do this, why am I still here wasting my time. I'm leaving." Khalid takes off angrily. As Khalid storms out of the stage, his abrupt departure leaves a trail of tension and disappointment in his wake, Manav's attention is immediately drawn to the children. The children's contrite expressions were directed at the stage who felt it was their fault that their kind guest got infuriated. Their dejected expressions weigh heavily on Manav's heart.

A heavy silence hangs in the air, broken only by the fading sound of Khalid's footsteps. But then, another set of footsteps resonates through the stage, overpowering the remnants of tension left by Khalid's departure. The children turned their heads, their faces lighted up as they saw Manav walking towards the centre-stage.

An uncontrollable wave of excitement washes over the children, and they erupt into the wildest cheer, the mischievous ones even letting out loud whistles. They unite their hands, dancing and shouting at the top of their lungs to show their support and cheer Manav up. The noise levels became alarmingly high, but the encouragement within it is nothing short of miraculous. The atmosphere transforms, becoming a haven of positivity and joy.

It takes a while for the children to tire from the constant applause and boisterous cheers but Manav, moved by their overwhelming support, doesn't attempt to silence them. As the room gradually quiets down, Manav breaks his nervous silence and begins his speech, stammering slightly in the beginning.

Despite his stutter, the children hang onto his every word, their eyes filled with anticipation and hope. With every word he spoke, the children gradually resolved into silence.

"Thank you warden for having us today, and special thanks to you all for that cheer.... Most of you told me that you have seen me on TV but I am not sure if you are aware why my pictures were shown...... I am not going to tell you right now how and why I became famous, You might need to grow up a bit before you understand all that.... there's still time. But I wanted to tell you a few things about me, because I feel you deserve to know what is waiting for you. Believe it or not I was or should I say, still am, one amongst you. This was my home till I was 12 and when I was here all I can remember is, I never wanted to leave. Seeing people coming here from outside and choosing who to adopt, mostly the fairest or the brightest, made me want to remain here as long as I could. I was scared to be with people such as those with dishonest smiles and selfish choices. Choosing children to adopt was beyond the scope of my understanding.....Many people think of me as brave and calm, some even mistake me for an intellectual ... but I am not, not even close.... Anyway, Eventually when I had to leave, a missionary took me in, gave me education, and I thought my life and I will change for good. I could never really take this place out of my mind as I started hating this place for letting me go, and I remember a belief starting to ingrain in me that everything Is Just Going To Get Worse From Here, and that my better days are behind me..... I felt secure behind these walls.... After leaving this orphanage and perceiving what the world outside had to offer, I created a wall of my own, in my own mind, believing it will keep me out of harm's way......But I Was So Wrong and that is why I Am.. So Not Brave..... Walls are not meant to keep you safe, I learnt it so late that walls are only meant to keep people apart from each other. I never let anyone in, never became a family or a friend to anyone, I could never fight the fear of letting my guard down. I never learnt the true value of family..... Though when I did, It came through an unbearable trauma, at an unbearable price.... Finally a family found me, and there they are."

He points out towards Aban and Sana and noticeably starts to shed a tear.

"After meeting them I realised the value of family, I realised that even if you have to go through an infinite number of unspeakable failures, It Is Still Worth It, It Is Still Worth Your Tries. Keeping myself behind walls was stupid, weak and cowardly because I kept myself apart from the people who deserved and needed my love and caring and probably even my protection...".

Manav's voice starts to tremble, his tears could not be held anymore, burdensome he continues.

"I should have come back here a long time ago and more often. For that I beg your forgiveness. I should have been your family, your friend, your mentor, your 'Anyone' that you needed me to be.... but that changes today. The man you're seeing in front of you .... belongs to you and he will always be at your disposal..... That being said, I think I have taken enough of your time for today but I must tell you one fact before I conclude, that never have I seen better morality and frankly better smiles than you guys, be proud of that, even if you forget, I'll be around to remind you of that."

As Manav's speech came to an end, a profound silence settled over the room. The orphans, still processing the weight of his words, refrained from their usual instinct of seeking answers from each other, the normal reaction of looking at each other for answers was completely absent. It was as if they were caught in a moment of suspended thought, hoping for more, yearning for the peace and assurance that Manav had instilled within them. None of them wanted the speech to end.

But then, Sana stepped to the rescue, who recognized the need to break the silence and lift the spirits of the children. She began clapping slowly and softly, and like a ripple in a pond, the applause spread among the children. It started off gently, almost muffled, but it quickly gained momentum and volume. Sana's infectious energy and beautiful laughter filled the room, igniting a wave of excitement and joy among the children. Their energy levels soared from 0 to 100 in an instant. With Sana's presence and her playful nature, the ambiance in the orphanage transformed completely.

As she made her way towards the microphone, a sense of anticipation and delight engulfed the children. They eagerly awaited her next words and actions, their faces flickering with anticipation and glimmer.

Sana - “I can tell how glad you all are to have found your long-lost brother. Congratulations to you all. However, don’t you think we still need him for something else? Who could guess? Correct guesses will earn rewards. So, how about we play a game? What is Mr. Manav missing?"

She triggered a ruckus, kids were jumping with their wild and witty guesses so loud and together that not one voice could be heard properly. Sana lets them vent out their energy for a few minutes while enjoying the surge of positive energy with an infectious laughter.

Sana - “All good guesses, but look at him carefully don’t you think he is missing a smile?"

Bewitched and enthralled by Sana’s irresistible energy and infectious charm, the children found themselves captivated by her aura. They were completely spellbound, unable to resist her enchanting presence. And so, when she prompted them to respond, they had no choice but to erupt in unison, shouting at the top of their lungs, "YES!!"

And she looked back at Manav in the most cheerful way, with sparkling eyes bathed in joy. Only a dead man could have ignored such an ambience that she was, no one could be blamed for getting overwhelmed by her personality. Manav couldn’t help sensing a particular fascination in the atmosphere that the orphanage had developed; everyone wanted to express their gratitude to Sana. She took over like Caesar, everyone’s jubilation was at her mercy. She confined everyone in a joyful habitat where everyone somehow felt safe and joyous. Despite his best efforts to hide his awkward smile, Manav had to succumb to her spell at some point. He was sitting there attempting vainly to conceal his smile, but everyone noticed it.

The transformative experience had not only brought out the inner-child in the orphans, but it had also tapped into the same childlike wonder within Manav and Aban. Aban, with his heartwarming Santa Claus smile, radiated joy and warmth.

Witnessing this beautiful moment unfold, Sana couldn't help but convey her silent message to Manav with a tilt of her head and a knowing smile. It was a non-verbal confirmation of her belief in Manav. She mouthed the words, "I told you so." This time, as Manav returned to the stage alongside Sana, his field of vision expanded beyond the physical presence of the orphans. His eyes seemed to penetrate through their outward appearance, bypassing any barriers or judgments, and connecting deeply with their hearts.

Sana spoke a few more finishing sentences, adding some more confidence from Manav that they all have a great future. She then invites them to march to their cafeteria for lunch.

Even after the assembly Sana didn't leave Manav's arm, she held onto him. They followed the kids to their cafeteria. On the way, Manav takes a diversion, and Sana follows him. Aban and Khalid didn't stop, they continued their walk towards the cafeteria. After reaching at a distance Manav turned back at Sana, he was disoriented to the core, if there had been an infra-red camera, he would have been alarming on the highest levels.

Manav - "It wasn't a 'win' for me that day, despite what everyone believes. I brutally murdered Hafeez. A good person wouldn't do that. I chewed over his neck until I stopped the flow of blood and air, and then I bit through his bones. I could have stopped but I didn't. Mikhail called me a 'Predator'. He couldn't have brought up the animal inside me if he didn't already know that I had it in me. It makes me sick to think over why he chose to save me at the cost of his own life. Was he looking to save what was good in me or was he saving something bad? You know your brother better than I did Sana. What do you make of all this?"

Sana takes a deep breath, comes a little closer and touches his forehead.

Sana - "Ya Allah!, You're burning up here. You must stop acting like all that was somehow yours to control, now calm down. Nothing will alter for the better or worse because of your presence or negligence. If it was supposed to happen, it will happen, and it did.... Manav, We all lost Mikhail. If I was there I wouldn't have brought your best or your worst for no reason, and as far as I know him, he wouldn't do anything important without expecting an important outcome. Maybe he brought out something in you forever or Just for That Moment. These are the only two possibilities that make sense, but now, there are no terrorists in front of you, you are safe. Now come on I laughed too much, I have to eat, I'm starving."

She pulls his arm and takes him to the loud cafetaria, all four of them eat together surrounded by the giggling children. They eat a hearty meal before leaving the orphanage. Aban has a long chat with the warden while Sana and Manav say their goodbyes to the children, promising they'll be regularly visiting them. As Khalid, Manav and Sana wait by the car, Aban is observed to be continually having a conversation with Warden. Manav asks Sana, "why is he talking to the warden?"Sana replies, "maybe discussing the donation." A few minutes later Aban came back and they all headed home together in the car. Khalid didn't seem very pleased, something was clearly bothering him.

Khalid - “Enjoy the attention Potter, Abbu has made you a headliner for tomorrow."

Manav - “What do you mean?"

Aban - “We all know he is sporadically bitter at his own will, let him be in his own head."

Khalid - “Why not tell him, it’s not something to be ashamed of, he should know.”

Aban - “Let us all peacefully travel to our destination Khalid, details do not matter, do not forget what I taught you about sadaqa.” Aban responds firmly.

Khalid - annoyingly he says, “Yeah, yeah I remember Charity is a central tenet of Islam: everything one has belongs to God and therefore a Muslim is obliged to share wealth with those less fortunate."

Manav was confused, he needed answers.

Manav - “What are you really talking about? Do you know what’s going on, Sana?"

To which Aban calmly replies.

Aban - “I donated to the orphanage, I don’t see any reason to further discuss that."

Khalid - “I disagree, 50 Lacs is not a small amount."

Manav - “50 Lacs!?My God, Aban, that is a huge amount, I don’t know what to say."

Sana - “Let’s leave it at that, Abbu doesn’t like to talk about his Sadaqa much." She whispers in Manav’s ears.

In the car, an unusual silence fills the air, accompanied by undeniable awkwardness. Sensing something amiss, Manav notices that the car seems to be veering off in a different direction. He quickly alerts Aban, expressing his observation that they may be taking a different route than planned. Aban, wearing a mischievous smile, assures Manav to sit tight and wait for a surprise. Manav’s suspicions grow as he wonders what surprise could possibly be waiting for them. His mind ponders the possibility of being taken to a rooftop to enjoy the city view once again. To his surprise, the car indeed heads towards the Porsche locality. As they approach the security, Aban rolls down the window and provides the security guard with the apartment number, "Suite 101." The guard notes down their details in the visitor logbook and grants them entry.

As they walk towards the building Manav asks, “Suite-101? That may have been a little suspicious,We could have come after a little dark, I am not acquainted with guards on duty at this time." Aban replies, “Not to worry." They pass by the guards at the reception as well, to add more surprise, the guards greet Aban as if they know him. Aban uses a keycard to enter the elevator, Manav was nothing but flabbergasted every moment every step. He asks in the elevator, “Do you have a friend here, how did you get hold of a keycard?" Khalid remained baffled in a bad mood but Sana and Aban were having a laugh, they happened to enjoy how Manav was completely out of air. “Just wait and watch”, Putting her hand over Manav’s shoulder she says, “I am sure you’ll like it."

As the elevator glides to a stop on the second-to-top floor, Aban leads Manav towards a door with a keycard in hand. With a swipe, the door clicks open, revealing a breathtaking sight. This apartment is no ordinary living space; it is a lavish penthouse.

Manav’s eyes widen with awe as he takes in the class and elegance that fills the penthouse. The space is grand and luxurious, boasting two floors, four bedrooms, and five bathrooms. A balcony adorned with a lush garden provides a picturesque escape. It feels as though they have entered a loft in the sky, a sanctuary that surpasses any expectation.

Settling down on a plush couch, Manav sinks into its comfort and confusion.

Aban - "So Manav, what do you think?"

Manav - "I've been to this building so many times but never entered into a house, It's amazing, how did you manage all this?"

Aban - "Through some friends and good luck, lucky for us that a fully furnished penthouse was available, I wanted to give this to you before we left."

Manav - "I want to be shocked but I feel like I do not have those sensations anymore What am I going to do with such a big house?"

Aban - "Didn't you notice the view? I thought you liked it."

Manav - "That's the only thing that's intriguing me to accept this, but four bedrooms?"

Sana - "Are you going to let us stay in a hotel when we visit next time, or in that box you call an apartment?" Jokingly she says.

Aban - "I can understand this may take a while to process in your brain but you seem a little unsure."

Manav -"I can't help thinking that if you had enough money to buy this, you must have had more to donate to that orphanage, I'm sorry but I'm just speaking my mind."

Aban - "That's quite alright Manav, that wasn't our last visit or last orphanage to visit There will be more times like this, I promise you that, by far, today was the most peaceful in a long time."

Manav basked in the feeling of importance that enveloped him, a sensation he hadn't experienced in a long time. For once, he allowed himself to envision a future where he was finally happy. As he sat on the couch, gazing out over the balcony, a peaceful serenity washed over him.

His mind, usually overrun with overwhelming thoughts, quieted down, leaving space for positive and uplifting ideas to take centre stage. He felt a sense of transcendence, as if he had risen above the challenges and uncertainties that had plagued him before. This moment of respite and joy offered a refreshing break from the constant stream of shocking surprises that had characterised his life in recent times. The good surprises he had encountered since meeting Aban and Sana had brought a newfound sense of relaxation and contentment. As Manav closed his eyes, succumbing to the tranquillity of the moment, he drifted off into a peaceful sleep. In this serene oasis, he found solace, allowing himself to completely let go and embrace the much-needed rest he deserved.

Manav woke a few hours later, about evening time. He noticed everyone freshening up. He got up to ask, "What are you all getting ready for?" While combing her hair Sana replies, "We are going to a club, Abbu is going to visit his old relatives and friends, get up we have to leave soon, Khalid is also joining us." Manav went a bit perplexed when he heard Khalid was also joining.

Manav - "Are you sure that's a good idea? He doesn't like me very much."

Sana - "You mean YOU don't like him very much?"

Manav - "Come on, you know what I mean, what's the point if he doesn't enjoy it."

Holding Manav's hand Sana poses a humble request.

Sana - "Please let him come, I know he is a little 'jughead' but he is my brother, think of him as a sick person, and why are you so uncomfortable with him, you're Manav who devoured the great Tabib. Act your personality Potter." She laughs like a baby, and Manav laughs too, however embarrassingly.

Manav, Sana and Khalid call a cab while Aban stays back at the new apartment. Sana asks the driver to go to one of the biggest privilege dance clubs in the city. Manav felt nervous, sitting in the front seat he looked back and asked,

Manav - "I've heard that place is really expensive and you probably need to be on the list, I hate crowded places."

Annoyed, Khalid replies,

Khalid - "You've heard it right, now will you just keep quiet and let us take care of things, keep your thoughts to yourself rather than jumbling us?"

Sana interjects.

Sana - "Khalid, behave yourself, he is just trying to help."

Khalid – "Help with what? We didn't ask for his opinion."

Khalid became a little furious.

Manav got ballooned up a little with annoyance.

"Alright" Manav raised his voice,

Manav - "I am sorry if i confused you, I don't want you to spoil your time because of me, so let's just enjoy from here on, I won't step on your toes and you don't step on mine, Are we good Khalid?"

Manav offers a handshake, Khalid takes a few seconds but accepts the greeting. After a forty-five-minute journey, they finally arrived at the dance club. Even before stepping foot inside, they were taken aback by the sight of the building. It was a spectacle of lights and vibrant decorations, displaying a level of grandeur that was truly out of this world. The mere view of the club was enough to infuse anyone with a surge of energy, inspiring them to dance the night away.

As Sana settled the fare with the driver, they eagerly made their way inside. The anticipation hung in the air as they were drawn towards the pulsating beats and the rhythmic allure of the music within. With each step, excitement and thrill began to bubble up inside them, ready to be unleashed on the dance floor.

Stepping inside the club, the group was greeted by a sight even more impressive than they had anticipated. The interior was vast, adorned with exquisite and intricate decorations that added to the overall atmosphere. The vibrant lights bathed the room in a kaleidoscope of colours, creating an electric ambiance. The pulsating beats of the music filled the air, simultaneously loud yet soothing, pulsing through their veins. As they made their way through the crowd, they couldn't help but notice the well-groomed and affluent clientele. Each person seemed to be in their own world, content and immersed in the rhythm of the night. The air was filled with an undeniable sense of sophistication and indulgence. Khalid led the way towards the bar, Sana and Manav followed.

Sana was trying to say something to Manav but due to loud music he couldn't hear much. She brings her mouth close to Manav's ears and asks loudly, "Do you ever drink?" Manav nods his head and says, "Yes, I do."

Amidst the lively atmosphere and their growing companionship, they found themselves at the bar where Khalid ordered a few shots. Initially facing some disappointment as the bar didn't have the specific drinks he requested, he eventually settled on a shot called the "Painkiller." They raised their glasses in unison, exclaiming "cheers," and eagerly gulped down the concoction. Manav, intrigued by the drink's cost, glanced at the menu and felt a momentary buzz evaporate at the realisation of its high price, it was priced at Rs.5000/-. However, he quickly dismissed the thought, he figured it was at someone else's cost, then what's to lose, he was in a different mood, he didn't look at the price again.

As they continued with their shots, the group found themselves growing more fond of each other. Khalid's mood lifted, accompanied by the infectious music that enveloped the club. The tapping of their feet turned into full-fledged dance moves, igniting laughter and singing from Khalid and Sana. Even the DJ occasionally lowered the music volume to let the patrons revel in their own voices. Sana's wild, carefree dancing, and Khalid's seemingly endless flow of drinks brought joy and entertainment to Manav, who wasn't very fond of his dancing skills and neither did he want to interfere and spoil the angelic dance moves of Sana.

About two hours later, as fatigue settled in and the DJ's music began to play at a lower volume, Manav and Khalid were ready to call it a night. Their bellies full after indulging in a satisfying meal, they longed to return to their new apartment and sink into a comfortable bed, drifting off to sleep like babies. However, Sana seemed to have different plans. Despite the late hour and the dwindling crowd, she remained on the dance floor, her enthusiasm undiminished by the repeating songs. Each new track sparked fresh excitement within her, causing her to dance with the same vigour as before. Khalid, in his inebriated state, realised he needed assistance and asked Manav to bring Sana and take him home.

Approaching Sana, he conveyed his admiration for her dance moves through his appreciative gestures and warm smile. Understanding the unspoken message, Sana reciprocated the smile.

Manav - "Come on let's go, Khalid is too tired and seems drunk."

In a surprising and unexpected move, Sana remains still as Manav reaches for her hand. Then, with a mischievous smile, she takes control of the situation and pulls him towards her, their bodies coming into closer proximity. She confidently places her hand on his shoulder and guides his hand to her waist. Manav, taken aback by Sana's boldness, feels a mix of excitement and uncertainty coursing through him. The sudden intimacy on the dance floor leaves him both exhilarated and slightly disoriented. With Sana leading the way, they sway to the rhythm of the music, their bodies moving in sync. Lost in the moment, the rest of the world fades away, leaving only the pulsating music, the electric atmosphere, and the intoxicating energy between them. Unable to resist, Manav allows himself to be carried away by the magic of the dance and the allure of Sana's presence.

Sana - "This is a duet song, care to dance with me Manav?"

With an embarrassing little smile on his face, Manav responds.

Manav - "Whoa, you are a good drinker and a dancer too, I wouldn't want to inferior your dance display."

Sana - "Come on, it's a dance club not a dance competition, I'll take the lead, just follow my body and have your body respond to me, it's very simple."

Manav was stupefied with the instructions.

Manav - "How do I do that?"

To which she seductively replied.

Sana - "Just feel the music and feel me."

In order to do that, he had to look into her eyes, which he was frightened to, because apparently he enjoyed it too much for his comfort. As the dance continued, Manav found himself torn between the fear of looking into Sana's eyes and the irresistible temptation to do so. He recognized that there was something mesmerising about her dreamy eyes, something that stirred an unfamiliar and exhilarating feeling within him. Her eyes seemed to possess a magic of their own, radiating warmth, kindness, and a hint of mischief. They held a captivating power, drawing him in like a fruitful distant planet in a vast universe, and its gravity pulling him towards it, Manav felt both captivated and afraid of being pulled into it, and what he might find if he delved too deeply into those alluring depths. The intensity of their connection, created through the language of dance, made him hesitant to take the leap and fully embrace the allure of her eyes. The vulnerability and potential depth they seemed to hold threatened to unravel his emotions in ways he was not ready for.

Yet, as time passed, Manav gradually grew more comfortable, finding solace and excitement in their synchronised movements. As Sana guided him with unspoken instructions. Slowly and gradually he became more and more comfortable and got the understanding of their bodies flowing together, swaying to the music. Sana's instructions were like music in itself, Manav had been breathless, not once he took his eyes off her.

Sana - "See, you got it, just feel every part of your body, trust me all the body parts can dance."

Manav - "So it seems."

Sana - "You were so nervous, I could see it on your face (Laughingly)."

Manav - "I was, but in my defence, your whole personality is intimidating."

Sana - "Is that so? Come on Manav, I don't bite. What is so intimidating about me? I am just a tiny little person."

Manav stays quiet for a while, after giving some thoughts he replies.

Manav - "You are a powerhouse"

Sana laughs

Sana - "Me? I am the queen of procrastinators"

Manav - "Then why do I feel thunderstruck whenever you touch me? Inside my whole body I feel a current that passes through every particle in me, and I can sense my physical form and see it the way you want me to see it. I feel like I just came into existence. My focus sharpens so much that I can feel every heartbeat. Not only can I whiff but taste your aroma in the air, and all of this makes me very happy. Maybe it's the alcohol but I want to tell you I have never been happier in anyone else's company."

All those beautiful words were said without a stutter, as Manav finally summoned the courage to look into Sana's eyes, he noticed a flicker of surprise across her face. The realisation that he had been hesitant to meet her gaze catches her off guard and momentarily shatters her usual air of unwavering confidence. For a brief moment, Sana's confident exterior wavers, revealing a glimpse of vulnerability. It is as if Manav's hesitation disrupts the usual certainty she carries within herself. precariousness replaces her usual poise, and she engages in a silent battle between her own vulnerability and the desire to maintain her composed facade.

However, Sana quickly regains her composure and reasserts her confidence, not letting this momentary glimpse of vulnerability overshadow her spirit. In the blink of an eye, her eyes resume their mesmerising twinkle, a smile playing at the corners of her lips. They continue their dance, their bodies moving in harmony with each other, while the shared understanding and connection between them deepens. The significance of that fleeting moment of vulnerability between them remains unspoken but acknowledged, adding a layer of complexity to their 'yet to be defined' connection.

Sana - "That's too much for a drunk man to say and a drunk woman to understand."

As Sana ruffles his hair and pulls him closer, their bodies mere inches apart, a palpable tension fills the space between them. Their breaths intertwine.. Just before millimetres between their lips she stops and probably in the most tantalising manner, she says.

Sana - "However......That's the silliest thing anyone has ever said to me."

Right at that moment, Manav stopped breathing and his heart started panting like a marathon runner. Suffocation was just about to kick off when Sana came close enough to block any air passage between them and says,

Sana - "But also the most passionate words I've heard, thank you Manav for opening your heart to me."

She then gently touches her lips to his lips and kisses him. The kiss may have lasted for a second, however, if before Manav had felt thunderstruck by her touch, this time he felt imploded, burnt and electrocuted. Hiding his jitters he replied.

Manav - "You are very welcome."

As the night carried on, Manav and Sana continued to dance, completely immersed in each other's presence. They were unaffected by the passing time or the surroundings, lost in the enchantment of the moment. Even with Khalid occasionally nodding off, their enthusiasm remained undeterred. Though it was well past 3:00 AM, they avoided acknowledging the late hour. Time seemed irrelevant in the midst of their enjoyment. However, as they glanced around, they noticed the dwindling crowd and the weary expressions of the club staff. It became apparent that the situation was becoming less desirable with the sparse number of guests and the exhaustion evident on the faces of the staff. Manav wrestled with the decision to suggest leaving, aware that Khalid was in dire need of a proper bed. Breaking the trance of the night, he mustered the courage to express his concerns, understanding that it was time to bid farewell to the club. Their shared understanding led to a consensus, and without a word exchanged, they agreed that it was time to depart. As they made their way towards Khalid, gently waking him from his sleepy stupor, the fatigue of the night began to weigh heavily on their limbs.

When it was clear that he could hardly crawl, let alone walk, together they took an arm each of Khalid. As they picked him up, He partially regained consciousness, began speaking incoherently. It was a struggle to support his weight and navigate through the crowd, his intoxicated ramblings and demands for another drink echoed in the air. It became evident that keeping him balanced and on track was proving to be a challenge. His erratic movements and random pulls caused Sana and Manav to strain in their effort to keep him on his feet. Despite their best efforts, Khalid's physical state, compounded by his height and drunkenness, made it feel as if they were carrying a heavy burden on their shoulders. They pressed on, as they slowly made their way towards the exit. Once outside, they found a place for Khalid to sit and wait for their driver to arrive. As Manav observed Khalid's wide open eyes and focused on his eyes, he couldn't help but sense a shift in Khalid's demeanour, he was in deep thought despite being in the state of drunkenness. Something seemed to be inciting a growing intensity within him, it was more than evident in his facial expressions.

Manav - “Is he OK? He looks very uncomfortable."

Sana - “I am not sure, Khalid - shall we take you to the restroom?"

Khalid did not move a muscle or blink still. Sana kept on asking him if he needed help, right about then the cab arrived and they both helped him get into the cab, unstirring Khalid was determined to keep his focus on where it was. They managed to get him in the cab and he closed his eyes right after settling himself on the car seat, he kept mumbling a few words which were hardly understandable however one word was quite clear, “Bastards." It occurred to Sana that Khalid might need to vomit, she kept her attentive eyes on him to make sure that he doesn’t blast off in the cab itself. Sana advises,

Sana - “We should take him somewhere and fill him with some fluids before going home. It will be a disaster if Abbu sees him in this condition, he would lose confidence over us being responsible in future and might worry. Let’s give it a try and see if his condition improves."

Manav - “I am not sure if any place will be open at this time."

Sana - “Let’s check with our driver, Is there any place on the way where we can get fresh fruit juice?"

Driver informed it’s possible to find some street hawkers near India Gate selling sugar cane juice, instantaneously they decided to head in that direction in the hopes of finding a refreshing beverage to aid Khalid’s recovery. They drove around the India Gate circle, scanning the surroundings for any signs of street vendors. After a while, luck was on their side as they spotted a street hawker selling various street foods. Although sugar cane juice was not available, the hawker offered them lemon drinks instead, which would still contribute to helping Khalid regain some sobriety. Grateful for anything that could assist Khalid in his state, they purchased the lemon sodas and handed one to him. As Khalid took a sip of the lemon soda, his glazed eyes momentarily shifted towards the iconic India Gate memorial. In his intoxicated state, he mumbles something, the words lost in his slurred speech. Sana, concerned for his well-being, moves closer and gently asks if he's alright. To their surprise, Khalid responds by pushing her away and beckoning Manav to come closer. Curiosity mingled with concern, Manav warily approaches Khalid, ready to listen to his drunken sarcastic insults.

Khalid - "Superb cover up isn't it? That's the grave of 84000 soldiers who died for nothing, not even when the country was theirs, born on this land and fought someone else's battle in someone else's soil."

Putting over his hand over Khalid's shoulder, Manav says -

Manav - "There are two ways to look at it, I see it as a memorial for the proud men who died to save their families."

Khalid - "It's a cover up and a compensation, that's all that is, and idiots like you all over the world pay to visit it. Remember one thing, the only battle there is in the world is for power and money and the sad part is that the ones who actually fight the battle never win, imprint that fact in your mind, you think their families would have wanted a monument or their men back?"

Manav - "I see that you're feeling better now, are you ready to go home?"

Khalid - "Don't treat me like a child, you don't get to do that being so naive as you are. None of you see how they have been feeding us with incomplete facts to slow down our evolution. Democracy was born before any of the modern Gods. I hope you can see for yourself how much religion is followed over Democracy, how the degree of religious influence in a democracy evolved. All of these monuments are nothing but distractions to keep our mind away from real facts, to slow us from our reach. You see, humans will be uncontrollable if they evolve with better abilities, that's why they need us as their resources, they need to .. slow our evolution to remain in control. That's what all of this is, you ignorant bastard."

Sana - "Ok, that's enough Khalid, behave yourself. Let's go home."

Khalid - "Don't you dare...

Khalid charged towards Sana with hostile intentions, Manav got in between and put his arms around his shoulders.

Manav - "You both can stop now, let's move, we are getting unnecessary attention, let's go before we find trouble."

As Manav helps Khalid back to the car, he notices a group of military men nearby. Pointing them out to Sana, they both acknowledge their presence with a sense of respect and get on their way. Once seated in the rear of the car, Khalid gradually starts to doze off, his head finding a comfortable spot on Manav's shoulder. As he drifts into sleep, Khalid mumbles to himself, his slurred words becoming a barely audible murmur. The exhaustion and effects of his intoxicated state manifest in his restless mumbling, a sign of his deep weariness.

Khalid - "One day you will see Manav, they will cut all the trees in the world and put them in a museum, and will charge us whatever they want from us to see them, you'll see.."

And slowly he passed out, Manav and Sana looked at each other and giggled.

Sana - "I wonder what one has to put in his drink to shut him up."

Only halfway through, Khalid again started feeling unwell and began coughing, looking at his condition, Sana shouts at the driver to stop the car, Manav helped him out. Khalid sprinted towards a bush and started vomiting profusely.

Sana - "Can you look after him, I need to call Abbu, I will be right back."

Despite Khalid's best efforts, there was nothing left to expel from his system except for the lingering uneasiness that came with excessive alcohol consumption. Manav continued to provide support, rubbing his back and assisting him in standing upright, knowing that Khalid's legs were betraying him in his weakened state. The driver, growing impatient, displayed his frustration by honking the car horn a few times. In response, Manav gestured for him to wait, After a few minutes, Sana returned. With Khalid still leaning on Manav for support, they communicated to the driver that they were ready to proceed.

Sana - "How's he feeling?"

Manav - "I think there's nothing left in his tummy, he is just forcing out air."

Sana - "Khalid, come buddy, we have got to go now."

She takes Khalid's other arm then they help him get back to the car, Khalid refuses to drink the lemon juice and just passes out again, Sana requests the driver to drive faster as getting him on a bed under a blanket seems to be the only cure.

Manav - "He would be so embarrassed tomorrow?"

Sana - “Him? No way, he loves his problems, the biggest one being his Ego."

Manav giggles hearing that from Sana.

Sana - “Yes, you can laugh, you’re lucky not to have sibling warfare... I’m sorry I didn’t mean it that way."

Manav - “I understand, you don’t have to apologise."

Sana - “Let’s get you home and some rest."

And she grabs Manav’s collar and pulls him closer, kisses him.

Manav - “Oh! You’re still drunk."

She smiles at him and says.

Sana - “Not today."

They hold on to each other’s hand till they reach the new house and somehow manage to get Khalid on his bed with his unwalkable legs. Aban saw everything but chose not to respond, he greets them and wishes them a good sleep. After taking care of Khalid, Sana walks towards Manav, with her sultry voice, flirtatiously she says.

Sana - “Oh poor baby, are you tired? I can tuck you in."

Manav - “Hmm, though I’m not a child but I don’t mind being a baby for tonight."

Sana - “Don’t get any ideas Potter, I’m just gonna tuck you in and say ‘good night’.”

Manav - “I wouldn’t dream of anything else."

A magnetic effect enthralled him, He moved closer to Sana and grabbed her by the waist. He then picked her up in his arms and carried her to his bedroom, where they crashed on the bed together. She did not take her eyes off him, even briefly, all the way to the bedroom, Manav did not stumble or stop, as if his senses were directing him, unhesitant of looking each other in the eyes, they smiled and gently gave each other a tender touch. Brushing Manav’s hair Sana thanks him.

Sana - “I want to thank you for today, you had no reason to help me or my brother out, I wasn’t sure if you would stick around."

Manav - “That would have been rude not helping out a damsel and her pony in distress, Why wouldn’t I? We are all family now, at least I thought we were."

Sana - “Pony? You called my brother pony, I think you feel he hates you more than he actually does but he’ll come around, just wait and you’ll see. However, let me ask you something. What does it make ‘Us’ then?"

Manav - “I’m not sure yet, it’s extremely odd what I feel about you."

Sana - “Odd? Well, what do you mean?"

Manav - “It’s a bit hard to explain, It’s like I’m attracted to my own angst, you terrify and bring me peace at the same time. Your aura contradicts with my senses."

Sana - “I can understand I am terrifying, but not the part where I bring you peace, I am not known for that."

Manav - “Well, we still don’t know much about each other, But I would like to."

Sana - “You’re expecting an intriguing backstory but there isn’t much to tell. I never felt ‘belonged’ to anything so I left home at a very young age, fortunately Abbu never caused any hindrance or let anyone be, then I travelled everywhere I could and now here I am, on the bed with you."

Manav - “Do you feel you belong here with me at this time, right now?"

Brushing his hair Gently, Sana comes closer and lands a kiss on him.

Sana - “You tell me."

Manav - “I want to remain in this moment forever, I never want to leave."

Ignoring Manav's trembles. Sana caresses his hair and says,

Sana - "Maybe we will, maybe we won't but do not doubt we will have more time. Tomorrow we will meet Jadd. He is the best grandpa one can hope for. You're gonna love him."

Manav - " Jadd?"

Sana - "That's what we call our "grandpa." His name is Khadim but you may call him jadd. He won't mind."

Manav - "Your whole family is so intimidating, can't wait to meet the senior most."

Sana - "He can't wait to meet you either. So have a good night's sleep Potter, tomorrow is a big day. Everyday with you is so fascinating. I can't wait to see what adventures you bring us tomorrow. Now if you could loosen your grip on me a bit would be very kind of you, else I will fall asleep here, and if Abbu finds out, our only escape will be the windows."

Manav smiles and says

Manav - "Sweet dreams."

Giggling every time they glance into each other's eyes after saying farewell and barely able to say goodbye, finding new excuses to start a conversation but failing because of their own concern for the other. It may have taken about 20 minutes for Sana to reach Manav's door, probably even more to close it. Before closing she leaves a remark in the most enticing way.

Sana - "I'm right next door, Potter. Don't be sad"

After Sana departed, Manav kept looking at the door in the hopes that she would return for one last conversation or even a kiss. However, when she didn't, he wasn't upset; instead, he smiled and looked up at the ceiling in anticipation of tomorrow. At what point he dozed off he couldn't remember but the sleep wasn't enough for him until he was woken up by the aroma of Aban's magical tea waiting for him right by his bedside. Just when he was about to pick the cup of tea, he was startled by Khalid.

Khalid - "We're starting in an hour, pack for a day or two."

Manav - "Good Morning to you too, I didn't think you'd be up for weeks after how much you drank yesterday."

Khalid - "Habit of drinking and habit of waking up early, not very happy with those habits but it is what it is."

Manav - "Well how early is it?"

Khalid - "It's 07:00, how much time do you need to get ready?"

Manav - "Less than an hour. Tell me, did you bring me this tea? Well, Thank you Khalid, I couldn't have guessed."

Khalid's tone remained constant and unaffected. Even when expressing gratitude for the support provided by Manav, there was a consistent quality to his voice that seemed untouched by the emotions he was experiencing. Despite his state, Khalid managed to convey his appreciation for Manav's assistance.

Khalid - "I heard you were very helpful yesterday, now we are even."

Both share a bit of a smile, Manav raises his cup and jokingly says "Cheers." Khalid walks out of the room and Manav starts to get ready. Just like he said, he was ready within an hour, he got out of his room where all of them were waiting for him. Aban greets him with a smile.

Aban - "Have we overstayed our welcome yet, young Manav?"

Manav - "Well it's your house."

Aban - "It is yours, paperwork will be dealt with by the time we are back, are you all set for the journey?"

Manav - "You were not joking when you said there will be 'Eventful days'."

Khalid - "He rarely jokes or smiles for that matter. I guess we should be thanking you for making him smile while you had him."

Manav and Aban made eye contact and nodded their heads with respect.

Manav - "You're more than welcome to hear the jokes I told him but I doubt they'll be useful. Are we not coming back here? You all seem packed to the fullest."

Aban - "I'm afraid not. All thanks to you our stay was heart filling and as much as it breaks my heart but we should keep the excitement for another time and probably for another place."

Manav - "It breaks my heart too, but yes another time and another place."

Aban - "Whenever you're ready, a starry night in a cold desert will be waiting for you, bounded by two oceans, I hear you have an interest towards abnormality."

As they bid farewell to Aban, they exchanged a firm handshake followed by an embrace, their closeness was evident in their physical connection. With his head resting on Aban's shoulders, Manav stole a glance at Sana, who stood by her luggage, her eyes reflecting a mixture of emotions. Big, moist, and seemingly devoid of their usual vivacity.

Throughout their journey to the airport, the silence enveloped them, little to none conversation passed between them. Both lost in their own worlds of personal memories and nostalgia, they shared fleeting smiles, aware that this was just the beginning of their story, not a true goodbye.

For Manav, the days spent with Sana had been unpredictable, emotionally charged, and significant. The memories they created together lingered in his mind. While he harboured concerns about Aban's father, Jadd, it was not the most pressing matter on his mind at that moment.

As they ventured into the depths of their own thoughts, their smiles reflected a mixture of anticipation and trepidation, Manav delved into each precious minute he had gathered over the past three days. The unfinished story they shared brought both excitement and precariousness.

The airport awaited them, a departure point toward a future yet to be written.

CHAPTER TEN

# DROUGHT

At the airport, the unfolding circumstances led to several awkward silences and interactions between Manav and Sana. Despite the inherent difficulty of their impending goodbye. Manav realised that this was the first time he had to bid farewell to someone significant in his life at such magnitude. While it felt tough in the present moment, he held onto the belief that with time he would learn to cope, live with the absence, and hopefully overcome the pain.

Despite the looming farewell, Manav firmly believed that the past three days were not memories to be tainted by sadness alone. They held precious moments filled with joy, connection, and shared experiences that he would hold dear in his heart for a long time to come. Those glimpses from the past few days were strong enough to allow him to relive the warmth and happiness they brought.

Amidst the intermingling of emotions, blank faces gradually transformed into smiles, albeit mild, but still conveying a powerful message. The subtle exchanges of these smiles spoke volumes, serving as silent reminders of the special bond forged between Manav and Sana during their time together.

As they waited at the gate, Aban took a seat beside Manav, observing his patience and the genuine joy he brought to their family. Aban couldn't help but admire how easily Manav had integrated into their family dynamics and how much everyone enjoyed his company.

Manav - "Should I be nervous meeting the head of your family?"

Aban - Laughingly he says, "You won't be nervous once you meet him."

Manav - "What kind of person is he? What does he do?"

Aban - "Let him answer all your questions, he loves a good conversation."

As the group boards the plane, Manav and Sana find seats together. The weight of the impending goodbye hangs heavy in the air, creating an uncomfortable silence between them. Manav, struggling with his own internal turmoil, finds it difficult to express his grief and the pain of parting ways.

However, after the plane takes off and the seat belt signs are turned off, Sana, sensing Manav's distress, reaches out to him. She gently takes his trembling hand in hers, offering a comforting touch and attempting to calm him down.

Sana - "I'm gonna miss you too, but I'll be orbiting over you every now and then. Just be sure to give me a good welcome."

Manav - "Just don't orbit as a comet, try and be a moon."

Sana - "When did you learn to talk like this?"

Manav - "I'm just trying to respond fittingly."

Sana - "So Abbu told me you are nervous meeting Jadd?"

Manav - "He told me not to, but honestly I'm a bit intimidated. I still haven't wrapped my head around your father."

Sana - “Well, with whatever he found out about you so far, he can’t wait to meet you. A word of advice though, don’t lie to him, it’s impossible to be deceptive with Jadd. He’s not someone who listens to voices or reads words, he has a talent to look through emotions. He can interpret what your eyes say."

Manav - “Thank you for easing my worries, that doesn’t make me nervous at all."

Sana - “Why are you always so nervous, we are all just people Manav."

Manav - “I haven’t been around many people, I never felt I belonged to any, I’m not a hater, I just don’t count myself as a people person I guess."

Sana - “He can heal you, only if you know where you need to be healed."

Manav - “What if I don’t know that."

Sana - “You can’t go to a doctor without knowing why you need one, I can only head you to the right direction, take the path, stay on the path or not take the path at all, is all up to you Manav, You are just getting ready, I am excited to see your unleashed version."

As they continue their journey, Sana lays her head on Manav’s shoulder, seeking comfort and sharing comfort. They occasionally engage in small talk, reminiscing about the events that unfolded and occasionally poking fun at Khalid and their plans for the upcoming adventure. The conversation brings a lightness to their hearts, momentarily easing the fatigue and melancholy that comes with goodbyes.

After landing, they embark on a long ride back to Jadd’s house. Exhaustion takes its toll on Manav, and he soon dozes off in the backseat of the cab. As his body jolts awake upon realising the vehicle has made a stop, he rubs his eyes, trying to shake off the remnants of sleep.

Before he could fully focus on his surroundings or appreciate them, his mind was still partially engrossed in the dream he had before Aban appeared, the same dream appeared in his subconscious while he took his nap — This time the dreamy-puzzle seems to have acquired more complex pieces. However, his attention was quickly diverted when he set his eyes upon the magnificent property he was standing in, that captivated every fibre of his being.

The structure before him resembles a mausoleum, ancient and steeped in history. The surrounding garden exudes an air of regality, an opulence typically found in centuries-old estates. Manav's keen sense of smell detects the presence of a stable or some kind of farm nearby, likely with poultry or dairy animals. The fragrances in the air transport him to a different time, evoking the essence of a vibrant village.

He might have turned his head for the fourth time to observe the captivating surroundings when he noticed a large man taking small and delicate steps towards them, his approach was quick yet deliberate. Initial intimidation crept over Manav, unsure of the man's intentions.

However, any apprehension quickly dissolved as Manav caught sight of the radiant smile that graced the man's face. In an instant, the man's warm and welcoming expression erased any lingering doubts. Manav's eyes widened as he witnessed Sana's excitement, her feet carrying her swiftly towards the man in a display of familiarity and delight.

Curiosity piqued and any weariness momentarily forgotten, Manav approached the scene, drawn by the infectious happiness between Sana and Jadd. While his surroundings still held an air of mystery and grandeur,

Jadd's presence and Sana's reaction served as a captivating re-introduction for Manav.

Sana - "Jaddu I missed you so much, how have you been?"

Khadim - "My dear kids, I have been waiting for ages. How were your travels? Look at how big you have grown."

Khadim takes a glimpse at Manav, and notices his precariousness. He then comes forward and holds him with both his hands and says.

Khadim - "I have been so disquietly waiting to meet you Manav. I have a feeling you are going to love this place." Holding Manav's face he says. "A great wonder what's in that soul, Almost like looking through a transparent opacity."

Manav smilingly says - "I have no idea what that means sir."

Khadim - "I don't know either why I chose those words, yet but we will find out, and you can call me Jadd or whatever it is you would address your grandfather as. Come on son, I have so much in my mind, I can barely carry my excitement."

After a brief meet and greet, Khadim leads them inside the heritage home that seems to come straight out of a Mughal folk story. Manav finds it impossible to take in the entirety of the property in one glance; even a fraction of the house cannot be comprehended in a single view. The sheer size and expanse of the home leave him wondering how many days it would take to explore every nook and cranny.

Once inside, Manav is enchanted by the captivating interior. The simplicity of the design is enhanced by classic paintings that exude a sense of inheritance and history. The walls are adorned with photographs, showcasing the lineage of ancestors alongside notable and recognizable personalities. Every step feels like a journey through a museum, delving into the rich heritage of Aban's family.

Modern amenities such as television sets and contemporary sofas are noticeably absent. Instead, the seating consists of large cotton cushions placed on the floor, evoking a traditional and authentic atmosphere.

The house is a sight to behold, with arches adorning every passage and turrets gracing every corner, imbuing it with a grand and monumental presence. The restoration work has been carried out meticulously, with certain parts of the house brought back to their original style, preserving the historical essence.

However, Manav notices that there are also areas of the house that have been left untouched, seemingly without any logic or pattern. While he struggles to understand the reasoning behind this decision, one thing is clear - the preservation of the house's beauty has not been compromised. The untouched areas still exude a charm and allure that perfectly complement the restored sections, creating a captivating blend of old-world magnificence and timeless elegance.

The juxtaposition of the restored and untouched areas adds a sense of intrigue and curiosity, intriguing Manav to explore and discover the stories that lie within the walls of this magnificent house. The preservation of its beauty and the seamless integration of old and new create an enchanting atmosphere that invites him to unravel the secrets of Aban's family history within these hallowed halls.

Khadim - "Have a seat, I'll get you all some homemade Arak, we have some fresh out of fermentation."

Sana - "Are we allowed to?"

Khalid - "Since when do you ask permission from elders?"

Sana - "Oh I'm sorry you look similar to a guy who's ass I had to carry when he could not digest his booze."

Aban - "Children, Show some respect to our guest and your Grandfather."

Khadim - "Relax, Aban, we are all in good spirits and trust me we will have some good spirits too. I hope you are not against some alcohol for celebration, Manav."

Manav - "I Couldn't refuse even if I wanted to, Sir, now I am thrilled."

Khadim - "Splendid, It will only be a few moments, Let me take away some age from this room so that you youngsters can relax, Aban join me Please."

As Khadim and Aban departed, leaving Sana, Khalid, and Manav alone, they couldn't help but burst into laughter at Khadim's cheeky joke. Although they weren't sure if it was appropriate to laugh at the time, the humour of the situation overtook them, and they indulged in a moment of shared amusement.

After their laughter subsided, Manav felt drawn to explore the room and its surroundings. The scent of old bricks and cement, mingled with the fragrance of raindrops that had attempted to seep through the bricks and cracks over the years, filled the air. The house had its own distinct atmosphere, one that welcomed Manav and invited him to take deep breaths, immersing himself in its unique ambiance.

Observing Manav's fascination with the surroundings, Sana picked up on his curiosity and joined him as he wandered alongside the display of old photographs. They walked side by side, admiring the captured moments frozen in time, each image telling a tale of the ancestral legacy that had shaped Aban's family. The combination of the laughter and the exploration of the house's rich history deepened the bond between Manav and Sana, forging memories that he hoped he would carry with them long after their departure.

Sana - Don't ask me who they are, to be frank I lost interest in my family heritage when I found out that my belief was untrue - That Khalid wasn't adopted."

Manav - Giggling he says, "I wasn't going to ask you, but it must be really important for Jaddu, why else would he preserve all these memories, and I think it's better for the person who was in the story to tell the story."

Sana - "Yeah, you better be ready with your story too, because one thing Jaddu likes the most is telling people his story and relating with the listener."

Manav - "How do you mean?"

Sana - "It's hard to explain, you will come around when it starts, it's not rocket science but just a little bit hard to explain, one of those scenarios where it makes sense when you are actually there. Abbu has been really looking forward to this, it was his idea."

Manav - "Your father really knows how to keep secrets, his daughter not so much."

Sana - "Well, 'Secret' not anymore, I'm just happy that you tagged along, first time we all felt like a family and not some sort of operative."

Manav, still processing the sudden openness from Sana, is taken by surprise as Aban, Khadim, and their caretaker Sajid enter the room, each carrying trays filled with an array of treats and drinks. The room was installed with delicious aroma of the delicacies, momentarily diverting Manav's attention from his curiosity about the house.

Without hesitation, the group gathers around the coffee table, and everyone takes a seat, prepared to indulge in the delectable offerings laid before them. The enticing smells permeate the air, stimulating Manav's senses and momentarily setting aside his intellectual queries in favour of the satisfaction his taste buds and nose crave.

Suddenly, Khadim steps forward and pours a milky-coloured beverage, Arak, into each glass. Manav, unfamiliar with this particular drink, is intrigued by its unique appearance. As Khadim raises his glass, a gesture signalling a toast, Manav's curiosity heightens, eager to learn more about this traditional alcoholic beverage and the significance it holds within Aban's family.

Khadim -"Let me toast to the fact that we are all here because we are all alive."

As they all share a drink and begin to savour the delectable meal Khadim had cooked for them, Manav observes that Aban has not had any Arak. He turns towards Sana and asks,

Manav - "Is Aban sober? He did not drink."

Sana - "Yeah because he doesn't drink, he is very strict with his regime and beliefs."

Khadim notices Sana and Manav whispering.

Khadim - "What's with the secrecy Children? You think Khalid is too immature to take a joke?"

Manav - "No, Jaddu. I just asked Sana why Aban didn't drink, I just wanted to make sure that no one on the table is offended by anything then I don't want to be a part of."

Khadim - "Not at all son, he has his own beliefs that I don't understand but he has my uncut respect, and I appreciate you calling me Jaddu. Felt wonderful, glad that we all could sit as a family."

Aban - “I don’t take offence at Manav, I don’t like messing with my brain, and most importantly, I never truly mastered the taste of alcohol."

Khalid didn’t seem to be genuinely enjoying the flavour; instead, he appeared bored and disinterested while they were all enjoying the small talk and "getting to know each other." Something kept preventing Khalid from laughing, and despite his best efforts, he finally breaks the stillness with restrained aggression.

Khalid - “If we are done with all the formalities, can we discuss about Mikhail now, none of you seem to remember why we are actually here."

Aban tried to respond to calm Khalid and divert everyone’s attention from the unwelcome distraction.

Aban - “You are tired Khalid, we can talk about it tomorrow, first thing what we will do."

Khalid wasn’t really ready, he seemed a little embarrassed being completely shut down by Aban, but it appeared he understood what he meant, so he stood up and left the dining room abruptly.

Khadim - "Poor kid, he is still tangled, Aban can you make sure he sleeps peacefully. I don’t want to be impolite by leaving my guest alone on the table, nor do I want him to sleep with unfavourable thoughts, so make sure that he doesn’t feel alone before he wanders off."

After finishing the food on his plate, Aban leaves to follow Khadim’s instructions.

Khadim - "Manav, I apologise. Even if he doesn’t appear friendly, he is harmless. I’m certain he didn’t mean any offence."

Manav - “None taken Sir, we haven’t spoken much but i do not completely disagree from his point of view, I was as ragefull as him, anyone will be if they have lost someone they love."

Khadim - What a wonderful thought you shared with us."

Sana seemed a bit surprised by Manav defending Khalid, she asks.

Sana - "And, when did you two become friends?"

Laughingly and crossing his fingers Manav replies.

Manav - "I hope so, but not yet. I understand exactly where he's coming from. His reaction may require justification, but the matter he is drawing attention to, does not. I remember how he looked at the India Gate and said that it's not a monument their families would have wanted but their men back, and also something about someone slowing our evolution, that didn't make much sense but at least when he opened up I saw another side of Khalid. I wanted to find out the truth behind Mikhail's murder as much as anyone of you, but I'm beginning to question, even after the truth, if I'll be able to stop grieving for him."

The room went silent for a few seconds, However, very skillfully Khadim stopped the elephant from entering the room. Smilingly he looks at Manav and says.

Khadim - "You have the blessing to see people through their armour, but didn't you find anything odd about what he said, anything at all?"

Manav - "It was a sincere curiosity; I cannot assert that Khalid's deliberations are exclusive to him; there may be others, and based on the evidence that is at our disposal, there may be a reason why these concepts continue to surface in people's minds."

Khadim - "Manav, your choice of words, 'Available at our disposal', that's very interesting. Have you ever wondered if we really have access to all of human history? Some chapters missing that we ought to have been aware of from the very beginning, something of great significance or importance concerning the entire human race?"

Manav - "That's difficult to say, I am not sure if it ever occurred to me, having said that I don't believe that any human in the world has been 100% aware of anything."

Khadim wasn't very pleased, he had a little disappointment on his face. He got up and asked.

Khadim - "Let me take you for a walk, come join us Sana."

Sana - "Oh! I'm beat jaddu, I know where you're taking him, I've been on those walks many times, I am sure you two will give each other good company."

As Khadim leads Manav through various rooms and halls, they eventually arrive at a grand chamber filled with photographs spanning across the wall. The condition of the room spoke of its age, with some items even describing its grandeur as belonging to yester-centuries. In addition to the pictures, numerous desks were scattered around the room, adorned with large albums and old paperwork. The drawers, in particular, seem to hold treasures, with materials peeking out from within. In the centre of the chamber, a sizable window allows the sunlight to stream in, casting a soft glow on the space. Positioned directly in front of the window is a large desk, almost resembling a presidential office. It is adorned with piles of files and an imposing reading lens, along with several unfamiliar pieces of equipment that piques Manav's curiosity.

The cold, dampened walls of the chamber, mixed with the century-old scent of the cement, create an atmosphere that feels like breathing in a whole different world. Manav finds himself drawn to the allure of the big leather chair seated behind the desk. Manav's desire to sit in the imposing chair behind the desk was undeniable. The authentic leather work and the straight-angled seating evoked a sense of authority and power that was hard to resist. He can easily imagine the commanding presence one would exude while seated on that chair. However, in an effort to contain his urge, Manav resists the temptation and instead takes a seat in one of the audience chairs positioned nearby.

Turning his attention to Khadim, who seems to have a wealth of knowledge about the history and significance of the room, Manav musters up the courage to ask his burning questions. With a curious expression on his face and a touch of anticipation in his voice, he directs his query towards Khadim, eager to learn and understand more about the contents of the files and the stories behind the photographs.

Manav - “So this room is what you must address as your family’s legacy, I suppose."

Khadim - “That’s not how I see it, whenever I enter the room it makes me feel like I am in an aquarium of dead fishes, a room of fossils if it pleases you."

Manav - “It does appear like that doesn’t it, why maintain it then? Who asked you to? Is it some kind of responsibility you need to carry over and pass over?"

Khadim - “Easy, easy Son! be easy on this old man, I have to keep the air in my lungs in reserve." Laughingly he says, “I wasn’t obligated to, and from what I can tell, just a few others have been in this room. I’m not even holding this up as testimony. I just did it. One fine day I started it and realised my achievement after I finished it. I could have done a million other things with my free time but I chose to do this. I looked up for every member in our family, even distant relatives and put their picture in the family tree, corresponding to their branch. I wasn’t searching for them, I wasn't missing them, you see first you have to know someone to miss them, so that's there."

Khadim finished his sentences but continued murmuring something Manav couldn't recognise.

Manav - With unsurety in his voice, "so it's a hobby, a curiosity I guess...

Khadim - "Let's just say that I am yet to find out the reason why I keep this Ridiculous ledger and pictures of all these dead people on this Ridiculously-high wall. This room is what makes me wonder, Manav, does our actions signify our thoughts, because if that is true, I happen to remember a blank brain everytime I enhance this room, does that make me evil?"

An utterly confused Manav asks himself first before he asks Khadim.

Manav - "Evil", Why would that make you evil?"

Khadim - "You know the common expression 'An empty mind is the devil's workshop'. That's what made me think."

Unsure whether to laugh at that joke or sympathise with a confused man's internal mysteries, Manav's expression looked like a boy trying to laugh in an extremely terrifying situation. Khadim might have felt rude though.

Khadim - "Well don't just stand there, say something"!!

Manav looked at Khadim, and really looked at him, breathed deeply before concocting a response. When he was prepared, he felt pretty good about himself because, in his opinion, he was about to lend a hand in the most significant way. With a contented smile on his face, he says.

Manav - "Like you said, I think you are yet to find an answer, but I also believe that it's more than just a hobby, it is a prayer. It's not a routine, more like a ritual. You come here when you feel you are alone but not looking for company in these pictures but to BE alone with them, you feel their unexpressed loneliness and their masked emotions tell a story ONLY to you, perhaps unfelt by any others in your family, and that makes you feel special, doesn't it? I really admire what you did here."

Khadim took a moment of silence reflecting on Manav's thoughts. He had the expression of a man who had lost or cracked but is an expert at concealing his bleeding wound, completely unnoticed by those who are unaware.

Khadim - "Every person that I find interesting enough to bring in this room, I ask all of them the same question, 'Why do you think I do what I do'? I hope you don't mind me trying to indulge you on one of my projects."

Manav - Not at all, it was a pleasure."

Khadim - "Would you like to know some interesting answers I have got so far?"

Manav - "I would love to."

Khadim - "One of them remarked I'm looking for someone who is dead, who can advocate me in front of the almighty on my judgement day and another was that I want myself to be remembered for bringing the family together, rest of them stood by their 'Hobby' conclusion. Those two were my favourite answers until today. You have the ability to see people like no one else can, you are truly blessed, you are Mubarak."

Manav grinned modestly at his virtual accomplishment, narrated by Khadim as a power like nothing else, Khadim's eyes and smile on his lips made it even more exciting for Manav, to the point his blushing colours on the cheeks were at the best of their 'Pink', and assumed a very elegant monarchy stance.

Khadim - "Let me ask you a question. You are only here for two days, so I can only speculate as to why Mikhail befriended you and deviated from the plan, so drastically that it resulted in his death. Let me be clear: I DO NOT hold you accountable. Mikhail was my grandson, my troublemaker, an introverted fighter, he had no friends. I can tell you that he DID have parental problems, that his mother passed away a long time ago, and that Aban was never present. That's how I perceived Mikhail before you entered the picture, but no one could make him do what he did not want to do. Calm but always paranoid, soft spoken but untrue to his words. Make no mistake Manav, I see people too, from whatever I just told you about Mikhail, does anything seem common between you too?"

As Khadim's question hangs in the air, his observations lead the atmosphere in the chamber to become deadly silent, Manav felt naked. The sound of strong winds battering against the ancient and poorly maintained windows adds to the eerie ambiance. The howling gusts seem to permeate the room, creating an unsettling effect that sends a shiver down their spines. Amidst the silence, the only audible sound is the rush of air gushing out from the tiny cracks.

Manav - "I never believed I was paranoid and untrue, I just thought I never cared."

Khadim - "Oh! But you are, and that is what makes you dangerous; it indicates that you constantly have ammunition for conflict and are geared to strike back, much like a predator; do you know why we all consider predators to be dangerous? They can all attack, defend, protect, and even destroy for pleasure because they are all paranoid.

Manav - "Why did you say 'untrue to my words'?"

Khadim - "Regarding that, pardon me for expressing this, but I do not initially find someone trustworthy who smiles a lot and exclusively speaks in sweet tones. Which forces me to ask you a simple and straightforward question:

Are you prepared to avenge Mikhail's death?

Manav turns his gaze towards Khadim, mustering every ounce of steadiness he can summon. His eyes meet Khadim's, his expression is one of unwavering determination and curiosity. The emotions that may be swirling within him are veiled behind an impassive facade, as if he is trying to hide his true feelings in order to maintain his composure.

With a silent yet powerful determination emanating from him, he says.

Manav - "Two days ago, if you had asked me that, I would have replied, 'When do we leave?'" However, in just a few days, a lot has changed. I believe that my life could be better if I stop seeking vengeance. I see hope for myself, and that gives me motivation to live my life without upsetting anyone, especially my newly found family. Does that make me selfish? Personally, I'm no longer entirely sure.

Khadim - "So you find yourself conflicted within?"

Manav - "I think that's an accurate statement."

Khadim - "The only thing anyone could say or do in that situation is to give you more time to think. Wait for the answers—they are out there—but you'll have to find them on your own, I can't help you on that, no one can."

Manav, feeling a sense of shame wash over him, briefly lowers his head, resembling a defenceless dog. However, to his surprise, Khadim responds with kindness and understanding. He reaches out and gently pats Manav's forehead, trying a gesture of reassurance and comfort. A warm grin spreads across Khadim's face, washing away any feelings of shame or inadequacy. Khadim continues

Khadim - "Mikhail really changed you, didn't he?"

Manav - "In ways I can't even begin to explain."

Khadim - "Can I share a story with you though, for the sake of killing time?"

Manav - "Of course, the story sounds so good right now."

Khadim - "Great, so here it goes. History has many stories revealing identities of people who started something significant but ironically we still don't have one hundred percent clarity on how communication or language came into existence. It is believed that there were these groups of people who we call Phoenicians, coming out of nowhere and established settlements all across the mediterranean. No one really knows from where they learnt it but controversial as it may be, theory holds that English, along with other Germanic languages, was profoundly influenced early on by Phoenician. Thus introducing to the world the deadliest weapon in history."

Manav was clearly confused however he just waited for the story to continue.

Khadim - "I can see you have questions."

Manav - "I would like you to continue."

Khadim - "Okay, let me ask you this, what is the motive of wars? Everyone has different theories, I'd like to hear yours"

Manav - "My theory? It's a bloody waste of time, no one has ever achieved anything useful."

Khadim with a little grin on his face continues.

Khadim - "Any war's aim has always been conquest; the weapon with the greatest capacity for destruction won. One might even argue that a few individuals' wretched intent, constituted the root of it, but once it starts to escalate, everyone involved seeks for opportunities on both sides. They look to spread their wings all over their enemy territory, but what if you could expand silently and make more of your enemy's people accustomed to your culture than to their own? In the name of education, their language and lifestyle was taught, leading them to believe that their literature and heritage were far superior than the native's. Does it ring any bells at all?"

Manav - "Are you referring to the expanding western culture? But I'm confused, wasn't that a choice made by the people? I'm not too sure if that was forced upon the populace. As far as my recollection goes, people found it practical or fashionable, maybe to be a part of something new, something bigger than earlier perceived."

Khadim - "Your response is precisely what I anticipated, and in truth, it's exactly what anyone would have said. But what if I'm right and everyone else is wrong? It's possible that I'm wrong and you and everyone else are correct. Still the question remains, isn't it?"

Manav - "I don't know, what do you think about all this?"

Khadim - "I asked the question, didn't I? Ok, let's forget about it, I guess I asked the wrong question at the wrong time but let's just say hypothetically, If i tell you that one man has actually succeeded not only making a fool out of the whole world but also is playing a God controlling everything since the beginning of time as we know it. Who becomes rich and who becomes important... One man decides. What would you say to that?"

Manav utterly confused asks - "I might ask some follow up questions..."

Khadim - "You are certainly free to do so, you are young, understandably you don't know everything, but with what you have learned so far about this planet, is it impossible that a small group has always been in charge of every significant decision that had global impact. Really consider and answer that, I'm interested in your thoughts."

Manav - “At this point I won’t be surprised if the world is ruled by Monkeys."

Khadim - “I was expecting a serious answer, though it looks like you won’t try to do anything about the man playing God? You will continue as you were."

Manav - “Yes, of course. I hate to break it to you Khadim but there are people like me who have no ambition of becoming rich or famous. Some of us just want to observe, live a simple life with least possible conflicts and leave.”

The atmosphere in the room started to get a little hotter when Khadim responded to Manav’s statement with an irritated silence and disgust. He scoffed and wandered his glances around the room, realising he offended his host, Manav took the high road.

Manav - “I apologise Sir, I mean no disrespect, I am disappointed in me just as much as you are, but unfortunately that is who I am."

Khadim - “No my son, it’s me who should apologise, I’m not disappointed for what you are, but for what you could have become, Looks like this world never left their grip on you. I have been pushing you way too far, forgive me son, I’ve been a terrible host. Let’s retire."

Before they said goodnight, Khadim wanted to show him one of his side projects, so they started walking towards the backyard garden. On the way, Khadim asks something that Manav had not anticipated.

Khadim - “Shall I have your luggage sent to Sana’s room?”

Manav was startled, he was utterly speechless, but regained his consciousness knowing that longer pauses might just raise more questions.

Manav - “Why? Is she leaving?”

Khadim - “Sana is not leaving, of course, but Manav, I must emphasise that you are not in an environment where you need to conceal your intentions. If I‘m mistaken, I really apologise, but it seemed like you two preferred each other’s company rather than being apart."

Manav - “We do, but I also don’t want everyone to be looking at us strangely. Let’s just enjoy our family trip without worrying about unforeseen conflicts."

Khadim - “If you say so, but let me assure you, there are no families in the world without conflicts.”

Manav was beginning to appear relentless, Khadim’s curiosity may have been a bit uneasy. However, he took a deep breath and soon assured himself that he was acting appropriately.

Manav - “If you say so. I believe there’s no harm in being honest with you. The other night me and Sana kissed, and before you say anything we do not have any intentions to hurt your family’s feelings. It just happened one time.”

Khadim - “I felt nothing wrong, You both are young and intelligent, so was I a few days ago." Smilingly he continues. “We have all been there Manav, we trust you, they say Love and Eggs are best when they are fresh, Enjoy it’s freshness while you can."

Manav - “Thank you, I’m sorry for being a little sensitive earlier.”

As the silence lingers and the atmosphere grows increasingly unsettling, both Khadim and Manav find themselves at a loss for words. The weight of the silence becomes suffocating, hanging heavily in the air like an unspoken tension. Neither of them feels compelled to break the silence, unsure of how to navigate the growing unease in the room.

Suddenly, an overwhelming feeling of confinement washes over Manav, reminiscent of the day he was once held hostage. The tense hallway and the weight of the atmosphere begin to mirror that traumatic experience. Despite his efforts to remain composed, the memories flood back, overpowering him and rendering him powerless. The accumulated stress and emotions become too much for Manav to bear.

Tears well up in Manav's eyes, his emotions overflowing like an overextended rubber band that can no longer hold. The pent-up pain and trauma release in a torrent of tears, betraying his efforts to keep it at bay. The room, once filled with an air of mystery and suspense, now becomes a witness to Manav's vulnerability and the depth of his emotional turmoil.

Manav - "I did not have the heart to talk about those moments to Aban or even Sana. For reasons unknown, those moments keep swirling in my head and I can't help it. You have no idea how it feels to lose the person you love, in front of your eyes."

Khadim - "What's going on Manav, you can speak freely here. No judgement. We are all humans here."

Manav starts to burst out a little bit

Manav - "He was a human too, taken away from the palm of my hand. My brother, the one who saved me from hell, and I couldn't do anything but watch his flesh shattered. Tell me can I ever take those images out of my head and live like a normal person?"

In a state of desperation and longing for solace, Manav finds himself resembling a beggar searching relentlessly for a helping hand. Khadim, committed to providing support, remains silent and maintains his unwavering focus on Manav. As Manav's cries grow louder and more desperate, it becomes evident that the attention of those around them is drawn to the emotional outburst. However, the room's unsettling atmosphere makes it unlikely that anyone would willingly enter and witness the raw vulnerability exhibited by Manav.

Sensing the intensity of Manav's anguish, Khadim takes a step closer to him, sensing that this act alone may be enough to bring Manav to his breaking point. And indeed, Manav collapses onto Khadim's shoulder, seeking comfort and refuge from his endless pain revolving in his head. Khadim guides him gently to a nearby chair, allowing him to sit and regain composure. He then offers Manav a glass of water and guides him to breathe.

Khadim - "Let's talk about humans for a minute, here read the title."

Manav - "The Invaders: How Humans and Their Dogs Drove Neanderthals to Extinction'. What is this about?"

Khadim - "Exactly what the title says, it talks about studies and proof on how it's a possibility that early humans killed their evolutionary cousins to extinction. The invasive instinct of humans had developed long before you can imagine. So many facts are lost in history like a broom on devil's footprints, making us all believe that God is still out there, but that's a discussion for another time. This book will give you a new perspective on humanity, probably solidify or disqualify your beliefs."

Manav - "So humans are responsible for the extinction of another species, I'm not surprised."

Khadim excitedly comes closer to Manav, almost whispering.

Khadim - "Manav, you need to realise that we are in danger from our own kind. Similar to monkeys' natural inclinations, we desire the highest branch and support people in positions of power. We are so paranoid that we take what doesn't belong to us that we start wars for personal gains, we kill people who have nothing to do with anything. Count the innocent blood, Millions perished, just like our Mikhail."

Manav kept silent, and kept turning the pages of the book.

Manav - "What are you trying to imply? I am unable to understand who's side you are on."

Khadim - "There are no more sides Manav, either you're the one with the gun or you are not."

Aban - "Even if you have the gun, the size of the gun matters."

As the emotional scene unfolds, Aban, with his commanding presence and unwavering voice, interrupts their conversation, making his way towards Manav. Despite his hands being tied back, Aban's calm demeanour remains intact. He walks softly towards Manav and tenderly caresses his hair.

Aban - "I knew Mikhail was still in there, I don't know if to envy you or pity you."

Manav - "Something is going on isn't it? Are you going to tell me now or waiting to add more suspense?"

Aban looks at Khadim with a smile and says.

Aban - "Nothing is going on my dear, we as a family have a habit of getting into healthy discussions. You are always welcome to join or just observe. I didn't believe it earlier but talking does really calm your mind. If you both are at all interested, I have a topic for discussion 'What drives a species to achieve their next evolutionary stage'? Any opinions?"

Manav - "I remember Khalid had something to say about evolution, it went all above my head but it felt like he truly believes our evolution is somehow controlled, that didn't make any sense."

Jokingly Khadim says

Khadim - "Let's not bring Khalid for this discussion, I plan to sleep peacefully tonight."

As they shared a laugh, Manav's curiosity was swirling in his strange mind, he randomly presented a topic.

Manav - 'Survival of the fittest' We should consider that idea for a moment. The ability to reproduce is the key to an organism's ability to adapt to its surroundings as effectively as possible. At present, our environment is favourable to our further evolution; yet, when it ceases to be so, it's possible that our future generations will develop a new type of ability. I really hope it's flying or breathing underwater, there is still so much we haven't explored."

Aban and Khadim weren't very pleased, with a fake smile he almost interrupted Manav.

Khadim - "That's really interesting but that theory suggests our surrounding environment is responsible for our evolution, what if knowledge of our full capability was the key to the next stage of our evolution. Do you understand how much knowledge is unavailable to us? What if that knowledge is not lost but hidden just to ensure that humans remain docile and submissive, think about in this way. We have evolved from our previous evolutionary stage for over 200 thousand years now, and with the endless capability that we have, what is our best innovation so far? Flying machines, mobile phones, all technology, but what about our own strength, why haven't our capabilities improved?"

Manav - "Interesting point, but our average life span has increased hasn't it. We have better control over diseases and war. Even if it is slow, in some way, progress is still ongoing."

Khadim - "That is the carrot Manav, stick doesn't work on us donkeys anymore."

Manav looks at Aban, who has all his attention to the ongoing discussion, then he stands up, keeps the book on the table and points a question to Aban.

Manav - "What are we really discussing here? Is there hope or not? For us humans?"

Aban - "That's where we are getting at, you see there was a race between two donkey riders, the losing jockey used the strategy of beating his steed with a stick to urge it forward, while the winner of the race sits in his saddle relaxing and holding a carrot on his baited stick, at first they scared us with the stick: with the wars and weapons but now there is a carrot: The illusion of democracy. We won't be able to adapt to our situation or environment till the time our pace is controlled."

Manav - "That's really deep Aban, but can I say something? You both are a gentleman and a scholar. I have never met anyone so wise and peaceful. With the inspiration I have got from this family, I came to realise that we can never win a war fighting hatred with hatred, if evolution is really in our hands then maybe it depends on reaching to an understanding that slight miscalculation of our perception about someone's actions or reaction is suppositional, you cannot control that. Like you just said, we have so much knowledge lost in history. Perhaps that is where the problem lies, we create perception without all the information, And, any conclusion based on less than enough information is the devil's work. We probably need to create a new history, maybe begin again. Everything anew."

Khadim - "I admire your positivity Manav, your childlike thinking and innocence, never lose that."

Aban - "I agree, let's keep the rest of our discussion on 'The Uncertainty Of Humanity' for another time. Go ahead Manav, get some rest."

Khadim - "Of course, how rude of me, keeping my guests occupied during their bedtime. Rest well, tomorrow I will show you my farm."

Manav - "Can't wait, I'm so excited."

As Manav enters the inviting and artistically adorned bedroom that Khadim had shown him, he is immediately struck by its grandeur. The room was adorned with sculptures and paintings, creating a sense of artistic beauty in every corner. The large, comfortable bed beckons to him, inviting him to surrender to its soft embrace.

The walls of the room had retained the appearance of a castle, adding an air of royalty and grandeur to the atmosphere. The warmth and pleasantness radiating from the room seem to be designed to evoke the best feelings within a person. Manav allows himself to sink into the plush cushions. The faint scent wafting from the unused blankets envelops him, bringing forth nothing but good vibes and a sense of tranquillity.

Just as Manav begins to unwind and succumb to the perfect setting for a restful sleep, a sudden and unexpected movement sends a jolt of fear through his body. He felt a sensation of something slithering inside the blanket and onto his legs. Startled to his core, he instinctively pulls his leg back, attempting to free himself from whatever it may be. However, before he can fully react, a pair of hands firmly push him down onto the bed, preventing his escape. As Manav's eyes meet the gaze of the person holding him down, he realises that it is Sana gazing back at him rather indecently. A naughty smile graces her face, though the circumstances leave Manav in a state of shock. Despite his surprise, he musters the courage to remain courteous and returns a smile in response.

Manav - "We practically are in a jungle, you cannot sneak into somebody like that, you almost gave me a heart attack."

Sana continues her intoxicating approach, essentially submitting her head on his chest while she whispers discreetly.

Sana - "I know who I am sneaking into. This predator knows its prey."

Manav - "And you have stalked me enough to plan a sudden attack anytime without warning, right?"

Sana - "Only because I know you must be thinking about me, so you see it's not that difficult for a jungle cat to perish a distracted prey like yourself, and make no mistake Potter, when it comes to hunting I'm a Snow Leopard."

Manav - "Wow, out of all the carnivores in the world, that is what you could choose, a snow leopard? It's kind of funny."

In a slow and deliberate manner, her voice takes on a whispering tone, however clear as crystal, ensuring that there is no room for misunderstanding.

Sana - "You tell me, you have known me for some time now. Shy, elusive and solitary in nature. Primarily active at dawn and dusk. Are there any other predators that match me?"

Manav - "Elusive and solitary maybe, definitely not shy. I can absolutely agree on being most active at dusk and dawn, are you here to hunt me little kitty?"

Sana - "Human, you are in my dwelling, do not patronise me."

Manav - “Not even in my wildest dreams ‘lady Shen’, to what do I owe this pleasure?”

Sana - “I was bored, thought I will hunt for amusement, what were you doing with ‘The Past’ for so long?”

Manav - “Did you just call your father and grandfather ‘The Past’? That’s funny. If you must know we were having an interesting conversation about history but something tells me you already knew.”

Sana - “Trust me you were not the first and I am sure won’t be the last, how’d it go? Do you find the future more interesting or the past?”

Manav - “Oh future all the way, undoubtedly. But I was certainly interested in his view of the world. It was almost as if he was trying to explain something to me, but I was incapable of comprehending much. I hope he doesn’t consider me to be a moron.”

Sana - “Well you are what you are, you shouldn’t worry about what people think.”

Manav - “Oh really miss ‘Perfection’ those are some wise words coming out of someone so small, you must come from a line of geniuses.”

They cuddle, tickle and giggle until it gets quiet as Manav’s concentration is compromised again. Even Sana’s silky hair didn’t affect him, his eyes were on Sana but clearly the focus somewhere else. When the laughter concluded the whole room was subdued with this strange hush feeling as if you have hid yourself under a blanket, not even daring to whimper or breathe or else you will be found. Sana couldn’t wait any longer, she kisses Manav and rests her head on his chest and asks, “what are you thinking?" Manav remained silent and kept looking at the ceiling with thoughtful eyes and a verge of a smile.

Manav - “I believed that I was the only source of light in this otherwise gloomy world. Sana, I wasn’t perfect. I wanted to pass away alone. At a moment that most people dread, I was making jokes, inflaming them to hurt me more, almost as if I believed I deserved it. I get a feeling that a righteous mind, even a little bit, won’t incite violence. Before I could feel the pain, I was getting excited wondering how bloody or creative they were going to be. Something was really wrong with me when I met Mikhail. That man has helped me in so many ways, almost everyday I find a new reason to miss him. He gave me hope, made me believe that good is somewhere hidden, but it is there. After all that he has given me, and what you have given me, I cannot make myself walk towards hatred anymore. I am sorry, I have to say this - I know you all have been planning to avenge Mikahil, and I have nothing against that, trust me for a very long time there was nothing else I wanted but to see those responsible die, but I don’t anymore. I just don’t want any of us to get hurt.”

In response, Sana holds his face between her hands very gently and says,

Sana - “Manav, whatever you decide, it’s your call. But at least pay attention to what they say. More time has passed for Jaddu and Abbu in this world than for you and me. Even though I first disagreed with them, I now realise that what makes sense to me doesn’t necessarily have to make sense to you. You can’t be certain without acquiring all that they have to offer. You don’t seem like someone who would enjoy looking back, so don’t give yourself anything to regret. However, if you’ve already made a choice, don’t change it; instead, consider what you could do instead of what "Mikhail" would have preferred."

She taps his head jokingly but gently, and delivers an adorable little smile, Manav had no other option but to reflect. Sana helps him take a few deep breaths to relax the situation.

Manav - “I see what you mean, but up until this point, I didn’t really care if I let anyone down; but, with all of you, I would be furious if I did. I feel forced to voice my opinion as a family, but I'm not sure where it ends."

Sana - “Then you wait for a dialogue to ingrain and see how it goes. Family doesn’t mean you have to agree with each other Manav, family is a place where you can freely share your thoughts without prejudice or judgement, it’s a place of understanding. Don’t worry too much, tomorrow you will have enough time to solidify your understanding.”

Manav - “What do you mean? Is something happening tomorrow?”

Sana - “Oh did I not tell you? Me and Abbu are going for an engagement, I thought you might not want to come unless you would like to meet my 70 cousins and their parents.”

Manav - “70 cousins? Are your cousins some kind of fish breed? But you’re right, I don’t think I will do well around so many people but I will be so bored without you. Is Khalid going as well?”

Sana - “Of course Khalid is coming with us, wait! Don’t tell me you have developed a liking for my brother?”

Manav - “To be honest I never hated him, he definitely seems to have a ‘bully mentality’ but not by choice. I may not like him but I don’t hate him either, I was just hoping for a familiar face as this place is all new for me.”

Sana - “Oh poor baby! Don’t be sad we will be back by afternoon, we are staying till the ceremony, it shouldn’t take long and I am leaving you with the best company possible, Jaddu is the best conversationalist."

Manav - "Well, have fun, will you show me what you're wearing though?"

Sana - "You will. Ok Potter, hope you are cosy enough because it's time to say good night, you and I have a big day tomorrow."

After sharing a few kisses and smiles, Sana leaves Manav's room, leaving him all alone with his thoughts. It was an ideal environment for a deep drift off, the cold room and the warm comforter was ready to melt him down to a peaceful sleep, but Manav's eyes were still not getting tired enough. Even in the pitch-black chamber, his eyes and thoughts were wandering in pursuit of something. He appeared to have had a fine day, but his mind continued to feel like a firecracker bursting off in all directions. The upcoming day, where he will be alone with Khadim, carries a hint of uncertainty. His age difference and the chemistry between them leave Manav feeling a bit uncertain about what to expect from the interaction. The time they have spent together was quite insufficient, and his gut feeling doesn't entirely align with Khadim's characteristics. Taking a few deep breaths, he tries to relax himself, and to accept the outcome of what tomorrow may bring, expecting himself to be on his best behaviour irrespective of the outcome. He acknowledges the wonderful space they are in and makes a conscious effort to appreciate the natural beauty and the monument in which Khadim resides. Hoping that his sense of unease won't overshadow the day, he allows himself to slowly drift off into dreamland, with positive thoughts taking root in his mind.

As the morning dawned, a biting chill hung in the air. Manav, roused from his sleep by the sound of frosty winds jostling to enter the room through small ditches, he sought refuge under the cocoon of his warm comforter. The bone-chilling cold outside deterred him from leaving the comforting sanctuary of his bed, leading him to drift back into peaceful sleep.

However, Manav's peace was abruptly interrupted with a sudden incident, he found himself shaken awake when his comforter was forcefully pulled away. The real shock came when a cold hand delicately brushed his face, trailed down his neck, and continued its chilling course over his chest. The intrusive touch sent a shiver down his spine, lightening him fully awake and alert.

The sudden intrusion reminded him of the torture he endured. With goosebumps and half-shut eyes he wakes up frantically to a rather mesmerising and pleasant view, he is greeted by a sight that captivates his attention and leaves him awestruck. Sana was standing before him looking like a princess from a fairy tale with her gold-toned embroidered attire. The ethereal beauty radiating from Sana envelopes the room, casting an enchanting spell upon Manav, his eyes glowed as if he had seen an angel, Her gorgeous white kurti transformed her image, making her look less like a tomboy and more like an ethnic Muslim woman. "So, how do I look?" Sana asks while whirling herself round to have him see her from all angles. Each angle made Manav just more speechless. Her Dupatta gave the illusion of wings of an Angel. While she was spinning herself around, only two ideas coiled in his mind, "either she was made for this dress or the dress was made for her." The flow of the white silk brushing down her radiant skin was unexplainable and somewhat torturing. She asks again, "Don't act dumb, say something." Looking at her beautiful eyes as deep as he could, spellbound he says,

Manav - "You look like a waterfall."

Sana was completely stubbed, “You look like a waterfall?" What does that even mean, smilingly she tries to think about it, but somewhere in her heart she wanted Manav to be the one to explain.

Sana - “I look like a waterfall? Never heard a compliment like that."

Manav - “It means your beauty is delightfully dangerous. Like a waterfall, it is beautiful from a safe distance, but if you venture too close, you might perish by its force."

Sana - “That’s deeper than I thought, but lovelier than I expected."

She comes closer to Manav, just before landing a kiss she says.

Sana - “How am I going to manage being without you all day, I didn’t plan that."

Manav - “Well, you did, now you are committed and I am not, I am just going to relax and yawn all day with your jaddu."

Sana - “He isn’t that bad Manav, just try striking a conversation, he might just surprise you."

Manav - “I am just joking honey, you have an exciting day ahead, can’t wait for you to come back and tell me all the stories."

They hug each other goodbye, as she was leaving Sana says.

*Sana - “And I can’t wait to come back and hear all Your stories, hope you enjoy your day of relaxation and illumination... Potter."*

CHAPTER ELEVEN

# SEA WAVES

As Manav settled back into bed, his mind started yearning for a few more moments of the magical comforting sleep, he preferred to confine within the warm embrace of the soft cotton. However, an unsettling realisation began to seep into his consciousness – the understanding that he and Jaddu were the only inhabitants of the vast house today.

The weight of this knowledge began to impede Manav's comfort, plaguing his thoughts and disturbing his peace, making him somewhat feel guilty for not attending his gracious host. He found himself lost in contemplation. In the stillness of the room, Manav searched for any small indication or random occurrence that could provide him with a reason to remain in the comforting cocoon of his bed. He yearned for a sign, a small reprieve from the weight of the isolation that surrounded him.

"He might still make me eat something, but at least he'll leave me alone for the majority of the day if I just remain inside and claim I have the flu." There were a lot of 'Eureka' and 'How can I be so stupid' thoughts before he gave up and just forced himself out of bed. The process of getting ready for the day was a process of slow pace, almost as if time itself was in no hurry to proceed. Manav meticulously groomed himself, ensuring his appearance aligned with the ambiance befitting the host's environment. He cleaned every nook and cranny, carefully tending to his personal hygiene. Yet, despite his efforts, a lingering feeling of dissatisfaction persisted. Nothing seemed to be "good enough" for the occasion.

With a sense of half-determined purpose, Manav set off on foot, walking in search of the kitchen, dining room, or any room that might offer a semblance of human existence within the house. The huge building had no escape from the clutches of palm-sized spiders and layers of ancient dust; however finding a human soul looked to be quite a struggle.

A few strolls later he understood that he was lost. The temptation to call out for help crossed his mind, but he swiftly dismissed it as an immature option that would not leave a positive impression. He decided to keep walking to new corridors and mark each pass, that was the best idea he could foster.

As Manav continued to explore the corridors, he took on a newfound sense of intrigue and fascination. Adorning the walls were various pictures, capturing moments from different eras, each one marked with a salutation and a date. Some of these photographs seemed to have been taken during the early years of camera invention, showcasing the evolution of photography throughout history.

Manav's curiosity piqued as he delved deeper into the stories behind these pictures. He wondered about the locations where they were taken, the significance of the poses chosen by the subjects, and the reasons behind their outfit choices. Each photograph seemed to hold a unique narrative, inviting him to unravel the tales they held within their frames.

He found himself intrigued in a thought, whether these individuals had specifically requested their children to preserve these pictures as mementos, a way to immortalise their memory and preserve their legacy? Questions swirled in his mind, as he pondered the intricacies of capturing memories through photography and the way in which these frozen moments held their own significance, to what extent, he had to ask, he had to ask someone, his quest to find Jaddu or anyone to answer these questions was becoming impatient.

The pictures started guiding him, he started remembering all of them, "I have seen this picture, I have come this way before." That's how he finally found a way out. He emerged through a door that led directly into a kitchen garden and down to a picturesque winery, Manav found himself at the perfect vantage point to take in the breathtaking view of the entire vineyard. The first light of the morning sun illuminated the dewdrops on the leaves, transforming them into glistening diamonds. The natural beauty and the divine glow of the sunrise left Manav in awe.

With each passing moment, he realised the immense value of witnessing a beautiful sunrise. While sunsets may possess their own calming charm, they can never quite encapsulate the sense of new hope and rejuvenation that a sunrise brings. This particular sunrise, seemingly designed exclusively for Manav by some divine force, instilled a sense of inspiration and anticipation within him.

Manav decided to continue his walk, venturing farther from the house. As he ventured deeper into the farm, he found the land expanding before his eyes, adorned with an abundance of fruit and vegetable plantations. Flowers of unparalleled beauty blossomed, some of which were entirely unfamiliar to him. It became evident that Jaddu has some deep understanding and appreciation for horticulture.

In a distance of a few kilometres, stood majestic mountains, their presence added the best grandeur of the scene, almost like marking it as a period of space. Manav couldn't take his eyes off and rested his gaze on the horizon, transfixed by the expansive beauty. Uncertain of which direction to explore first, he felt overwhelmed with a multitude of choices before him. Every direction seemed to offer its own mystic charm and hidden treasures to explore. Manav felt a sense of adventure and curiosity building within him, urging him to embark on a journey of discovery. Suddenly, the absence of companionship became starkly apparent, he started feeling lonely as the desire to share such an expansively beautiful universe with others touched his heart, he couldn't help but feel a sense of loneliness creep into him. Beauty and wonder could be found in solitude, but Manav couldn't help but yearn for the joy of experiencing it with others. Philosophical thoughts on the nature of solitary exploration captivated his attention, momentarily distracting him from the awe-inspiring beauty that had initially captivated his gaze.

"She has left me for a few minutes and I already miss her."

Manav wasn't a couch potato, he had his share of exploration, however things that never really registered earlier in his mind were raising serious questions, and he really needed someone to talk about them. The air was both warm and cold, which was an odd sensation. "It is I who has to decide to carry back the warmth or the chill back to the castle." He finally decides to find Jaddu and maybe show some courtesy to his host. He heads back to the villa, a universe in its own kind, a universe of history rather. Bidding adieu to the heavenly landscape, he drags himself back to the castle.

This time, Manav moved through the hallways with considerably more ease than before. He carefully checked every room, occasionally calling out Khadim's name, but receiving no response. His heart sank a bit, realising that his search for company might be in vain. However, a glimmer of hope sparked within him as he thought of Jaddu and the possibility of finding him in his "Family picture room."

Drawing upon his memory of previous visits, Manav recalled the familiarities and details to lead himself to Jaddu's cherished room. With much more confidence than before, he navigated the winding hallways, trusting his instincts to guide him. Despite the vastness of the house, he managed to find his way to the room where Jaddu had displayed his beloved portraits.

He finally found the room, and there he was – Jaddu, staring at the portraits just as if he never left the room. Relief washed over Manav as he realised that his instincts had led him to the right place. The loneliness he had felt during his exploration began to dissipate.

A sense of familiarity and comfort enveloped them both as they looked at each other and wished each other 'Good Morning', surrounded by the memories captured in each portrait. Manav and Jaddu, like old friends, happy to be reunited, the joy in their eyes reflected their happiness revealingly.

With a smile on his face, Manav stepped closer to Jaddu,

Manav - "I thought I'll find you here, I hope I am not interrupting."

Khadim - “Not in the slightest my dear, I saw you leaving to the gardens, you looked quite content and enjoying yourself. I didn’t have the courage to interrupt you."

Manav - “Oh you did? I was just making myself familiar with the surroundings, I must say I have never seen a house so close to nature. Is this a holiday home, a farmhouse, a castle? It’s really hard to decide. It’s a beauty, Jaddu."

Khadim - “You are so kind. I prefer to spend some time here after I wake up. I like to remind myself to be appreciative of the gifts God gave me - My family."

Manav gently smiles and asks

Manav - “I can understand, this room does have a gravity of its own. If I were you I would have done the same."

Khadim - “Now that you are here, would you like to help me with something?"

Manav promptly replies.

Manav - “I would be honoured to”

Khadim - “I was wondering where to put your picture in this family tree, but I can’t decide and I also do not have a photo."

Khadim suddenly appeared flashing a mischievous crooked smile. He pointed towards a particular portrait, drawing their attention to a scouting ancestor who had decided to hold a rifle while posing for the photo.

Curiosity piqued, Manav and Jaddu looked closely at the portrait, taking in the sight of their ancestor proudly displaying the rifle. They couldn’t help but chuckle at the audacity and playful nature of their family members. It was a fascinating glimpse into the past.

The ancestors that gazed back at them from the photographs seemed to be not just frozen images, but vibrant characters with tales woven into their very beings.

Khadim - "Something like this would suffice."

Laughingly Manav says.

Manav - "Any picture of mine is not commanding enough to be on that wall, look at the aura and grace on their face, decades apart and they can still give any personality a run for their money."

Khadim - "In a family, your achievements become dull. Even a person with gravity in his personality such as yours, is meaningless. In a family everyone is equal. That is what I believe and that is what I have taught all my children. You are equal among us and you are equal among them."

Manav - "So you were not joking, you really want my picture on that wall?"

Khadim - "We will be honoured to, and you are family now so why not? We always have remained with our own. But this time God conspired and brought us all together. We rarely brought anyone from outside. When Aban brought you here, I felt like I was meeting someone who belonged to me, am I making any sense?"

Manav - "More than you know Jaddu, Let's do it." Is there a studio we can go to?"

Khadim - "No, but I can call a photographer, go wear a nice kurta. If you don't have one go get one of Khalid's, he won't mind."

Manav - "I am so excited that I am not even worried about his reaction."

They chuckled for a bit and Manav left the room to get ready. He sprints to Khalid's room and opens up all his bags to find the shirt that suited him the most. He found a light-teal-coloured shirt and sprinted back to the picture room.

Khadim - "That was really quick, and look at you, you look like a freshly bloomed flower."

Manav smiles compassionately.

Khadim - “The photographer is on the way, let’s go have breakfast by then."

Manav - “No sir, I don’t want to risk any gravy spillage on Khalid’s garment, I’d rather get the picture clicked and then have breakfast."

Khadim - “I don’t think so, you do not want to mess up your picture my lad. Your excitement is what’s spilling all out on the floor ."

Manav regards Jaddu’s joke however there were thoughts spiralling in his mind, his focus was more on the wall with the pictures.

Manav - “Jaddu: I want to apologise for my behaviour last time, I was a little arrogant, I was in my own world after I met everyone, those were by far the best days of my life, I’m afraid my behaviour might reflect ungratefulness”

Khadim - “What are you talking about? You have been nothing but a gentleman since I have met you, come here let me help you."

Khadim reaches out and hugs Manav, and surprisingly knocks his head firmly enough to make him feel a little prick.

Khadim - “I just knocked the negative crow out of your head to make some place for the cheerful koel, feed her well and she will sing captivating melodies for you, on your command."

Manav laughs adorably, but nothing compared to Jaddu’s. The moment was delightfully embarrassing.

Manav - “Sir, yes Sir. I’m having a really good time and somehow this room is getting more and more interesting. I have to give some thought to where I want my picture to be but I need your help. What can you tell me about him?"

As Manav and Jaddu started deciding where to place Manav’s picture, Manav’s curiosity got the better of him.

He pointed at each intriguing picture, eager to learn about the personality, background, accomplishments, and even the failures of the individuals depicted. His thirst for knowledge and finding a connection with their shared history was palpable.

Jaddu, patient as always and full of stories, began to narrate with increasing excitement. With a twinkle in his eye, he painted a vivid picture of each person's life, making it sound like an enchanting children's storybook. He animatedly described their personalities, delving into their passions, dreams, and the adventures they embarked upon. He didn't shy away from mentioning their failures and challenges, for he believed they were an integral part of their journey.

Amidst the storytelling, Jaddu would occasionally interject with a playful joke, teasing Manav about placing his picture next to Sana, evoking a blush and a shy smile in response.

Khadim - "How about I place you next to Mikhail?"

Manav pauses for a moment, his gaze lingered on Mikahil's smiling picture. Mikahil, his hero, the one who opened the path for a new journey, the one he admires the most. A rush of memories flooded his mind, and for a moment, he relived the precious moments he had spent with him.

a sense of guilt overshadowed Manav's thoughts. He couldn't help but question whether he truly deserved a place next to his hero. The weight of his own perceived failures and shortcomings weighed heavily on his heart, creating a spiral of self-doubt and reflection.

Unable to maintain his gaze on Mikahil's picture for more than a few seconds, Manav knew that lingering too long would unleash a flood of thoughts and emotions that he had been trying to evade. The guilt that had been haunting him for some time now threatened to consume him once again.

"I think I finally know why you are doing this, with all these pictures of your family. Maybe it really does what you say it does to you. But I feel there is more to it."

Khadim interestingly sits himself on the desk and asks Manav to carry on.

Manav - "I think you are trying to understand the beginning and end of your family tree. Perhaps you have already given up on the beginning but now you are figuring out where it will lead you to. It's not a hobby, it's like a curse, an ambition that has made your mind its home and you cannot be peaceful until you have done what it asks you to do, I don't think you really like it, you are just preventing your mind from going haywire."

As Manav observed Jaddu's reaction to his theory, an eerie silence filled the room. Jaddu remained motionless, his eyes fixed on the papers and pictures scattered across his desk. The weight of Manav's presumption seemed to hang in the air, causing him to question whether he had unintentionally caused offence.

Just as Manav gathered his thoughts to offer his apologies for any miscalculations or misunderstandings, Jaddu's demeanour shifted. Slowly, he lowered himself onto the nearest chair, appearing to be overwhelmed by an unspoken emotion. His silence persisted, but a faint smile graced his lips, adding intrigue and ambiguity to the atmosphere.

Manav - "I apologise, I may have crossed a line."

Khadim - "Apologies are quite unnecessary Manav, if anything, you have given my thoughts a new direction, exactly what we have been expecting from you. Do you know what Aban said while he was monitoring you, he said to me, 'He seems to believe he is the devil on the side of the angels but in actuality it's the other way round, even with his amass potential, he doesn't pose a threat to anyone, he likes to keep the poison within rather spit it out'."

Manav - "I can assure you Jaddu, I didn't mean to spit any poison, I was concerned that this habit is consuming you, you have such a beautiful garden, this whole house is like a castle in a fairy tale, and yet you spend most of your time in this room, excavating the past."

Khadim - "You are so kind hearted Manav, that you don't see the evil I am trying to understand, your kindness overlooks my compulsion to understand why it is necessary for some humans to mark their names in the history books, why is that they cannot perceive that the desire to be remembered after they have gone is an obsession, and not passion."

Manav - "I don't understand Jaddu."

Khadim - "It's quite simple actually, I believe that history is a time machine. But every book has an author, through their eyes we see the events, the emotions, the rights and wrongs. Who is to say that at a time when being important in society was the only way to survive, there must have been a tug-of-war between the intellects to be the first at something. I wonder how the environment was, the big question is how much can I believe in them."

Manav - "But you have your gut feeling, your own conscience, something has to make sense to you before you believe in it, and then I guess we verify."

Khadim - "Verify? Some of the books written are thousand years old, what does your conscience say about it? And how do you verify?"

Manav - “Well Jaddu, there is a reason we haven’t talked about your gigantic book shelves in your gigantic library, I’m not really a book-reader. However, assuming we are talking about the religious books, I’m not sure if you’ve heard, I haven’t inherited any beliefs. I was an orphan in a place that could barely afford one hot course meal a day. They weren’t really keen on teaching us who the one true god was."

Khadim - “I am aware, I do feel sorry for you son. Sana has the potential to find your parents, but when we insisted, she said "you might not like it."

Manav - “She is right, I have made attempts of my own. I can tell you I did not fail, but it doesn’t matter to me anymore. Let me assure you that is not the reason why I am a non-believer."

Khadim - “Everyone believes in something, it’s like a seed. It takes time for it to bloom into a beautiful flower or a monstrous tree, but it takes work. You have to nourish it, look after it, protect it."

Manav - “I am yet to find out what my plant will grow into, in that case."

Khadim - “That brings me back to your point, “verifying a knowledge." I sense we are moving to an interesting conversation, how about some Arak to fuel our inner inspirations."

Manav’s naughtiness was on the tilt of his chin, he was practically waiting for him to ask, possibly because he was much more relaxed with Khadim today than before. Khadim calls upon a helper and asks for two glasses and a bottle of fresh Arak. After gulping a few sips Manav could feel his muscles getting relaxed and his eyes and shoulders loosening up. With every sip, he found it more and more simple to be brutally honest.

With the Arak coursing through his veins, Manav felt a deep emotional attachment to everyone and everything in the room, particularly towards Khadim. It wasn't a matter of unawareness, but rather a shift into another dimension of consciousness, where the weight of reality faded away. Memories, objects, living beings, and even the laws of gravity no longer held the same significance. Manav couldn't help but wear a constant smile. He was captivated by the cognitive nature of the conversation that unfolded.

Manav found himself questioning the familiarity of it all. Why did this environment feel so strangely familiar to him? Yet, instead of allowing the question to perplex him, he embraced the mystery and celebrated it in the present moment.

Manav - "My main point is that, while not all knowledge is passed down from generation to generation, the majority of it undergoes verification before it is made available for the general public."

Khadim - "But is that really entirely accurate though? Not just from one generation to the next, but also from one culture or society to another, knowledge is passed on. Who is to say that the leaders who led and educated each culture didn't make a few adjustments for their personal satisfaction?"

Manav - "I don't deny the possibility, History negationism is a sad reality, It happened all over the world. Take an example of book burning, denial of holocaust, revising textbooks and even religious books to hide crimes on a genocidal level. It's all true, so is the fact that it has all been revealed by real historians and scientists".

Khadim finds Manav's argument so appealing that he smiles attentively. Impressed beyond his expectations, he keeps his glass on the table and asks.

Khadim - "Ever heard of a little game called "Chinese Whispers?"

Manav - "I know what you're talking about, and certainly, in some circumstances, revolutionaries from each age of prophets have interpreted all that surpassing knowledge, but it still goes on, right? Every day a fresh explanation is offered, isn't that how it should be?

Khadim - "I couldn't agree more, writings, even a thousand years old, fit perfectly in the void of new realities that we discover even today. But you're not thinking big enough, how about we forget the misinterpretation of a short period in time, and expand it's spread from a country or a continent."

Manav - "How large are we talking about, you mean more than centuries and millennials?"

Khadim - "How about from the beginning of time and the whole world as we know it."

Manav took a moment to think, his experience and knowledge or his brain capacity wasn't enough to fathom what his thought process was taking him to. Khadim said something that was beyond any possibilities but his confidence to confer on it was highly compromised.

Manav - "If you're saying what I think you are saying, that means that data of our existence is completely falsified and the world was misinformed, is that what you are saying, wouldn't that be a hack of all time?"

Khadim - "Hmm, allow me to say this, without denying any scientific findings, the passing of information has been vastly controlled by individuals who had nothing to do with physics, maths, botany or even astronomy. Have we been really that independent in our society where whistleblowers are perceived as normal? Have they been considered as revolutionaries or some loud-mouth-attention-seekers who people laugh at? And before you even bring it up I agree that some of them have been recognized and are the pillars of the modern world but indulge me for a moment Manav, and tell me with absolute confidence, is there any chance, whatsoever, that a real revolutionary, a real rebel who could have changed the course of history, his footprints were wiped away from every known cognizance. Is there even a minute part of your mind captivated by this question?"

Manav's inebriation required constant refills, everytime Khadim came up with an argument, he was so much enthralled by it, he had to turn every page of his knowledge and experience to be responsive enough not to look stupid in front of the intellect of Khadim.

Manav - "Doesn't Science always find a way to reach the needful? It's like life, it cannot be caged, sooner or later all is revealed, maybe not in our lifetime."

Khadim - "If not in our lifetime then what's the point living the rotten truth, they won Manav, whoever deceived you, they Won. I know it is too much to take in one gulp. Allow me to paint an analogy for you. You wake up one day and find out that you are the only human in the entire planet, the rest of the species in existence are just a few steps behind you in the evolution cycle to become a complete homo sapien, I'm sure for the man that you are, you will certainly help the other beings, help them organise, help them find food, help them socialise. Now imagine each and every human being in existence getting a chance just the same as you are. If the under-evolved hadn't been so fortunate to have come across someone like you, I'm willing to wager that the chance you get won't be handled as gracefully, some of them would treat the 'left-behind' as slaves and perhaps even kill for fun.."

Manav - "Maybe someone like me would be rather scared of the ones left behind."

Khadim - "There is a good chance of that too, Now see Manav a good argument should unravel every fact, that's why I went that far, but we both know history is filled with people who wanted to be remembered, their dedication was not always towards the betterment of society, some or probably most were obsessed to be written about them to be immortal - like Jesus, Alexander or Genghis Khan. When a standard is set, be a good or a bad example, a challenge instigates in us to cross that line, doesn't it? Hasn't that been Man's desire all throughout history? Now, to win, you either become better than everyone or make everyone else less efficient. A widespread false knowledge with unrecognisable deceitfulness must have slowed down the evolution that we should have surpassed a thousand years ago. Just think about the pyramids, which have existed for thousands of years, but still there is no book that says 'How to make pyramids', where did all that knowledge go? How many people have perished from starvation in the more than 12,000 years that we have been producing food? Manav, even though the world is far from perfect, each year we celebrate the New Year without realising that the same amount of money could have saved the life of at least one new person. Ignorance was a bliss some generations ago, not anymore, ignorant men are impious villains."

At this point Khadim's tone was becoming more stern and louder, his voice got deeper and deeper, attaching every bit of emotion in his tone he started browsing pages from one of the books on the table and asked Manav.

Khadim - "You do know what the term 'Historical negationism' means?"

Manav - "I'm Sorry I do not anymore."

Manav looked vulnerable, he had no energy left to even sit straight. Just as Khadim began to explain, they heard noises. In comes the rest of the family, tired and exhausted but as soon as they saw the expressions on Khadim and Manav's face, everyone knew something curious was going on, Khadim takes the first step to welcome everyone.

Khadim - "Ah, what a surprise, we were expecting you at a later time but what a joy, come join us. We were under a gripping spell of curiosity, right before you interrupted us."

Sana comes over to Manav, and without any hesitation greets him with a tiresome hug and a kiss, tells him how much she missed him and how exhaustful the event was.

Sana - "So let us in, what have you been discussing about?"

Khadim - "I was just about to read a paragraph from a book about 'Historical Negationism', but let me explain what it is exactly. In simple terms it means that powerful and the higher class of the society decides what the masses should read and learn, in some forms of history it was done deliberately and publicly but in some cases it was proved long after since all actions were executed in secret, just to keep people busy and occupied so that the masses never can make time to do what is necessary. I have several books for you to read from - This one's about China, this one from Japan, we all know what happened in Nazi Germany, this one about Ukraine. Aha! There it is, one of my favourite books - "The Gulag Archipelago. Allow me to read the quote I love - "We forget everything. What we remember is not what actually happened, not history, but merely that hackneyed dotted line they have chosen to drive into our memories by incessant hammering."

The sound of crickets from the garden, the wind gushing through the imperfect closures, even a little movement of the bodies and even their heartbeats was breathtakingly audible, such was the presence of 'a dark silence' in the room. Truth, at times, is like a nail piercing through the most sensitive part of your body, which, halfway through, takes the form of a broadsword, and very slowly it leaves but the pain stays behind forever, but we are taught to move on, and only move on. Even the wisest of them all - Aban, had his head down, seemingly recollecting memories affiliated to the ongoing discussion. Sana stood by Manav, however Khalid was not as uncomfortable as everyone else was.

Khalid - "What's the point of all this? We are wasting time, he doesn't care. I already told him, showed the picture, the monuments and the grand cover-ups behind them, but he was laughing at me, he didn't believe me."

That triggered Sana.

Sana - "First of all he did not laugh even once and second of all, you were cock-eyed after consuming all the alcohol from the club. Do you not remember how he helped balance you up and held your hair so you don't fall in your own vomit? The ever-thankless cry baby Khalid, you haven't changed a bit?"

Just as anyone expected, Sana and Khalid started quarrelling like any other siblings. Aban was still quiet and it started to bother Manav a little, After all he was the hero father of his hero and while a topic of discussion that had paramount value to this family, was at its peak, he still didn't look like he wanted to share any insights. Khalid and Sana's tone in their argument was getting louder, Sana will call him something and Khalid will come up with something even more meaningful to embarrass Sana, this went on for a while until a steady, deep and fervent voice echoed the halls voicing out a question in a tone as definitive a tone can be, even Aban couldn't avoid paying attention to it.

Manav - "How can anyone control evolution, controlling evolution means restricting nature. How can nature be restrained? It's impossible..... Isn't it?"

Everybody had his attention, however Khalid could only be more annoyed, he left the room irately, mumbling hateful words, not loud enough for anyone to hear though. Aban walks up to Manav, looking into his eyes, he puts his hand over his shoulders and makes him sit on a chair. Manav began to sob a little at this point, absolutely astonished by the knowledge he couldn't even begin to fathom.

Aban - "Sit down Manav, I will explain everything."

Manav - "I don't know what to think, Maktaba, Please help me get rid of this... whatever that is happening in my brain, I have a headache, I can't think straight Maktaba, Please help me."

Khadim interjects.

Khadim - "Any medicine that goes in your body has the same effect, at first your body is confused with the alien inside, then it accepts after it understands the medicine's purpose, what you're going through is completely normal."

Aban - "Do you know Manav, from where the word "War" is derived from? In old high German language the word Werren which literally means to confuse or to cause confusion, in the old English dictionary the word Werre means the same, the seeds of war were often sown by political entities or rival factions, leading to open and declared armed conflicts. That's how it all started, young men fought on behalf of old aristocrat moguls seeking to maintain or expand their riches and influence. The sacrifices made by these brave soldiers went unnoticed by the very individuals they fought for, while the moguls clink their glasses of champagne in their villas, are you with me so far?

Manav - “That reminds me of someone we both know very closely."

Aban - “We ‘knew’! That’s the correct word Manav, Mikhail is not with us anymore. And you know exactly the cause of that, it’s because of the uncertainty of humanity. The extent of our species is threatened by our own existence, we have enough nuclear power to destroy our own planet, many times over, are we really in safe hands? If we do feel safe with all these actual facts, how real are we Manav?"

Manav - “I’m still gasping for a proper breath, right now all I can think is; if what I believed in before meeting any of you was true, everything seems unreal now."

Watching him break down, Sana approaches him, ruffling his hair she says.

Sana - “Listen Manav, We are all real, even that jerk Khalid, and you are just as real to us as Mikhail was."

While she was trying to comfort him another familiar hand touched his shoulder, Aban brings a chair right next to him and says,

Aban - “I have been collecting intelligence all my life, that is the direction I chose in my studies, or training, such was the life I had chosen. The hardship, the long nights that never ended. Finally when It all started to make sense, it was like a puzzle in which every puzzle-piece was a puzzle in itself. When I pieced them all together, I saw the big picture. Do you know what was missing in that “Big Picture?" Everyone like you and me, people who don’t make sense, people who don’t have a name, people who are nothing but just a number in a population amongst those who make us build stairs for themselves and once they reach the top, they are destined to rule over people like us, and thus follows a series of men destined because of their inheritance. Someone inherited their family name, their wealth, someone inherited their race, the skin colour or anything that was the paradigm of the time. It's like a wheel of fortune where people like you and me will never have their names on."

Manav - "I remember having the same conversation with Mikhail, it's all coming back to me. I told him how I wanted to just die, how fed up I was seeing this wheel of fortune. Long ago the kings were gods, then the prophets and now the richest of the society decide our fate."

Aban - "Next gods could be army chieftain or something new, humanity after all these years shouldn't be this unpredictable, don't you think?"

Khadim - " So you too have felt something, haven't you, Manav. I was aware from the beginning that there is no need for us to spell it out to you or sugarcoat matters of war-profiteering."

Sana - "War-profiteering and planned Famine, Millions killed in Bengal, Chalisa, Doji bara and Agra byBritish Policies. I was about to bring up that point, how many wars were instigated, how many men died for the profit of corporations run by another set of men who have hegemonized our lives for generations, re-written history, who knows how many times and for how long. Ask yourself a question, where are the innovations humans had shown promises in the past?"

Aban - "Especially medically."

Khadim - "I agree, but these are facts Manav. The architectural brilliance of pyramids, the astronomical knowledge that men had gained thousands of years ago, are still in pursuit, Why? Until you believe in them there is no point addressing them, you see why we are bringing this to you, not because of the hatred we have for the world but for the mere reason that we believe it could have been handled in a much better manner only if the greed of some powerful men wasn't an obstacle to us."

Sana - “I know it's overwhelming."

Manav - “Yes it is, It's a lot to take, not that I haven't thought about it but it's not easy to absorb all this enlightenment."

Khadim - “Maybe because you are made to believe you are not good enough beyond a certain potential."

Manav - “Maybe, but that doesn't surprise me. ‘Survival of the fittest', right?"

Aban - “And who decides who is the ‘fittest'?"

At this point in time, Manav had nothing but headaches all over him. He couldn't fathom what was in the room. Even though there were only four souls in the large room, he constantly felt as though he was in a crowded hall. The room felt exceedingly loud with voices that weren't originating from those four souls as if all of the readings, conversations, and fleeting thoughts he had in the past had come crashing down all at once. It reminded him of the time when Mikhail pitilessly braved him up to kill Hafeez. But what are these souls trying to make him do? He kept his head down as it became too heavy for his shoulders to carry, time and again he would look up to all three of them with a nervous smile hoping to hear something that would vitalize him, and have a better understanding of what he learnt so far. Though it felt like he waited for it for a million years, a soft and sympathetic touch on his scalp uplifted not only his spirits but his head too. The touch of Sana was so affectionate that he closed his eyes like a baby getting ready for a nap, she comes closer face to face to him and says.

Sana - “Maybe that is enough of a history lesson for now, would you like to take a nap? I know I do."

Manav - “Maybe that’s a good idea, but I don’t want to be rude to Aban and Khadim." He whispers.

Laughingly Khadim says, “The drink is doing its job, it’s relaxing, you don’t misunderstand it, you’ll see how restful the nap will be."

Sana takes him along to the bedroom, as soon as he reaches the bedroom he just sits on the bed holding his head. A while later Sana enters his room all changed and refreshed, she sits beside him and puts her hand over his shoulder, quietly combs his hair that made him feel better, she makes him lie down on the bed. As he relaxes himself flat, his eyes closed, covering his eyes and forehead with his arm, he reminisces his memory of Mikhail and decides to share with Sana.

Manav - “He said what he does is a distraction, and it pissed me off. I almost felt like taking his tongue for that, what did he mean by that?"

Sana - “Who said that?"

Manav - “Mikhail, he said what his people do is a distraction, the real plan is in hiding, I wish he was here today, I really need him to clarify it for me."

Sana - “What else did he say?"

Manav - “A lot, more than I ever conversated before, but that clicked, ‘the distraction’ part, why did he say that?"

Sana - “I don’t understand, but that’s not the name he came up with for our faction but distraction sounds way cooler."

Manav - “Your faction? What do you mean you guys are some kind of gang within a gang?"

Sana - "We have to survive Manav, where we come from, if we don't have a purpose we are useless, and being useless means most likely death."

Manav - "What was the name he came up with?"

Sana - "Agents of Gradation. You know like - Wind, Glaciers, River, Rain and Sea waves. He was fascinated by how Natural calamities impact the environment, how they refresh everything, like restarting a computer.."

Manav - "I did not know that. Though, it suits you all you know. Just as mysterious you guys are, 'Agents of Gradation'.

Sana as she embraces and kisses him, says.

Sana - "You take a nap, don't think about anything, I have to check on Abbu and jaddu."

Manav - "Will you be back later?"

Flirtatiously she says,

Sana - "Yes Potter, can't keep you apart for too long, but don't wait, I'll be here before you wake up."

Manav - "I'll try but don't know if I'm tired enough, but go ahead, you know where to find me."

As Sana left Manav started to lose himself in his thoughts. He continued to reflect on the discussion from various angles, trying to find a conclusive understanding. However, each time he approached a conclusion, there seemed to be a hesitancy within him, as if he subconsciously avoided reaching a definitive answer. Perhaps the complexity of the subject or his own reservations, prevented him from fully acknowledging the elusive truth. "This door, this whole world was introduced by Mikhail. Now it hardly makes sense or am I too stupid to see it through. I must be wasting their time terribly."

Doubts started to creep in, causing Manav to question his own intellectual capabilities. He wondered if he was missing something or if he was simply too foolish to comprehend the deeper significance of it all. In his self-deprecating thoughts, he began to believe that he was wasting their time, disappointing them with his lack of insight or understanding.

"How disappointed they might be, maybe they are discussing I am not what they thought I was. I shouldn't be surprised, a few more added to the list of my dissatisfied customers. God, it still feels like a dream, the life before this was too dismay to be true, and this - A father and grandfather, A child-like brother who seems to be in dire need of assistance,, always. And a woman who chose me, though I was the one who fell for her first, if it isn't a fairytale then what is it, and to make it all more interesting, we have a castle in the country and a tower in the city, so unreal, all of this."

As Manav contemplated the complexities of his thoughts, he acknowledged that his mind wasn't quite ready to retire for the night. There was still a multitude of calculations, puzzles, and connections that needed to be made within the labyrinth of his mind. His conscious efforts to analyse and piece together the fragments of his thoughts were tireless. However, despite his conscious intentions to stay awake, his subconscious gradually took over. Fatigue settled in, lured by the comfort of the cosy surroundings and the gentle sway of the weather outside. The feathery bed seemed to pull him in, as if embracing him and coaxing him into a state of blissful slumber. Manav succumbed to the allure of dreamland, even if it happened inadvertently.

As Manav suddenly awakened around 5 in the evening, a sense of panic surged through his body. It wasn't due to any external disturbance but rather a startling realisation that his bed was drenched in his own perspiration. His body felt clammy, and his breathing was laboured, as if he had just experienced a harrowing ordeal. Confused and disoriented, he stared at the soaked bed, questioning what had caused such excessive sweating. He checked for any signs of bedwetting, but finding none, he attempted to calm himself and regulate his breath. As the realisation of the dream came crashing down on Manav, he recognized that it was not just any dream, but a haunting nightmare. The details flooded his mind, painting a vivid and terrifying picture of the prison he had been trapped in within the confines of his subconscious. In this dream, he was in a peculiar prison, the windows stood out with anomalous features. Positioned unusually low, below the usual height, One has to force himself/herself to bend down or sit to catch a glimpse of the outside world; you can't stand straight and gaze outside. However, the thick walls surrounding him obstructed his view of what was close by, limiting his perception to objects and scenes in the distance. Each side of the prison presented its own horrors. One side was consumed by fire and its destructive aftermath, while another exhibited a pale white wall made of ice. The third side was filled with buildings, shops, and streets, but an eternal night shrouded the surroundings, accompanied by distant cries for help and sounds of suffering, but there wasn't a single soul to be seen. The absence of visible life added an eerie and unsettling dimension to the scene. The fourth side offered no respite or solace either, showcasing a sky devoid of clouds, celestial bodies, or any signs of life, not even birds. It was a vast expanse of emptiness that only amplified the sense of hopelessness and eternal confinement.

In his dream, Manav had been trapped in this nightmarish cycle of repetition endlessly, yearning for something different, anything but this, anywhere but here.

He waited there until the sweat dried, then walked into the halls, he saw everyone together laughing, chatting in the dining room, everyone greets him with excitement.

Aban - “Look who finally woke up, welcome back my friend."

Khadim - “I trust you had a wonderful sleep."

Sana grabs his hand and brings him to the group.

Sana - “So this is what we were talking about, who should take over this fort and jaddu will decide but you will have to impress him with what you will do with it."

Manav - “Nice, that’s interesting, who won?"

Sana - “Not yet, you didn’t get a chance, tell us what will you do?"

Khalid interjects.

Khalid - “How can he get a chance, he already got the apartment, that’s not fair."

Aban - “Keep it together Khalid, show some sportsmanship, and we are just playing."

Manav - “I got the apartment? What do you mean? Aban, did you really do that?"

Aban - “I did Manav, all arrangements are done, you have your own house now, it was nothing but a gift."

Manav - “No Aban, as much as I would like to, I can’t accept that, I don’t deserve it."

Sana - “Let’s not have discussion on that Manav, it’s yours. We liked it and we thought you should have it."

Manav - “No Sana, it is too much, you all have given so much to me already, and I couldn’t. I didn’t even stand up to the cause that had meant everything to me a few days ago. I know you were planning something, but I was not good enough to be a part of it. You gave me a life to remember by, that is more than I could ever expect."

Aban comes closer, puts his hand over Manav's shoulders and comforts him.

Aban - "We weren't planning anything, we met you we liked you and understood why Mikhail chose you, and we are happy that you could join us, now that we are going to part our ways, we need more than memories to remember these moments, that house is yours and do you really expect us to fit in that box of yours when we visit again?"

Manav - "But please tell me you understand, vengeance was the only thing in my mind but now you all are my family, and I want to try and stay away from any cause that could hurt it."

Khadim - "We do, I was hoping you could lead us, and you did exactly that, we never felt this solidarity in us, you made us all feel like a family again, we should thank you for that and not the other way around."

With a growing sense of acceptance, Manav realised that his companions were determined not to hear a 'NO'. Despite his initial reservations he gave up on their arguments eventually. In a moment of surrender, he embraced them warmly, and they began discussing their exciting itinerary. Although Manav's flight was scheduled to depart four hours after theirs, he made a decision to leave with them anyway. The thought of parting ways and missing out on the shared experiences was unbearable. In the remaining hours leading up to their departure, a palpable sense of joy filled the air. The memories of their shared meals, tantalising the taste buds and leaving an everlasting impression, brought a smile to their faces. They delighted in the recollection of cool and comforting drinks that had quenched their thirst, the beautiful weather that had embraced them, and the insightful conversations that had flowed endlessly. The touch of warm companionship, the breathtaking views they had witnessed, and above all, the indescribable feeling of being in the presence of such genuine connections, were moments they vowed to cherish forever.

As Manav wrestled with the inability to find the right words to express his sentiments, he realised that sometimes silence and gestures can speak volumes. He knew that his eyes held the unspoken gratitude and love he felt for them, and he hoped that they could see it reflected in his gaze. However, even a blind man could interpret the tender, heartfelt emotions conveyed by his puppy-like eyes. Khadim, ever thoughtful, had prepared a special surprise for each of them, a small memento to open once they reached their destination. He explained that souvenirs were not only meant to bring back memories but also to serve as a reminder of their ultimate destination or purpose. It was a symbolic gesture, reminding them that they are all welcome, anytime. To everyone's surprise, even Khalid seemed to be in good spirits. He exhibited improved manners and was noticeably less sarcastic than usual. As they gathered their luggage and prepared to leave, Khalid went above and beyond, offering to assist Manav with his belongings. This unexpected act of kindness momentarily shifted the attention to Khalid, surprising and pleasing everyone, especially Manav. After a few heartfelt prayers and goodbyes, they made their way to the airport.

At the airport Aban borrows Manav from Sana and takes him a little further for a private talk.

Aban - "Son, I don't know if things will be difficult or easier after you met us but I hope in the lifetime of your own, we did bring a few moments of happiness and peace to you."

Manav - "I'm glad my paths crossed with your family's, and I've been wanting to tell you, all along but I was too nervous to share, I have been a fan long before I met you. Thanks for reaching out to me, my life has never been better."

Aban - "You never know, there is still so much to come, you're always welcome to our humble abode, your home is not the only home you got ."

They embrace each other in Arabic tradition, Aban leaves Manav to make his way towards his boarding gate. Then Manav forwards himself to the toughest task on his to-do list, he walks towards Sana with a heavy heart, Manav summoned the courage to approach Sana, knowing that he had a difficult task to accomplish. Watching each of her perfect hair as he made his way towards her, he couldn't help but be captivated by her once again. Her lustrous hair, flowing in the wind like a mermaid's tail in the water. The flawless curve on her cheeks when she smiled, added to her ethereal beauty resembling a crescent moon. Looking at the sublimity of the skin tone and her lips, exuded a divine perfection that defied description. The wave in her walk seemed to unfold in slow motion, as if she walked on air. When she reached out and placed her hands gently on his shoulders, an electric current surged through his being, leaving him enchanted. And the most intoxicating of all was the scent of her hair, a fragrance that held the power to captivate his senses completely. Sana possessed a natural allure that made her a perfect and effortless seductress. She mumbles something in his ears but he didn't hear anything, as much as he tried not to look bewitched but there was little to no success, he was blushed to the cherry and eyes flooded to the brink. It was no surprise it was too emotional for a freshly-fallen in love.

Sana - “When will I see you again?"

Manav - “You know where to find me, and If I am not around I’m guessing you will still locate me."

Sana - “You are famous, Potter. You’re not that hard to find."

Manav - “I’m going to miss that self-confidence of yours, and certainly being called ‘Potter’."

Sana - “I hope you know what you signed up for Potter, you got off easy this time, anyway off I go. I will call you from my layover airport. Drop me a message after you have landed and take care I’m going to miss you so much, you have no idea."

Manav - “It would be hard to stop thinking about you."

Sana - “You could never."

Their good-bye-talk went on for a while but it was never enough. As they went their separate ways, Manav and Sana couldn’t help but steal one last glimpse of each other, their eyes filled with a mixture of hope and longing. Every few steps, they paused and looked back at each other, unable to resist the enigmatic aura that surrounded them. The farewell embrace held a sense of loss and optimism, but Manav couldn’t deny the bittersweet reality that one last glance can never truly last.

With her departure imminent, he found himself unable, or perhaps unwilling, to let her fade from his sight. Her presence was etched in his mind, her enchanting allure captivating his every thought. Even from a distance, from the airport taxi, he could still envision the fatal curve of her smile as she turned to steal that final glance. The combination of all her attributes created an unmeasurable beauty.

Yet, as he finally tore his gaze away and began to walk away, a recognizable smile graced Manav's face. His heart felt light, and the air around him seemed fresh and invigorating. Gravity no longer seemed forceful, as if the weight of the world had lifted. The faces around him were filled with happiness and beauty, and even the birds organised in a sequence of single notes producing a melodious, satisfying, and soulful tune. The usual sounds of irritating crows were absent, but even if they had been present, Manav's focus would have remained fixed on the overwhelming sense of tranquillity.

CHAPTER TWELVE

# GLACIER

After landing, while he was on the way home, his cab driver kept asking him if Manav had heard the news. Manav continued to politely ignore his queries because he wanted his mind to linger a little longer in the memories. Each and every moment of the last few days, he was able to project in front of him, as if watching his own movie as the protagonist. However, every movie has a climax, it ends.

He had to divert his focus when he noticed the disordered crowds all around him, the heavy traffic, and the fact that everyone on the road was either using their cellphones or gathering in a cluster and watching television in front of stores. Curious Manav took out his phone and started looking for headlines and latest news. There was only ONE breaking news. Reacting to the news, Manav's blood briefly evaporated upon reading that the Prime Minister had been the target of an assassination attempt. Though the attempt failed, however, when he kept reading the details in the news, something kept bothering him. Like an 'earworm' there were some catchy memorable details that the news specifics kept triggering in him. It was really bothersome to know what had happened obviously, however now at least he knew what the cab driver was talking about. Manav was initially thrilled to move into his new home, but his sense of anticipation was now significantly diminished by his unexpected return to a frantic scene.

Manav sprints back to the apartment, he could not bother freshening up or make himself comfortable, the first thing he did was switch on the news channel. It was obviously a big story, and every channel was offering their take on it; some proclaimed war, some said it was an act of sympathy, and so on, there were as many conclusions as the number of news channels. However, Manav's curiosity was triggered by the way the attempt was carried out. He discovered that the Prime Minister was the target of a sniper shot during his address, and that shortly after, when security was transporting the PM back in their protected vehicles in accordance with protocol, en route an explosion occurred, which he luckily missed. A few hundred metres from the Prime Minister's podium, the investigative team discovered an automatic long-range weapon in the slums, which was still pointed and locked on to the PM's location. They also discovered explosives with active remote detonations, concealed on the road where the PM's convoy was travelling. The explosives and the rifle both were mechanised to be triggered remotely. It was going to be dark times and Manav could not believe that something of such gravity could happen in the current era. For a moment he thought, probably Aban and Khadim are right, we are all doomed but then he gave a little bit more attention to specifics of the news, the gravity pull began to be stronger.

As Manav connected the dots, uncovering unsettling details, his mind raced to make sense of the situation. He discovered that the explosives had been found along the same route he had taken with Khalid and Sana.

Furthermore, the automated gun used for assassination, had been placed in the very slums where he had walked with Aban, evoking a mix of relief for having escaped potential danger, but also a concern, circling around his mind that he may have overlooked crucial details.

The news provided further information about the explosion's location, and when Manav saw photographs of the scene, a wave of unease washed over him, almost as if his skin left his body. It was the exact spot where Khalid had felt sick and had to stop the car at Sana's instructions. Reluctantly, but unable to deny the connections, a conclusion began to form in Manav's mind - a conclusion he didn't want to accept or confront. His heart and mind waged a battle within him as he grappled with the reality that unfolded before him. He would randomly stand up and down every now and then just to remember there was no need for him to get up or sit down.

In the midst of his conflicting thoughts, Manav's phone startled him with an incoming call from an unknown number. Despite the unfamiliar number, there was something strangely familiar about the voice when he answered.

Aban - "Hello Son, have you reached home safely?"

Manav was slightly surprised, according to the itinerary, Aban was not supposed to land for another 6 hours, he expected Aban ought to be in the air by now.

Manav - Shouldn't you be on the plane?"

Aban - "I am, but with a slight change of plans, this is a private jet."

Manav couldn't construct a sentence, he happily avoided the customary pleasantry of asking any unnecessary formalities, so he asked what he was really compelled to ask.

Manav - “I believe you must have heard the news, why do I have the impression that you had something to do with it?"

There was a moment of silence that allowed Manav’s eyes and brain to revolve around a bit; however Aban responded before any of his nerves went into action.

Aban - “Why do you seem surprised, I thought we had an understanding."

As the moment passed on, Manav’s impatience and anger grew exponentially. The lack of a definitive response or resolution only exacerbated his frustration. Every passing second without clarity fueled his impatience, pushing him closer to the edge. His mind spun with a mix of emotions - anger, annoyance, and a desperate need for answers.

Manav - “We had no understanding other than keeping peace, what did you do Aban?"

Aban - “I told you at the very beginning ‘In peacetime Sons bury their fathers, when fathers bury their sons it’s war’ and WAR IT IS my son."

Manav - “How could you do this? I thought you were a peaceful, honest and a wise man. This is not the way, do you have any idea what you have done?"

Aban - “Calm down son, though we are in this together but we have ensured that none of it leads to you."

Manav - “NO WE ARE NOT! You have acted entirely on your own, I never intended such a thing, and I have no stake in it."

Aban - “So you say, but know this, we greatly benefited from the information you gathered while conducting your own research; you could have been a fantastic agent, but you opted for the former. You held on to the instinctual behaviour that prevents us from moving on to the next stage of evolution. If not today, then someday, you will realise this, but not before you are eradicated. I can assure you that we have never failed because we are perpetually prepared to sacrifice and you are not."

Manav - "Like you sacrificed Mikhail?"

Manav's impatience and frustration intensified as the silence stretched on, leaving Aban on the edge with the comment about Mikhail, Manav felt he had the upper hand. However, to his surprise, Aban did not allow the silence to linger for much longer. Before Manav could assert any upper hand in the situation, Aban spoke up, breaking the silence. With the silence shattered, the power dynamics shifted.

Aban - "If I have to, I will do that again, and none of my children will think twice."

Manav - "Was he even your son?"

Aban - "Careful what you say next, I will not tolerate misbehaviour."

Manav - "Or what? You will kill me too? or at least failing in what you were planning to do, You and your children failed, he survived both your attempts"

Aban - "I didn't fail You brattish boy! I have succeeded in what others have been failing for decades, I just showed the world that the 'God' can bleed, I just penetrated the most secure wall. People will see me rather as a champion who broke the chains and hacked into the arrogant who thought they could rule over me."

Manav kept quiet, all Aban could hear was cleansing breaths or probably gasps. But he didn't make Aban wait much longer for a response.

Manav - "I think I have heard enough, but this surely wasn't about Mikhail, it's a competition of arrogance between you and your fabricated foes. I'm sure in your wisdom you will find something to trump my argument but I wish you luck. Despite how difficult it is to accept your betrayal, I will continue living in a world where I befriended Mikhail, even alone but a world without deception. In those brutal moments of rigour Mikhail created a new 'ME' who believes in compassion over distancing, and family over loneliness, I will keep him alive as long as I breath and not for one moment I will let myself believe that he was even remotely related to anyone of you, you're not half as brave as your son"!

Aban - "Well that case, this brings us to 'Goodbye', any last words Son?"

Manav - "You will hear my last words but not today, until then, I have two things to say to you - Do Not Ever call me Son, and Second - Please don't die."

Aban - "Don't die? Well, you can't be concerned over something that cannot be controlled."

Manav - "Oh! I am not concerned, I just want to see your dying eyes and hear your last breath."

Just when Aban was conjuring a sentence in response, Manav abruptly ended the call, cutting off any chance for further conversation, and sat wherever he could settle, looking towards the horizon through the balcony of his new apartment, gifted by a terrorist. It was unknown how the new circumstances would impact his life, he was scared and angry, unable to contemplate what was affecting him the most. As the pieces started to fall into place, his mind could now picture what must have happened, all the lies and the scheming played against him was just raging him more. Knowing the truth didn't matter; he was obviously betrayed and made a fool of, but that wasn't what concerned him. He couldn't help but wonder whether not "playing the part" is the reason behind his loneliness. "Why does this keep happening to me? Should I have just gone along with them? Or was I not good enough for them?" He couldn't comprehend the reasons, his tears were trying a way out but even alone, he felt ashamed of crying all by himself or Perhaps he believed that the perpetrators didn't deserve his tears. Time was paused, he couldn't wait for tomorrow or the next day, anything but today or this moment. The sunset afar through his balcony window must have been the most beautiful of all the sunsets he has seen but it was rather irritating. "How long does it take for that damn thing to go down?" Darkness became more pleasing and comfortable all of a sudden and the light was making his skin burn. He succumbed to titillating sensations that were simultaneously scorching hot and freezing cold under his skin, almost as if a nuclear fission reaction were occurring all over him. Even after the sun went down, he maintained the same position, not even once taking his eyes off the horizon, almost like waiting for an answer, begging for an explanation. Even the vastness that the horizon had to offer, it didn't have what Manav was looking for. In his current state of mind it was unlikely if he himself knew what he was looking for but something, anything would have sufficed.

His eyes were getting tired enough for sleep, but he didn't even want to blink, his fear was what may happen if he takes his eyes off his life for even one second. His mind wasn't full of questions but rather judging the divinity of the cosmos. The horizon in front of him was moving in cycles turning bright then dark, he might not be sure how many cycles he witnessed before the limitations of his biological clock gave up and alarmed him. After he used the bathroom, very much unwillingly, for a quick moment he glared at his reflection on the mirror. The realisations of all the recent incidents started hitting him back so hard and fast that he couldn't believe what a fool he was played for even after being so cautious, he wanted to feel bad and say bad words to himself but his own reflection was pitiful in its entirety. Suddenly he had the urge to call Aban again and speak to everyone, especially Sana. However, the wheel of his desires had a conclusion in itself, "What am I going to say, what do I want to hear?" He somehow collected himself and brought himself back to the earlier position, glaring at the horizon. He couldn't feel hungry or thirsty, he was dangerously weak but he didn't want to shut his eyes even for a second. The peculiar reason he didn't want to sleep was,"If reality can be like a nightmare, what would a nightmare be like?" Though it was an insane thought, nothing was 'careful enough' for him, he must have been the most paranoid person at that moment.

As Manav's frailty overcame him, his physical and emotional exhaustion took its toll, causing him to faint. Unconsciousness descended upon him, ushering him into a nightmarish realm where he had no control over the twisted scenarios that unfolded. In his dream, Manav found himself reliving the moment when Aban had first visited him, a knocking sound echoing through his mind. As he watched himself in the dream, an unconscious Manav desperately tried to send a message, reaching out and pleading for his dream-self not to open the door. However, the dream-Manav remained oblivious to the warning, caught in the relentless cycle of his subconscious.

Unbeknownst to him, in reality, Manav was being carried by unknown individuals who had entered his apartment. The knocking he heard in his dream was, in fact, the pounding of those unidentified individuals on his door. Weakened by three days without food or water, he was too feeble to recognize that he was now being kidnapped. Disoriented and unaware of his current circumstances, Manav believed he was still trapped within the confines of his dream. The shock of the impending unravelling of his reality, was yet to be realised, as the events spiralled towards an unknown and dangerous outcome.

To be continued..... Anthroposcene and Enceladus.

www.ingramcontent.com/pod-product-compliance
Lightning Source LLC
LaVergne TN
LVHW091254150826
845673LV00006B/1412

*9798891866652*